BEDROOM
ROULETTE

Other books by BroadLit:

TruLOVE Collection:
When Love Goes Bad
Falling In Love...Again
Losing It For Love
Forbidden Love
When Love Sizzles
Love In Strange Places

Second Acts Series— by Julia Dumont
Sleeping with Dogs and Other Lovers
Starstruck Romance and Other Hollywood Tails

Infinity Diaries — by Devin Morgan
Aris Returns, A Vampire Love Story

Age of Eve: Return of the Nephilim — by D.M. Pratt

BEDROOM
ROULETTE

By Anonymous*

*The stories presented here were first published as "true stories" . . . at a time when it was necessary to hide the true identities of the women associated with these tales to avoid scandal. We have chosen to maintain the veil of the authors' anonymity to protect the innocent . . . and the not so innocent.

The timeless love stories from
True Romance and True Love live on.

Edited by Ron Hogan

A BROADLIT BOOK

BroadLit

February 2013

Published by
BroadLit ™
14011 Ventura Blvd.
Suite 206 E
Sherman Oaks, CA 91423

ISBN # 978-0-9887627-0-1

Produced in the United States of America.

Visit us online at www.TruLOVEstories.com

This collection is dedicated to all of you who are looking for true love or have already found it.

TABLE OF CONTENTS

INTRODUCTION
by Ron Hogan

W hen the TruLoveStories website went live, the first section I started exploring was "A Century of Love," which features True Love and True Romance stories from the 1920s up through the last decade. When I got to the 1970s section, and the story "My Mother's Lover Is My Husband," I knew I was in for a wild ride, but the cover to the May 1970 issue of True Love promised even crazier stories: "My Best Friend Stole My Baby," "Every Week My Doctor Drugs Me," and the "shocker of the year," a partner-swapping tale called "You Give Me Your Husband and I'll Give You Mine."

I joked on Twitter that the folks at TruLoveStories should turn me loose in the archives so I could come up with a whole anthology's worth of crazy love stories from the 1970s. It turns out they were paying attention—and here we are!

A few years back, I wrote a book about Hollywood in the 1970s called The Stewardess Is Flying the Plane! In it, I talked about the ways in which the films of that decade show us how the "countercultural" trends of the late 1960s became increasingly mainstream, presenting subjects that were previously taboo to larger and larger audiences. American society was in flux: Watergate and Vietnam had caused many people to lose faith in the government and other authority figures; the sexual revolution threatened the stability of marriage; the feminist movement shifted the balance of power between men and women. And each week, new films would come out that reflected these tensions, wrapping them in stories that (ideally) engaged their audiences.

It wasn't just about the movie theaters, though.

I don't want to oversell this idea too much as far as these stories are concerned. The fact is, if you look at an issue of True Love or True Romance from the early 1970s, chances are the contents will ultimately reinforce the status quo. Marriage is good; marriage with a kid, or one on the way, is even better. The hedonistic pursuit of pleasure comes with consequences, but if you're lucky you can clean up your act and start making a better life for yourself.

Some of the ways in which these stories deal with the counterculture are predictable. Dirty hippies using drugs and sex to lead innocent, if mildly rebellious, girls astray is like the '70s equivalent of a melodrama cad twirling his mustache. Sexual experimentation inevitably leads to shame and regret—the heroine who let another woman's husband into her bed may have had mind-blowing orgasms, but she'd feel dirty about it for a long, long time.

The more time you spend really digging into these stories, though, the more surprises you'll find. I was lucky enough to find a story in which the hippies living out on the commune aren't portrayed as sex-crazed monsters. Often, when gay and lesbian characters appear, the narrators refuse to condemn their behavior. (Granted, being held up as objects of pity isn't much better, but it's a start.) And though some of the women in these stories meekly accept the blame for all the hardships they suffer, other women can be seen taking charge of their lives, refusing a relationship with a man unless they can have it on equal terms.

There are also a few stories here that are just so far out there, with such crazy plots, I absolutely knew I had to have them in this collection. As you read these stories, though, don't think of them as just wacky pop culture artifacts from the past. Sure, some of this stuff comes off a bit silly now, but beyond the entertainment and nostalgia value, you'll get a glimpse at a pivotal moment in American cultural history.

I'm something of a late bloomer when it comes romance fandom, and my points of entry into the genre were basically Regency historicals, which tend to deal with aristocratic characters, and the "chick lit" of the early 2000s, which was often about middle class women in large cities striving for both personal and professional success.

The stories from early '70s True Love and True Romance come from a much different place. Characters tend to come from small towns; if they wind up in a big city, it's quite likely something bad will happen to them there. If the women are old enough, they're usually housewives; women who do work are often stuck at the secretarial level—and, in any case, they're probably only working until they get married.

For the most part, these are working class stories, with strong aspirational qualities. (There are some stories with middle class settings here, but they can feel a bit staged—fantasies of what life might be like for white-collar workers living in apartment buildings in big cities.) The men are doing their best to provide a stable home for their loved ones, and the women are doing their best to be supportive of their men. Their financial security is by no means guaranteed—and those money problems can be a powerful source of conflict.

These stories are like a snapshot of what was on America's mind in the early 1970s, and as I continue to explore the TruLoveStories archives, I'm going to be very interested in how the stories changed over time, to see what their creators portrayed as the biggest threats to "true love" and happy marriages. I've already found more great '70s stories than I could fit into this one collection, and I'm about to plunge into the 1980s next...

BEDROOM ROULETTE
The Game Suburban Housewives Play

"Bedroom Roulette" is a riveting story, but it's also a very troubling one, especially when you get to the ending. To 21st-century readers, the way that Donna accepts responsibility for the pain she experiences before she and her husband agree to get their marriage back on track isn't just implausible, it's likely to be offensive—no matter how much of a positive spin she tries to put on her decision. This is not one of our collection's feminist moments.

That morning as I dressed for my last day at work, my mind played a crazy trick on me. Here—just when I seemed to have everything going my way—I wondered if that's really what I wanted after all. I mean, I was gripped by this heavy, oppressive feeling that maybe we were making a terrible mistake; that we should have waited for a while before buying a house and moving all the way out to Westwind Dell. After all, it was a long way from the city and both Greg and I had lived in the city all our lives!

And on top of everything, I was quitting my job as assistant buyer in Barkley's department store! My dream had come true—to be a fulltime housewife taking care of her own cute little home!

This is one of the happiest days of your life, Donna Eldridge, I told myself silently —and sternly—as I put the finishing touches to my hair that morning. "You are very happy. You and Greg have planned for this day for a long time, since even before your marriage three years ago! And now the big moment has come.

Except that I didn't want to quit my job! Not really. Not deep inside, though I would never have breathed a word of it to Greg. I loved my work at Barkley's, loved the people I worked beside. But it had taken every cent we could scrape up to put a down payment on the house and there wasn't a chance in the world of getting a second car. No way I could get back and forth from Westwind Dell to the city, twelve miles away.

Greg came out of the shower, a towel wrapped around his waist. At the sight of my big, handsome husband, some of my secret doubts melted away. Greg swept me into his arms and pressed me against him. "Boy! Would I give a lot to see your mother's face today, honey." He threw back his dark head and tried to mimic my mother's slight nasal voice. " 'Marry Greg Eldridge, Donna, and you'll have to work the rest of your life and live in a two—bit apartment! What can he ever give you'?' "

Greg crushed me against him and nuzzled my neck. "I'd love to see the old—to see your mother's face, Donna, when she realizes she was wrong about me. Not only have I provided her beautiful daughter with a house of her own—but she can also quit working!"

He was pretty proud of himself and had good reason to be! I kissed him deeply. "Honey," I murmured, "I would love you anyway. What do we care about Mom's opinion?"

He drew back and his face clouded for a moment. "I care! I don't want her thinking you could have done better marrying that college creep—"

"Forget it, Greg," I told him shortly. Bob Ambrose has no place in my life." "He was only the guy you would have married if I hadn't come along," Greg said, half—teasingly.

I turned my back on him and studied my appearance in the mirror. My last day at work, I was thinking. My last day!

Greg's arms snaked around me from behind. "Well," he whispered, "I've never had to take second place to Ambrose in the loving department—"

"Nor in any other way either, you clunkhead!" I laughed, pulling away and picking up my purse. "Honey, I have to fly. I don't want to be late on my last day at work."

"C'mere, sweetheart. Give your old man a kiss sexy enough to last four days."

I threw my arms around him, pressed my lips to his, and put everything into that kiss.

"Hey," he whispered huskily, caressing me, "sure you have to rush away?"

"Positive! Take care of yourself and I'll see you on Tuesday! Now be careful driving."

It was crazy, but I felt glum on the ride downtown on the bus. On top of having to quit my job, Greg would be gone for days. He's a long haul trucker, and, with all the expenses we have, he takes on extra trips whenever he can. Now that we have our house, Greg won't rest until he gets a truck of his own; until he's his own boss!

My mother might never believe it, but she was so wrong about Greg! Just because he didn't go to college— like Bob Ambrose, her best friend's son— Mother's convinced Greg will never amount to anything. What she didn't count on was Greg's drive and ambition, his determination to succeed. A determination that sometimes frightened me!

Once I reached the department store I didn't have time to brood about it. We were busy all morning and afternoon. But when the store closed at six that night, they threw a surprise party for me. Tears filled my eyes when all the guys and gals I'd worked with for five years, gathered around to tell me how much they'd miss me. I was given tons of stuff for our new home.

"You'll come out to visit me, won't you?" I kept saying over and over. "Promise to come see us in Westwind Dell."

"I wonder if my polluted lungs could take all that fresh air," somebody quipped. But most of them promised they'd visit.

I cried all the way back to our apartment. I just couldn't help it. But at the same time I scolded myself on being so silly. I was happy! I really was! I had a darling little home of my own in the clean, country air. I didn't have to go to work every day. We could have a baby!

Wonderful!

Thinking of that cheered me up. I had, plenty to do, believe me.

The following Friday we were moving out to Westwind Dell!

When that day arrived, Greg and I were in a tizzy, as most people are when they move. We didn't have that much furniture, but still, it was after nine that Friday night before we could stop long enough even to sit down. I fixed us a drink while Greg shoved the last piece of furniture in place. We weren't exactly organized, but at least we could move around!

When I walked into the spanking new living room with our drinks, Greg took them away from me and pulled me into his arms. "Happy, sweetheart?" he murmured.

"Very. Oh Greg, I-I'm so happy I could explode!"

And I was! All my former doubts and misgivings had faded in the excitement of moving. And now that we were in our little house, dozens of decorating ideas were rattling around in my brain. Best of all, this was where we would start our family. Our first baby would be brought to this home.

"I'm so happy I c-could cry," I told him. And, dope that I was, I did cry.

Chuckling, Greg pulled me down on the couch and started kissing me like crazy. You guessed it! We ended up making love. I prayed that maybe our baby would begin that very night.

But it didn't! I wasn't really disappointed, though, because I had a million things to do getting us settled. I made drapes for the living room picture window, sewed slipcovers for our second-hand couch, and rearranged the furniture until I had everything just right.

And I got to know some of the neighbors!

Our house was on a dead end road, Walnut Lane, the last house on the right. Directly across the road were two almost completed houses, with only the finishing work and landscaping still to be done.

My next door neighbor, Fay Godowsky, became quite friendly. The minute her two kids left for school, she'd pop in for coffee. Fay was five years older than me, which made her twenty-eight. Her husband, Chet, was a mechanic; he worked in the city. After talking to her, I found out that all the husbands in West—wind Dell worked in town. After all, there was no work around our brand new development.

Most of the other wives were young too. I met a lot of them at a party the Godowsky's threw for us a month after we moved in. They seemed a nice enough bunch of people, the men all hard-working and eager to get on. The girls were full of decorating ideas, talk of their children, and the high prices in the only nearby shopping center, Westwind Mall.

Most of them seemed to be living on a tight shoestring, with little money left over for recreation or nights out in the city. I noticed, too, that a few of the women drank quite a bit and did a lot of whispering among themselves.

But that first couple of months flew by happily and by the time the weather grew really hot, we were settled. One day I sat back and surveyed everything in satisfaction. Sure, there were plenty of extra touches I would have liked to make, but they could wait. Greg had started talking about buying that truck of his own again and we tried to set a little money aside for that purpose.

So, with everything done that could be done, I had a lot of time on my hands. I called my friends in Barkley's, inviting them out, but most of them were busy or had no way of getting to Westwind Dell. My mother had moved to Florida the previous year, so she wasn't planning on a visit until Christmas. And my sister Ellen, and her husband were in Ohio.

Suddenly I—was getting up every morning, staring at my immaculate house, and going crazy. It was especially bad on the days Greg was away.

"Listen, kid. I know exactly how you feel," Fay Godowsky assured me one morning over coffee. "Most of us out here are slightly batty. You mean you haven't noticed?"

I thought back to the heavy drinking and the strange whispering and hesitated, "Well — "

"Sure you have! And no wonder! What's to do in this Godforsaken paradise?" She made a face. "None of us can afford a second car. The kids are at school all day. The houses are new and easy to clean. So what do we do?"

I lifted my hands helplessly.

"I'll tell you what we do," she went on, "we gossip too much and drink too much and — and, well, flirt with the milkman and the salesmen!"

"Oh sure!" I laughed. "I'll bet!"

"You think I'm kidding, don't you?

My own smile faltered at the sight of her solemn face. "Let me tell you something, Donna," she went on. "This development was built by the happiest construction crew in the country."

"Fay! Come on!"

"I'm serious, Donna. You know there's still a lot of building going on around here. Look at the two unfinished houses across the street! Well, ever notice how somebody — one of the girls - is always running across the road to take cold drinks to the men, or to invite them to drop by for coffee at lunch time?"

I stared at Fay, too stunned to utter a word. She laughed at the expression on my face and added wryly, "Listen, doll, some of these coffee breaks go on for hours!"

After she left, her words stuck in my mind like glue. Try as I might, I couldn't shake them off. I couldn't settle down either. After dusting the house for the third time that day, I paced to the picture window and looked out. The landscaping crew had moved to the house across the street. The place was finished except for the yard work. Now there was a bulldozer slowly moving over the yard. But it wasn't the machine that caught my eye—it was the big, bronzed guy atop it, his muscles rippling in the sun!

I turned away quickly, swallowing down the strange panic in my throat. The trouble was, I told myself, that Greg and I had been so busy for the last few weeks we hadn't had time for any fun. And every couple needs some recreation. I made up my mind that on Saturday we'd go into the city for dinner and dancing. I even called Sue and Norrie Greville, good friends of ours to double-date.

"It's over a month since you've been out to visit," I scolded Sue before hanging up. "I'm disappointed."

"Honey, after working all day I don't even feel like driving to the supermarket at night," she said with a sigh. "Besides, seems that Norrie always has something to do where he needs the car."

It was much the same story we got from all our city friends. Still, now that we were settled, we could go into town more. When Greg got home that Friday night, I told him about our plans for the weekend, sure he'd welcome a fun break as much as I would.

I was wrong!

"Dinner and dancing!" he groaned. "Honey, we can't afford it! It'd blow money we can save toward the truck, you know how expensive a night out is—"

"But we need a break!" I objected. "And it'll be years before you can get a truck of your own."

Greg looked crestfallen. "Years? Listen, Donna, I mean to have that truck next year! Once we get some money saved, I can make arrangements

"I've already told the Grevilles!" I was almost crying.

"Well, cancel it!" he snapped. "We can't afford it. And from now on don't make any arrangements without consulting me first!"

"How can I consult you when you're never around?" I yelled. "I see more of that—that bulldozer across the street than I do of you!"

"Oh, great! I'm only breaking my hack making money so you hare a window to look out of."

We glared at each other and I burst into tears and flew up to our room. He came up a minute later and slipped in and down on the bed beside me. "What's wrong, sweetie?" he whispered. "I thought you'd be happy in a nice house of your own."

"I am happy, Greg! Really I am. Only - oh, I wish I'd get pregnant! What I need is a baby to love while you're away."

"Well—" his arms closed around me, his lips on my ear, "—maybe I can do something about that."

I was so sure I'd get pregnant after that weekend! On Monday I got up early and drove Greg to work, as I always did when he started a haul, but since most of my friends worked, I spent the rest of the morning wandering around the stores. I was in baby department after baby department, drooling over all the darling little clothes. In my mind I began to fix up the spare bedroom for our baby. Blue and pink?

White and yellow? Which one would be cuter?

But I didn't get pregnant that month! I could hardly believe it. And I was plunged into a deep depression that wasn't helped when I got a letter from Mom. The picture of our house was 'nice', she wrote. A good 'starter' house of the type she'd seen in dozens of developments. She hoped it wasn't too much of a strain to keep it up on a truck driver's earnings. Oh—and she'd just had a long letter from her friend, Nancy Ambrose. Bob had been made a junior partner in a law firm. No, he still wasn't married. He sent his love —

I threw the letter on the old desk in our bedroom. Later that night I came upstairs and found Greg reading it. He glared at me, his face red. "Your old lady just never gives up, does she?"

"Oh, forget it, Greg."

"Listen, tell her to forget it! Tell her you don't give a damn about Ambrose. Or—maybe you like to hear about him; to know you still have his love?"

"Stop it!"

We went to bed without speaking and lay apart. I longed to reach out and put my arms around Greg, but I didn't. I had my pride too!

The whole weekend went by without us making love. Then Greg was gone from Monday morning until Thursday. When he got home Thursday night, it was to say he was leaving again in the morning, hauling an extra load to Michigan. He'd be gone three days.

"The extra money will come in handy, Donna," he said. "We can save it for the truck."

I tried very hard to swallow my disappointment; to forget my loneliness. I could see that, more than ever, Greg was determined to have that truck and start his own business, so he could spit in my Mother's face. It was no use to tell him to forget Mom; that her opinion meant nothing to me. Stubbornly, Greg would still go on trying to prove her wrong!

Soon he was taking on all the extra trips he could get. And soon he began to begrudge every cent we spent on anything that wasn't absolutely necessary. We kept trying to have a baby, though. Greg wanted a child as much as I did. But I couldn't seem to get pregnant.

One day, when I was really low, Fay took me to another girl's house up the street. Sandy was a tall, willowy redhead with restless grey eyes. Her house was filled with other girls, all chain-smoking and drinking highballs. I was about to refuse a drink, but shrugged. Why not? What did I have to stay sober for? I had no kids and my man would not be home for three days. I needed something to pull me together!

The subject soon got around to how bored and restless they all felt, how dull and nerve-twanging it was stuck in our development. How they hardly saw their husbands anymore since it was late by the time they got home from the city. Some of the men, to make ends meet, even had two jobs and stayed in the city all week!

"The construction guys are beginning to look better to me all the time!" Sandy laughed, but her eyes weren't smiling. "Ditto for the magazine salesmen and that cute TV repairman from Reads'—"

"Yeah," one of the other girls grinned, "I noticed he was in here for quite awhile last week. How many TV sets do you have anyway, Sandy?"

"Only one. But there was something else he stayed to fix."

Everybody thought it was hilarious except for one blonde who snapped, "D'you mean, Chuck Elliott?"

Sandy nodded.

"Why, that sneak, he was in my place just the day before!" the blonde raged. "I thought we had something going—"

"Sorry about that," Sandy chuckled. "I didn't know, Eve, or I'd never have, well, you know."

A chunky girl spoke up. "What we need, the way things are out here, is a few rules."

Fay snapped her fingers. "I've got a great idea! We'll play Bedroom Roulette! All we need are some dice. Whoever rolls the highest number gets her pick of the men. All the other girls must keep hands off!"

My mouth sagged open. This couldn't be for real!

"Hey, crazy!" the others were yelling, their eyes alive now with excitement. "Go get some dice, Sandy. We can roll for that dream driving the bulldozer down the street."

I knew they were all tipsy, yet I still couldn't believe it. But when Sandy returned with the dice, they gathered around her eagerly. I wanted to run out the door!

Fay, noticing the look on my face, whispered, "It's only for laughs, honey. Don't get so uptight. I don't think any of the girls really go the limit with a guy. It's only a lot of talk, to kill time."

She stuck a fresh drink in my hand. "It's all up to you, Donna. You can go as far as you want. But you'll have to agree about one thing—it's better than sitting in your house staring at the four walls!"

She was right about that! And how! Without the friendship of these girls, I'd go out of my mind. And I'd lose their friendship for sure if I started acting like an uptight square. So I raised the glass to my lips and drank half of it. The chances of me getting the high number were slight, with so many girls in the house.

I got a nine, though!

I just stared at the dice while Sandy yelled, "Hey, sweetie, that's the highest yet! How lucky can you get?"

My face turned hot and red and I kept my head down. I felt far from lucky! I broke out in an icy sweat as another girl rolled a four, then another got a seven. Only two left to roll! If I had to make up to that blond giant on the bulldozer, I would—Oh no—*I wouldn't!* Or would I?

The next girl rolled an eleven!

Everybody roared. All I could do was let out a squeak, like a mouse who had narrowly missed the trap. I was so relieved I was actually able to add my congratulations to the "lucky" Joan. Only Joan didn't want the guy on the bulldozer. The other girls couldn't believe it.

Joan, with a rueful grin, explained, "Listen, after living with my Freddy for six years, that guy over there is just too much man for me!"

"Well, who'd you have in mind honey?" Sandy prompted. She sounded happy that the big guy was still up for grabs.

"I kind of dig the guy from Walton's Appliances. He's delivering a stove to the house across the street from me tomorrow morning."

"Wow! There's your chance. We'll all be watching from Nancy's window."

"But what do I do?" Joan wailed excitedly. "How do I get him interested?"

Sandy took over. "First ask him into your house to tell you all about stoves. Make sure you wear your tightest hot pants. Then ask if he'd like coffee, or something ... "

I felt slightly sick and turned away. A few minutes later, as it neared time for the development kids to get home from school, the group broke up. But not before they'd made arrangements to meet the following day.

On the way home I couldn't help asking Fay, "Do they really intend to go through with this? I mean, you know—" I broke off in embarrassment.

She gave me a long, appraising look, then laughed softly. "In something like this it's every man—or girl—for herself. It's up to the individual how far she'll go."

I didn't say anything because anything I might have said would sound square.

Fay put a hand on my arm. "Look, Donna, nobody is going to get hurt—not the husbands, kids, or anybody. It's all for a little excitement, that's all. And what do you think our husbands are doing in town all week?" Her tone hardened. "You think they're deaf and blind to all the cute chicks who work around them?"

"My husband drives a truck."

"Hitchhikers are getting cuter all the time. They sure help to pass the time on the long hauls—"

"Fay!"

"Okay, sorry. But face it, Donna, Greg is a very attractive guy. And he's away from you so much ...”

Her words roared in my ear after I'd gone into the house. "Greg is a very attractive guy. Hitchhikers are getting cuter all the time—"

Could he? Would he?

No! Not Greg. Still, we hadn't been so close lately. Often, we were too angry at each other to make love. And once more Fay's remarks tortured me and I began to wonder about all those extra trips Greg was taking on. Sure, he said it was for the extra money. That's what he said.

With a choked sob, I pressed my hands over my ears in a vain attempt to block such disturbing thoughts from my mind. I paced around my spotless living room, paused before the picture window that faced the new house across the street. The big blond bruiser was getting off his bulldozer. When he got to the ground, he stopped and stretched, bare to the waist. His bronzed skin rippled; the hard muscles bulged. With a man like that to tease me every day, my husband had to, be away—

I jerked back from the window when he suddenly looked over. Did he catch a glimpse of me? Oh God, please no! What's happening to me anyway? I was as nervous as a cat. Now, if a man as much as looked at me I got all kinds of crazy thoughts in my mind.

Somebody knocked on the door!

For a wild minute I froze, standing there in the hall. I just froze!

It's him! Him! A maddening little voice screamed inside me. Go on, open the door. You'll find out!

I forced my stiff legs along the hall to the front door. And all the time I scolded myself on being so ridiculous, acting like a nut.

Taking a deep breath, I pulled the door open.

It was him!

Well, I just stood there. Maybe my mouth was open, I don't know. He was even bigger close up; bigger and more overpowering with that tan and blond hair and vivid blue eyes as clear as the sky on a summer day.

He held out a plastic jug. "Mind filling that with cold water. ma'am? It's mighty warm out there and I've run out of drinking water."

Ask him in! Invite him into your cool, quiet home for a drink! It was almost as if Sandy or Fay or one of the other girls was inside my head, telling me what to do.

I took the flask, managing a smile. "I'd be glad to."

I could feel his eyes on me as I walked away; feel them peeling back my skimpy clothes ...

You're becoming unhinged! I scolded myself. He's doing no such thing! The trouble with you, Donna Eldridge, is you're alone too much. You have too much time to think! At the rate you're going, you'll soon be as desperate as all the other girls around here!

I filled the plastic jug with cold water, dumped in a handful of ice cubes, and took it back to him. A huge paw reached out for the jug. "Sure looks good," he said. "A man can work up a mighty big thirst in the sun—"

But all the time his eyes were going over me, lingering on the low top of my sundress, sliding down to my legs. "Yeah, a man can work up a real big thirst."

Suddenly I was shaking. I couldn't swallow. There was a hand gripping my throat. I started to close the door at the same time as he drawled, "Much obliged, ma'am."

I nodded, closed the door, and sagged against it. I was out of breath, trembling, my heart was pounding like crazy. So when the doorbell rang again I almost flew apart.

But this time it was Fay and she came in, all eyes, "Wow! Did I see what I think I saw? Was that delicious brute over here?"

I let out a long breath. "He wanted water—"

"And you gave him wine! Right?"

"Wrong. I gave him water."

She gaped at me so that I had to laugh. "I was petrified," I confessed. "up close he's—well, he's too much."

"Honey, you can *never* have too much of a good thing," she lectured sternly. "And to send him away like that," she shook her head, "you must be nuts!"

She hurried home to fix supper and I was left alone. I didn't feel like making dinner for myself. I wasn't hungry anyway. And who wants to cook for one person? The long night lay ahead and nights out in Westwind Dell can be quiet— quiet enough to hear your heart beat!

I went to bed early, but tossed and turned. Finally I took a leaf out of the other girls' book and got up and mixed myself a drink. Two drinks later I went back to bed and lay counting the flowers in the wallpaper. Greg, please call, I was crying desperately inside. Please, darling, please—

But when I drifted off to sleep it wasn't my husband I dreamed about. It was the blond giant across the street! Once more his eyes possessed me: once more he reached for the pitcher of cold water I held out to him. Only this time his big hand closed around my wrist! And this time I was crushed against that bronze body until I stopped breathing. Suddenly those tempting lips were on mine!

And— oh God! — I *liked* it! I sobbed for more!

I woke up with a start, hot as if I had a fever. I was so ashamed I wanted to die! "Oh Greg," I whispered aloud, "I need you so! I want to hear your voice, to hold you close. I don't want this house. I want you!"

That Friday when Greg came home I had a special dinner ready for him. He was exhausted. It had been a long haul. I was hoping he'd be a little fresher so we could talk, because I had something important to say. But he fell into bed after the meal and dropped right off to sleep.

For one second— just one second—I was furious. All week I'd needed him desperately, and he came home only to sleep. Surely most men his age would be anxious for love after being away so long. Suspicion crept into my mind and I heard Fay's cynical voice saying, "Greg is a very attractive man. Hitchhikers are getting cuter all the time.

Pain slashed into my heart and I whimpered, but the next moment I pushed such thoughts to the back of my mind. I had Greg right here and though we couldn't make love, at least I could snuggle close to him.

Next morning, at breakfast, I tried to talk to him. "Honey, I've been thinking—wondering if we did the right thing by moving out here."

"What'?" he was startled.

I swallowed and tried again. "I—I was just wondering if we were wise to move all the way out here, Greg, so far away in the country."

He slammed down his knife and fork. "What are you trying to say, Donna?" he asked tightly.

"Just that I wonder if we did the right thing," I repeated lamely.

"Sure it's the right thing! Why wouldn't it be? We have a nice new house out in the fresh air," and he stressed the word "fresh." "Away from pollution and city dirt and crime. Why wouldn't it be the right thing?"

I wished I hadn't opened my big mouth! "Oh—" I hunched my

shoulders, "— it's just that with you gone so much I'm lonely."

"Well, you can't have it both ways! Grow up! Surely you can keep busy while I'm gone, and once we have kids you won't have time to think about it."

"But I can't get pregnant!" I burst out.

He sighed. "Well, go see a doctor. Do something! But quit complaining, will you? I came home to rest."

"Is that all, the only reason you came home?" I shot back.

"Oh boy!" he threw his hands up in the air.

The following Monday I made an appointment to see a doctor. When I went a few days later, he gave me a battery of tests and a complete physical. I had the results a week later. There was nothing wrong with me! No reason I couldn't have a baby!

"Now it's your husband's turn," Dr. Cairn smiled. "The trouble could lie with him."

I told Greg that Friday and his reaction stunned me. "There's nothing wrong with me!" he bellowed. "I could father ten kids. Look at my brothers! Every one of them has at least three!"

"Greg, that has nothing to do with you, honey, "I said gently." It—"

"I told you I'm fine!" He gripped my shoulders and his fingers dug in. "I'm not about to see any dumb doctor! I suppose you think I'm less of a man than that fancy lawyer you used to date—Ambrose!"

"Greg, don't be silly!"

"Then quit hinting that I'm not all there! I can deliver everything your fancy Ambrose can—a house of your own and all the babies you want. And forget about me seeing a doctor!"

"Greg, listen, this is so important"

"You listen to me! Start acting like a wife and less like a baby! You have nothing to complain about."

Tears filled my eyes. I opened my mouth, then realized there was no point in arguing. Greg's mind was closed and I'd never, never get him into a doctor's office. His silly pride wouldn't let him! It was obvious that he didn't really care if we had kids or not, or if I was lonely, or anything else! All he cared about was putting up a big front to the world, and to my Mother in particular.

We didn't speak the rest of the day, nor did we make love that night, though I was aching for the warmth of his arms around me. Sunday, one of his bachelor city pals came out and they went fishing. I was seething! I didn't kiss him goodbye when he left on Monday morning. I stayed curled up tight in bed. But the minute I heard him drive away, I burst into tears and cried myself sick. Oh God. I thought, what are we doing to each other? Doesn't Greg love me anymore? Doesn't he want us to have a baby?

I finally got out of bed, showered and dressed in shorts and a stretch top. I made coffee but had nothing else. The girls were meeting for coffee and Bedroom Roulette in Fay's house that morning once the kids left for school; I decided to go over. I had nothing better to do.

The usual crowd was there and across the road the blond guy was innocently riding up and down on his bulldozer, his bronzed back gleaming in the sun. Little did he realize so many girls were standing back of the drapes drooling over him.

"I'm going to win that boy doll today!" Sandy announced. "I just know it! Honey," she spoke to him through the window, "you don't know the treat in store for you."

"I found out his name!" Fay announced triumphantly. "It's Steve. Nice, huh?"

Sandy arched her slim body up to the window. "Steve, honey, come to Mama —"

Fay produced the dice and everybody crowded around the table, giddy with anticipation. Some of the girls weren't interested in Steve. To them, he was "too much." One thought he was hard, even mean. And Joan said, "Ever notice that nasty glint in his eyes when you pass him?"

Sandy laughed and tossed back her long, red hair. "Honey, it isn't his eyes I notice, believe me!"

"Come on, let's go!" Fay urged. "He won't keep forever."

Sandy gripped the cup and rolled. "Wow," she breathed. "Ten!"

I was second to the last. Finally the cup was in my hand and I rolled. I watched the dice bounce, roll, finally settle. And I kept staring even after that.

Twelve!

"You win!" Fay yelled in my ear. "You get to make it with Stevie boy, you lucky thing!"

"Say you don't want him. Please! Pretty please!" Sandy groaned.

I looked out the window at the bronze god across the street. Last week I would have said I didn't want him. Even two days ago. But now?

"I'll take him," I told them quietly.

"Go get him, Donna!" Fay laughed. "Here,–" she grabbed the pitcher of gin and lime and thrust it into my hand. "Go quench his thirst!"

I stumbled out the door clutching the pitcher close to me while the other girls crowded up to the window to watch. I tried to saunter along casually, but my legs were shaking and my stomach had dropped clean away. As I started across the street, Steve suddenly turned and saw me. I couldn't move. I just froze!

For a minute he stared, his blue eyes taking me in slowly from head to toe. Then, very casually, he raised his arm in a salute. "What you got there? Whatever it is looks good."

I forced a smile on my stiff face; forced myself to straighten up so the 'stretch' in my sweater really worked. "It–it's gin and lime," I stammered. "Want some?"

For a minute he didn't answer. He just sat there staring. Then he grinned, white teeth flashing against the tan. "Why sure. I'll be right over."

With a terrified glance at Fay's window, I almost raced into my house, the gin and lime sloshing all over me. Steve followed, his big body blocking out the sunlight in the hall so that it was dark for a moment. I led him into the living room and excused myself to find glasses. When I came back, he frankly appraised my legs.

"Your husband isn't around much, is he?" he remarked after gulping half his drink. "What does he do?"

"He's a long haul trucker." And for some reason I blurted, "He's driving a lot of extra trips to save enough money to buy his own rig."

"Oh yeah?" Hot blue eyes on my sweater again. "And what do you do while he's out slaving?"

I poured fresh drinks. I was matching him gulp for gulp. "Oh, I keep busy. There's always something to do."

"Right!" his lips twisted in a grin, "there's always something."

We looked at each other and it was right there in his eyes, big and bold as he was! I tried to tear mine away: tried to get up and run, but I couldn't. And then, in a flash, his huge paw was reaching for me, closing around my wrist, dragging me onto the couch beside him. "Yeah," he growled before crushing his mouth to mine, "I guess for most dolls like you there's always something else to do. Some other guy to trap." His kiss took my breath away. His embrace practically broke my ribs. In a flash, it seemed, I was fighting him off— and getting nowhere!

"No!" I screamed when I was able to jerk my mouth from his. "No— please!"

"Cut the act," he grated. "I'm onto wives like you, so save your breath, baby. I had a woman just like you—and now you're gonna pay off for what she did to me!"

He clutched my bra in one hand and, with a sudden twisting motion, ripped it away.

"Stop it!" I yelled, my nails clawing for his face. "No! No! Help!"

Somehow I did manage to get at his face, but only for a moment. Then, with a roar that almost lifted the roof off, he struck me across the side of the head. I went sailing across the floor, knocking a lamp table over, and struck the wall. Everything around grew suddenly dim. I saw him coming toward me, then his figure became blurred and finally faded into darkness.

I woke up in the hospital with Fay and Sandy sitting by my bed. "Oh Donna, honey, are you okay?" Fay cried when she saw I had come to. "How d'you feel? The way you were yelling, we thought he was killing you."

"That's when we decided to call the police," Sandy put in. "He was a madman!"

I tried to move and gasped with pain. Fay smiled wryly. "You have a broken rib, Donna, and a badly bruised face. Oh, we feel so bad, Donna! It's our fault for getting you to play Bedroom Roulette!"

But it wasn't their fault! A grown woman doesn't have to do anything she doesn't want to. So when Greg arrived and started to sympathize with me, I stopped him. I hated myself enough as it was, especially after the police told me that Steve's wife had recently betrayed him—after he'd worked himself to the bone to give her the best things in life. Just like Greg was working for me—

"It was my own fault, Greg," I found courage to say. "I asked for it."

And I told him the whole story, even the part about my discontentment and loneliness; how I'd never really been happy in Westwind Dell. When I finished, Greg was silent a long time. I could tell he was deeply hurt and I hated myself for being the one to do it. Finally he looked up. "What would really make you happy, Donna?"

And without hesitation, I said, "Having, you around more! Fixing it so you don't have to work so hard!"

Very slowly, he nodded. "I guess I've been a fool, Donna. Some of this is my fault. You see I—I wanted to prove to the world, well to your mother, that I could give you anything that fancy Ambrose guy could give you. Honey, I was so jealous of your old boyfriend, it drove me batty!"

Tears filled my eyes when I realized how much I'd let my husband down. I should have worked so much harder to let him know I loved him; loved him more than anything and anyone in the world!

I took his dear face between my two hands and kissed him deeply. "I love you," I whispered. "You, Greg Eldridge. And the only thing I really want from you is your love in return."

"You have it, honey! You know that, don't you?"

We were in each other's arms, hugging and kissing the close way we used to. And in that wonderful moment I felt sorry for Steve, and forgave him. And I knew I wouldn't press charges. Someday, with a little bit of luck, his bitterness would disappear and he'd know the kind of special love we have!

We sold the house in Westwind Dell and moved back to a city apartment. With the money from the house, Greg bought into a trucking business. And as soon as I became more relaxed and happy, I got pregnant!

We have no plans to move back to the suburbs. Our life is happy here and our apartment is roomy and within walking distance to everything—especially to our friends' houses! Best of all, Greg is no longer on the road. He works out of his own office now, and I'm always waiting with welcoming arms every night when he gets home." THE END

OUR NEIGHBORHOOD
SEX TEAM
We all played every game

I admit; I saw this title in the True Romance archives and I was sure I'd found a story that would deliver either wife-swapping or key parties. The title turned out to be completely misleading, but "Our Neighborhood Sex Team" is still one of the wildest stories I read while I was doing my research for this collection. A narrator who's trapped in a loveless marriage with an abusive alcoholic, living next door to the neighborhood slut, surrounded by gossiping housewives—and an ending you're just not going to believe.

Even before we get to that ending, though, "Our Neighborhood Sex Team" goes to 11, as Nigel says in This Is Spinal Tap, and stays there. This the sort of story that makes people laugh at romance, and now that it's had a chance to sink in, I'm no longer 100% certain that the anonymous author wasn't trying to tell us what's ridiculous about the genre by sneaking in a deliberate parody. Well, if it is a joke, it's an awfully entertaining one.

When I opened the door to Kay Worth's house that afternoon I had no idea I was taking the most important step in my life. I handed Kay the two loaves of banana nut bread she had ordered from me, and she ushered me into the living room.

"Here she is, girls," she said to the six young women sitting around and sipping their coffee. "Ronnie Dines, the best little baker in town." She took a whiff of the freshly baked bread, rolled her eyes ecstatically, and they all laughed. She introduced me to the gang, saying, "You little old tired housewives—if you want the best baked things you ever tasted, give your orders to Ronnie. You can tell your husbands you baked his favorite pie."

A cute girl, looking every bit the newlywed, said, "I'm your customer for life! I can't bake a lick."

Another asked, "Where do you live, Ronnie?"

Before I could answer, Kay chimed in, "Right down the street, next door to Tammy Storm."

One girl moved immediately on the sofa and patted a place for me. "So you live next to Tammy," she said. "Tell me, has she calmed down any? Or is she still chasing every man she sees?"

I thought my face had caught fire, and they laughed. "I don't really know what you're talking about," I said.

Someone else said, "You must have heard that Art Storm took her off the street!" And another asked, "Do they still tear up the house and break the furniture when they fight?"

I shook my head. "It seems all love and devotion as far as I've ever seen. I had no idea—"

"Oh yes," a pretty blond girl chimed in. "I used to live on that block myself. Believe me, they had some knockdown drag-outs!" Then she added, "Tammy was a lovely neighbor, though, when she wanted to be, and she certainly managed her children well, but I couldn't miss what went on there—the battling with her husband over the men who came to see her."

I felt completely bewildered. A lot of men did go to Tammy's house, but men came to my house too—the insurance collector, the furniture collector, the laundry man—so I hadn't thought much about all that traffic to Tammy's.

"Art checks on her constantly. Five times a day he runs in to see what she's up to!" someone else chimed in.

Yes, Tammy's husband came home for lunch, and other times when his job took him by the house, I thought. It had seemed natural enough—till now. Even so, you shouldn't trust hearsay, I told myself sharply. Then a girl called across the room to me, "Does he still call her a tramp? My husband's heard him more than once, over the phone. They're on our party line."

I shook my head. "I only know how it's been when I've seen them together. I've never heard anything but 'honey' and `darling' and such."

"Well, maybe she's settling down—but I can't believe it."

Kay came in carrying a piled tray. "Leave Ronnie alone!" she scolded. "I could have told her about Tammy, but I thought she'd find out herself."

"She's been nice to me," I said lamely, and they all laughed.

The blonde said, "And to your husband too?"

Kay sliced the banana bread, spread it with cream cheese and marmalade, and it was so good I got a standing order right then from every girl there, which meant a lot to me.

Ernie and I had bought a new house in that nice part of town, and I was doing everything I could to help, even to taking orders for home-baked bread. All day, every day, the smell of baking was through my house. Ernie hadn't been too pleased over the way I'd scurried around the neighborhood giving out free samples until the orders started coming in; he was less pleased now that baking kept me so busy. "You work too hard," he said. But it wasn't hard, just confining, and I cleared at least five dollars a day.

"If you get tired and worn-out," he said, "you'll look old and ugly, and I'd rather have a young, pretty wife than the finest house in the land."

"If I get old and ugly, tell me," I laughed, "and I'll throw the stove right out of the window!"

That was just my way of kidding, because it was a new stove and something wonderful, and I was paying for it out of my baking money. I was paying for our new furniture too, because Ernie didn't make such a lot—hadn't for some time, not since we'd left the coast and come back home. Ernie had been sick then, and we'd ended up stone broke. He'd been lucky to get a job with his uncle driving a junk pick-up truck. When Ernie and I found ourselves in such a mess, I'd gone to Uncle Hugh, who was a junk dealer, and asked him to put Ernie to work.

"I don't want Ernie to stick at this job," he told me. "It's no more than a bare living, and I want something better for you." But somehow, Ernie had stuck at that job.

I didn't like it. Not the hardship of it, but the humiliation of it. "She's too proud," my father complained. "She sends Ernie to work every morning as neat as a pin. Slaves, washing and ironing his clothes. Yes—the trouble with Ronnie is she's too proud."

I fought against Ernie staying in that job because it seemed like we were sinking deeper and deeper into a place, class, job, that's wished on you for life and can't be changed. My childhood had been just horrible. Daddy cruel, mean, and working only now and then, and Mom working all the time. I had to stay home, do all the chores and take care of the younger children, so all the education I managed to get was through sixth grade.

I met Ernie in a diner when I was working as a counter girl. At seventeen I married him. We both worked in restaurants for awhile after we were married, then we left town and went to the coast. We made good money there, doing factory work, but, as I said, Ernie's health broke down, so we had to come back home.

I guess it was worrying over the poor present and no-good future that gave me a nervous breakdown. That and Ernie's drinking. I knew he drank when I married him, but it was only after we came back from the coast that he began to go on regular binges. He'd beat me up and spend money that put us deeper in the hole, and I got to where I just couldn't take it and cracked up. I had a terrible time pulling out of it, and Ernie was scared. Maybe he thought I was going to quit him.

"I know it's been hard, honey," he kept telling me over and over, "but things are going to be different."

He made all sorts of promises when I was getting over that breakdown. "I'm going to stop drinking, get us a nice house in a nice part of town, and you can spend your time prettying it up."

He didn't stop drinking or get another job, but he did get the house. Uncle Hugh found it for us, and he let Ernie have the money for the down payment. Just several hundred dollars, because the Storms, who owned the house, were indebted to Uncle Hugh for some favor he'd done them. Besides, they owned several houses on the block and wanted to sell off everything except the house they were living in, which was next door to ours.

It was just wonderful, having your own house. There were three rooms and bath on each side, and the rent from the other side paid the notes on the place. What we'd been paying for rent went toward our debt to Uncle Hugh.

Tammy Storm, my new neighbor, was beautiful, gay, and always so smartly dressed that she looked like a fashion model. I wanted her to like me, but I couldn't feel easy with her, somehow. Right away, though, I liked her husband Art a lot, and I knew he liked me. How could I help it, the way he went out of his way to do things for me when we were getting settled? It would be awfully nice having him for a friend, I told myself. Not that Tammy hadn't been nice to me. She had, and sitting in Kay's living room, listening to all this gossip now, I was horrified. I could hardly believe it, and still. in a way, I did—because things that had looked awfully queer jumped at me now.

Like the time I'd walked in Tammy's back door, like she'd told me to do any time, and found her all wrapped in a man's arms. She was wearing sheer shortie pajamas. She'd said. "This is my uncle, Ronnie darling!" At the time I'd thought it was funny, because I'd never seen anyone act like that with an uncle. And then she had a couple of "cousins" who dropped in often.

And then there was that man who came dashing from her house one night into my yard—and right up to me because I was hanging some dish towels on the line. "Let me go into your house for a minute, won't you?" he panted. "I'm a friend of Tammy's. We grew up together and she's the same as my sister, but Art doesn't like me, and he's on his way home. Tammy said you'd let me wait here. If Art catches me there, he'd blow the roof off. But he'll go back to work pronto when he sees she's alone."

Well, it sounded awfully odd, but even so, I told this man he could wait on my porch. Tammy appeared in a few minutes, laughing, and full of apologies.

"Ronnie, what must you think? Believe it or not, this boy's wife is my best friend."

She took him back to her house for coffee and made me go with them. Ernie was off somewhere drinking, and I was alone, so I went. Her friend left after awhile, but I was still there when Art came in again. There was a sort of queer look in his eyes, but it vanished when he saw me, and when he went off he seemed sort of relieved, "He hates to work at night," Tammy told me. "Honey, he's so jealous it's pitiful, and he has no reason—no reason at all!"

Well, I just thought, she's flighty, and let it go at that. But now—All at once, I felt terribly sorry for her husband. He loved her, and he was simply crazy about his children, a little boy and girl. Tammy seemed to love the children too, but I remembered her laughing, "They're my meal ticket, honey! Even if Art and I broke up, he'd still support me royally for their sake. Children are a great help to a woman, Ronnie. You should have some."

Poor Art, I thought, while the gossip still went on around me. And then the party was breaking up at last, and I was glad. I didn't want to hear any more. Reba Charin gave me a lift home, and Tammy was in her yard. She saw me get out of Reba's car and came over, right straight.

"You're new out here, Ronnie," she said, "and you don't want to get mixed up with the wrong bunch. That Reba Charin is the very meanest person on this earth!"

I said a bit shortly, "She certainly doesn't seem mean."

She stared, amazed. "Darling, it sticks out all over her! Oh, I'm glad I'm not that way. A boy at the airport told me this afternoon, there isn't a mean bone in my body. I'm just back from the airport. Ronnie, I'll never be content till I have a plane of my own! It's the most gorgeous sensation, flying! It gives me a feeling of power, like an eagle ready to swoop down on its prey. Art's against my having a plane, but I will yet! I'm even getting myself a pilot's license, did you know? I'll fly you over the town someday."

"No thanks." I said. "I'll stick to cars."

She had a mind like a grasshopper. "Reba was driving a pretty car. Where did you meet her?"

"At Kay Worth's," I said, and I thought she would explode.

"That idiotic Thursday afternoon club? I wouldn't belong to it for anything in this world!" She went on to lay out the whole bunch. They were all liars with no social standings. Every one of them had more social position than Tammy, I couldn't help but think. Art Storm was all right in every way, but he didn't stand high socially. I hadn't ever thought of social position, having none myself, but the way Tammy carried on got me thinking of it, and I knew what she was saying was prompted largely by envy or downright viciousness.

"Don't worry," I said. "I won't get mixed up with them. They're so far above me socially, they wouldn't think of including me in their group."

And then she struck out at me. "You do very well, darling, for the wife of a junk collector. Very well indeed."

I saw red, but I said, "That's something. To do well for your position, whatever that position is, is really something. If everyone could say that, the world would be a better place."

"How right you are," she said, and turned back into her yard.

Ernie came home drunk that night, his first big drunk since we'd been in the new house. He made such a disturbance the people on the other side called Art to come right over and stop it. He came in a hurry, but Ernie was uncontrollable. "Look," Art told me, "I know the boys at headquarters, and I'm going to have Ernie locked up till he's sober." He dragged my husband out of his car and took him off to jail.

Immediately, Tammy came over, very cool and reproachful. "Darling, if we'd had any idea your husband drank, we wouldn't have sold you the house. This is a respectable neighborhood. I don't think it's going to stand such carryings-on. If it doesn't stop immediately, you'll be asked to move. "

I said, "Haven't you been here several years? Have you been asked to move?"

"My husband doesn't drink," she informed me haughtily.

"I understand you've been known to raise a roughhouse for other reasons!"

She jumped at me then, and slapped me across the face. I was so amazed I just stood staring—but only for a moment. Then fury got me, and I landed on her like a ton of bricks. Maybe I'd have killed her if a passerby hadn't come running and pulled me off her. Tammy was screaming and cursing me when Art got back. "What's the matter?" he cried. "What's going on?"

Tammy talked and I talked. I said the fights I'd been hearing almost nightly in the Storms' house topped tonight's little fuss in ours. That started Tammy screaming abuses about me again. "She's little and shy and pretty, and thinks she can get by with murder. She's pulled the wool over our eyes!" she flung at Art, "but she's not fooling me. If she thinks I'm going to stand for what she did to me, she's crazy!"

Art tried to lead her out of the house, but he finally had to carry her. She was screaming like a maniac.

I wanted to see Art and thrash this out with him. I couldn't go over there, but I had a feeling he'd come here, and he did. as soon as Tammy quieted down.

"I-I can't do anything with her," he sighed. "God knows I've tried." He couldn't seem to stop talking then. "I was crazy in love with her at first—now I stay on for the children. I could maybe take them, but they're hers too, and it's a terrible thing to take a woman's children from her."

"I'm sorry," I whispered. And then apologetically, "I guess I shouldn't have mixed with her, but when she slapped me I just saw red. I'd been hearing things about her, and—" I stopped, embarrassed.

"I know she's talked about," he said wearily. "It humiliates a man. She's never been the least bit of help. This property came to me from my father. She's gone through everything—just about. I was a fool, I let her pull me around like that, but I loved her. Then later, I tried only to hold her steady—for the kids."

"I'm sorry," I murmured.

"Life's funny," he said. "Here I am trying to make a go of it with Tammy, you're trying with Ernie. I'd give ten years of my life to have you for my wife, Ronnie. From the minute I laid eyes on you, I was crazy for you."

"Oh no! No—"

"It's nothing to be ashamed of," he said. "I just love you—"

I could hardly breathe. I said, "I don't see how you can love me, Art. I'm not beautiful like Tammy—"

"You're beautiful," he said, "in your own way. I like you, besides loving you. With Tammy it was never like that."

That lifted me to the sky. But I said, and meant it, "Maybe we'd better give up the house and move away—"

"No!" he said violently. "At least you can be here where I can look out for you! Maybe you'll get to feeling for me the way I feel for you. Maybe we'll be able to work out something."

"Oh no!" I said. "No!"

"Are you so terribly sold on Ernie?"

"No," I said, "but he's my husband."

"And Tammy's my wife. But we could change all that! Maybe for everything I've got, she'd let me go. She wouldn't let me have the children, of course. They're hers —she loves them, and as long as she has them, she can get money out of me."

I said, "I like you a whole lot, but I don't love you, and there's Ernie. He's my husband and—I guess I'll have to stick with him."

"I'm not after an affair with you. I'm after you for keeps, Ronnie. Up to now I've stuck with Tammy because of the children, but there's no sticking for me if I can get you."

He had me in his arms then, kissing me—and I couldn't begin to tell what those kisses did to me. They tore me away from everything I'd always held to, and I thought that nothing mattered except to give in to those kisses, and the storm of feeling they aroused in me. I could feel the wild beat of his heart. But it wasn't love with me, the way it was with him. It was passion, the most overwhelming passion I had ever known, and in a frenzy of nerves and terror and desire, I began to cry. I tore myself out of his arms. "Stay away from me! Don't you touch me! Because if you do, I won't be able to resist you!"

He swept me back into his arms, held me against his heart. He kept kissing me until I couldn't think, couldn't see, couldn't do a thing in the world but feel! And while I was like that, he took me. And I was dead—dead to everything except him!

When the passion had subsided and the radiance had died, I tell you I wanted to die! But Art looked as if he had just come alive. "You're my girl now!" he exulted. "I'm married to you now, Ronnie! Do you hear me? I'm married to you!"

"No!" I said. "You're married to Tammy, and I'm just as bad as she is."

"No!" he said. "There's been no one but Ernie with you. You loved him, married him, now you're through with him. You're going to love me and marry me!"

But I cried bitterly, "I begged you not to touch me!"

"I want to take care of you, love you, work for you!" he said. He was so sweet, so gentle. It was wonderful having someone want to shield me.

But in the dead of night, wide awake, I faced the fact that if I broke with Ernie, it would be the ruin of him, I was sure. And if Art broke with Tammy, it would be his ruin, too. He'd lose his good name and his job, and he'd lose his children—Tammy would see to that! Oh, he might win their custody, but he'd lose them a different way.

Of course—and the thought shook my heart—we might have our own children, but there was no guarantee. All these years I'd told myself it was Ernie's fault that we had none, but how did I know it wasn't mine? And even if Art and I had children, he'd still want the love of those he had now. And the memory of this night would he with us always, turning uglier with the years. He'd had one unfaithful woman, and I couldn't see how he'd better himself marrying another.

You're going to stick to Ernie and try to be a decent woman, I told myself. I slipped to my knees beside my bed, and asked God to forgive me and to help me go straight the rest of my life.

It was daylight before I went to sleep, and at nine o'clock Ernie came home. He was in an ugly mood because I'd let Art turn him in. He threw me on the floor and flayed me with his belt until I thought I'd never be able to walk or lie on my back again. I gritted my teeth, choked down my screams, and took it. I felt that I deserved punishment from Ernie. But that night I had it out with him.

"I'm not taking your abuse again—ever," I told him. "You're going to stop drinking, get another job, and treat me right—or I'm leaving and I won't come back!"

"Then leave me," he said. "When the urge to drink comes, I've got to drink."

"I'm not staying with an incurable alcoholic," I said. "that's final—I've had it!"

"You've got some other man on the string!" he accused.

"I'm not out for another man. I'm out for security and decency—with you, Ernie, if I can have it." Well, we made up and he made some fine-sounding promises. "Just live up to them," I warned.

Art phoned me the next morning. "Meet me in front of the courthouse. I've got to talk to you."

"Okay," I said. "There are some things I must say to you, too." I got myself prettied up and drove to the courthouse. His car was parked there, and when he came up to me his nearness unnerved me completely.

"Ronnie—" he began, and I said, "no—let me do the talking!" And I gave it to him straight. "We have to forget that night. I'm—crazy about you, but I don't love you." I told him all the things I'd recognized after he'd left me that night. "I'm just as bad as Tammy," I finished.

He put his hand over mine, but I jerked away from him violently. "Don't touch me—I'd give in to you, so don't you so much as touch me again—ever! If you come around or touch me, I'll hate you —I'll end up killing myself! I mean it, Art! I'm ashamed and sorry and—scared."

"Darling," he said, "please—it'll go right for us, somehow." His voice was like a kiss. "Try not to worry so much. Just remember I love you!"

How I got home, I don't know. That day, and all that followed, I worked like nobody's business. But no matter how I drove myself, Art beat continually at the closed door of my mind. "Think of me," he begged. I swore I wouldn't—and now look at me!

The worst part was living next door. I had to see and hear him sometimes, coming and going. And each time my heart swelled and called out to him. I wanted him in a way I'd never wanted anybody or anything in all my life!

I got so jumpy that Ernie and I quarreled again, and he went on a drunk that nearly cost him his job. But instead, and for my sake, Uncle

Hugh kept him, and switched him to work that called for office duties, too. He still drove the truck, but he had an office with a girl to keep records, answer the phone, and such.

"What kind of girl is she?" I asked Ernie. "To work in that isolated place with a bunch of men—most of them drinkers?"

"She's okay," Ernie spoke up gruffly. "Not too young or pretty, but okay."

Uncle Hugh told me more about this Nettie Crane. She was unmarried and was a pretty heavy drinker herself, but only after hours. "She's real tough," Uncle Hugh said. "When she speaks out, the boys jump."

I only half-listened, having other things on my mind. I knew Ernie wasn't going to improve his status any, but I could stand that if he'd quit drinking. He griped over anything, but if I complained whenever he kept back a good part of his pay check, he'd give me a back-handed slap in the face.

I saw Tammy all the time. We passed each other without speaking. But she did everything she could to aggravate me. One day I invited Kay Worth and her crowd for lunch, intending to serve in the backyard. The table was all set up when Tammy had a man come to take her leaves and burn them along with heaps of smelly trash. We had to gather everything up and go in the house.

She found more ways to torment me! Fire trucks came screaming to my house three separate times. The phone would ring a dozen times a day, and when I answered there was only dead silence. Packages were delivered C.O.D.—things I wouldn't dream of buying. I didn't take them, of course, but storekeepers began to get down on me.

After that, the stream of men started. Men to demonstrate household appliances, real estate men with "appointments" to show me property. I knew Tammy was in back of it all, but I didn't know how to stop her. Then one day my phone rang and a deep, deathly voice breathed, "The doctor, the ambulance, and the undertaker will come for you—soon." I hung up, trembling. This was too much! I called the chief of police. "It's Tammy Storm, I'm certain of it," I said. "I don't want to make trouble for Art, but can you stop her? Please!"

"I'll stop her, all right," he said grimly. "I know Tammy from way back—" He was still on the wire when I heard a siren.

"Listen!" I cried. "She wasn't fooling!" He hung up, and I ran to the door. It was the ambulance, all right, and inside of three minutes, the doctor and undertaker arrived. The whole neighborhood came running, and I was beside myself!

Suddenly a police car came dashing up, and the chief himself got out. He dispersed the crowd, sent the ambulance and the others away, and marched himself next door to Tammy Storm. What he threatened her with I don't know but the plaguing stopped, and our local newspaper came out with a piece on the front page exonerating me of all the things laid at my door. But it didn't name Tammy, out of consideration for Art.

After that, she simply paraded around her place where I'd be sure to see her, especially when Guy Tolan was there. Guy was a pilot and very good-looking. He had a regular run, big passenger planes. Kay Worth said he also had money, and that Tammy was out to marry him.

"You mean, she'd give up a man like Art, just like that?" I gasped.

Kay shrugged. "Art's not so much." The most awful rage laid hold of me! Art is all, I thought, that any woman could ask of life. And it wasn't passion that made me like that. It was love. Outraged love.

I just sat there in Kay's kitchen, drinking coffee, and there was tumult within me. I was in love with Art! And what was I going to do about it now that I knew? When I got home, I was limp with exhaustion, and every nerve in my body was screaming.

Tammy took the children to their dancing lessons that afternoon, and while they were gone, Art came to see me. I don't think I'd have answered the bell if I'd known who it was. His nearness set me shaking like a tree in a hurricane.

He came in and closed the door, and I backed away from him. "Ronnie," he said, "how is it with you now? About me?"

"I'm still powerless against you," I said, "so don't touch me, Art." He came toward me. I kept backing away, and my hand reached out and caught a heavy candlestick. "I love you!" I said. "I love you! But if you touch me, I swear I'll bash your head in!"

He stopped and looked at me strangely. "Loving me, you'd crown me, Ronnie?"

"Yes," I said. "Because if I didn't—you know what would happen. And that's not going to happen to me again, ever."

He dropped into a chair. "All right," he said heavily. "I won't touch you." Then, abruptly he said, "I'm going to get free of Tammy. Loving you, I can't stay with her."

"No!" I said. "If there's a break, let it come from her—if you want your children to love and respect you."

"What are you talking about?" he asked.

I said, "Guy Tolan."

His face went brick-red. "I know she's been hanging out at the airport," he said, "but I thought she was getting her pilot's license. I didn't know there was anything with Tolan."

"There's a lot you don't know, Art," I said, but kindly, because I couldn't bear to see him shamed.

"I'll catch them," he flamed suddenly. "I'll divorce her!"

"Your children!" I pleaded. "I want them to love you like they do now."

He got up, prowled around the room. "To stand around waiting—"

"If it's coming," I said, "let it come. Wait!"

The fury and outrage left his face. "Then will you get your divorce and come to me?"

"It's what I want," I said. "I warned Ernie I wouldn't stick if he didn't mend his ways, and he hasn't."

"Does he abuse you?" he demanded.

"Yes, but it doesn't matter."

"It does matter." he said hotly. "Ronnie, quit him! Now!"

"Not now," I said. "If we wait, it'll all work out."

I was a wreck when he left, wanting him so desperately and holding back even from the touch of him.

Ernie came home late that night—not drunk, but all lit up, and in good humor. He looked the way he used to look when he was courting me. "At last," he beamed, "things are beginning to look bright. The world's a mighty nice place, do you know that?"

"It's a very pleasant place to me right now," I said.

He laughed. "If you'd unbend a little, stop being a prude, you could get some good out of life. But all you want is this house all paid for, fine furniture, and a husband with a white collar job. Pride —that's what you've got in big chunks, and doesn't the Bible say 'Pride goeth before a fall' or something like that?"

"There's a difference between pride and self-respect, Ernie. I don't care so much about pride, but I'd like to keep my self-respect."

The rest of that week, Ernie was in the same strange mood, never really drunk, but not sober, either. "Come on," he said one night. "I'm joining a crowd, going bowling and on to the fight. Come with me, have a couple of beers—act human and womanly, for a change."

"I don't want to bowl or go to a fight," I told him. "I've been baking all day and I'm tired to death. Somebody's got to pay for this house and all that's in it."

"I'm sick and tired of hearing about ` this house and all that's in it.' Know something? I'm not sweating my life away over a house when the woman in it doesn't give a damn about me."

I couldn't say a thing then, because that's how it was. But Ernie had made it that way, a long time before I'd met and fallen in love with Art.

It was the very next day that Uncle Hugh came to see me. "Ronnie," he said, "Ernie's gone on that girl Nettie Crane. I opened my mouth and sort of gasped, and he went on. "I-I-well, I caught 'em together in the shack at the junkyard. You know what I mean. You don't need that louse, Ronnie. Divorce him. I'll testify for you."

"Thank you, Uncle Hugh," I said.

Ernie was delighted when I told him I was going to divorce him. "I wish we'd split up way back," he said. But when he was leaving with his clothes and things, he stopped to say, "You're okay in your own way, Ronnie—but your way's not my way, see? And a fellow has to go his way."

"You're right, Ernie," I said. "Good-bye and good luck."

I cried that night, though, because my marriage had been such a failure. Next day, on my knees working in my pansy bed, I heard Tammy on the other side of the fence. She said to someone, "Yes, her husband's left her. And it's a sorry woman who can't hold a junkman. I'd die of shame!" I thought, she'd die of shame if she knew I've beaten her time! But I didn't feel triumphant.

"What'll she do now?" Tammy's visitor asked, and Tammy laughed. "Go on with her baking and scrubbing and cooking. You know how soft Art is—he's reducing the payments on the house because he's sorry for her. Well, my sympathy is for poor Ernie. How he stood that vicious little drudge so long, I'll never understand."

She talked everywhere, but it didn't turn people against me. Everyone was kind to me, and the divorce went through without any trouble. The day it was granted, Ernie and Nettie were married. I didn't care the least bit for Ernie, but it gives you a queer feeling to have the man who was your husband marry someone else the very minute he's free of you.

Next day Tammy spoke to me for the first time since the night of our trouble. "You, poor thing, you look like a hag!" she said sweetly. "Well, it's a crushing experience, I guess, being divorced. But Ernie's holding up, I want you to know. And his new wife's hitting it high. Everyone's being lovely to them. Guy Tolan, you know, is giving them supper tonight, at Crosby's. Art's out of town, so I'm invited. And late this afternoon I'm giving them a plane ride—did you know I have my license now? Guy's renting the plane for me. Nettie and Ernie are all excited about going up." And then, as malicious as can be, she said, "Along about five-thirty I'll buzz over your house. Watch for us!"

Sure enough she flew over my house, and so frighteningly low I thought she'd take the roof off. In a flash she was gone. She gained altitude, came back and began stunting. She put a show on, coming and going, circling and swooping, and the roar was something awful. And then, there was one terrible minute when I thought she was going to land the little plane right in my backyard. What is she trying to do? I screamed inside myself. And then I knew she was in trouble. The plane was making horrible choking sounds. It barely missed my house and plunged into Tammy's—clean through it—and crashed in the other side!

Never in a nightmare could I have dreamed anything so hideous! The noise! The flame gushing up! The air filled with fragments! And Tammy's house all smoke and fiery fury. And the heat, the burning heat!

Without thinking, I'd thrown myself face down on the ground, and I guess that was all that saved me. Burning debris rained down all around me, and then I heard the sirens wailing as the police cars, the fire trucks, the ambulance, raced into our street. I struggled to my knees, to my feet, and tried to run. And all I could think of was poor Ernie! It was a wail in me like the sirens. I'd lived with him for years; I'd once loved him. Now he was dead.

I guess I fainted then, because the next thing I knew, I was in the hospital. When I came to, babbling questions, the nurse on duty said, "I'm sorry, Mrs. Dines, they're all dead. Mrs. Storm's house was destroyed and yours burned to the ground. It's the most horrible thing that's ever happened here."

"Yes," I said dully.

"And poor Mr. Storm!" the nurse said sadly. "What a shock for him. He was in Austin on business. You know," she hesitated, "he must have thought you were on the plane with them. When they reached him by phone and told him, he asked, 'Mrs. Dines? Not the new wife—the other one! What about her?' They told him you weren't in the plane. Then he called the hospital and said he was flying back immediately. It's God's mercy his children were at their grandmother's. At least he still has them."

I wanted to stay awake until Art came, but they gave me a shot, and I slept the night through. When I woke next morning another nurse was on duty. She told me Art had been here. "He sat in this room for three hours. Mrs. Dines," she said.

My room was filled with flowers. Kay Worth and her crowd, all the people I baked for, wanted to visit me, but the doctor had given orders I was to be kept quiet.

I lay quiet, but in my mind and heart, there was no quiet. If I'd let Art go ahead and get his divorce, I mourned, this wouldn't have happened. He'd have had it long before I had mine, and Tammy would have been somewhere else.

I said that to Art when he came. He'd put the nurse out and taken me into his arms, and I went all to pieces. "If I had let you go ahead," I sobbed, "Guy would have taken Tammy away—"

"No," he said, "it wouldn't have been any different. Tammy would have stuck around to goad you any way she could. She was down on you because she knew I was strong for you." He went on after a minute. "The way things are now, the children can remember her with love. They like you, will learn to love you. No, you weren't wrong to make me wait. You were right. We've played square with everyone, Ronnie. so there's nothing I'm ashamed of."

"I'm ashamed of myself," I whispered. "For what I did, that night."

"You've got nothing to be ashamed of," Art said, almost angrily. "What we did—we couldn't help. It was an act of love, not a sin. I have no regrets, Ronnie. You loved me even before you gave yourself to me. But you were afraid to admit it to yourself because you were a decent woman. You fought the impulse that drew you to me because you didn't want to be like—Tammy." He shut his eyes, as if to blot out the unhappy memories that must have suddenly flooded him. "Knowing that you wanted me and needed me," he continued, "gave me the courage and the strength to carry on. I would have waited for you forever, but now that isn't necessary."

He held me tenderly, running his hand gently over the back of my head. "You forget," he went on, "how you held me off—because you thought it wasn't right." He smiled. "I loved you all the more for the strength of character you showed. I was miserable and needed you, but you fought for your principle—and won."

My lips found his. We clung together for the longest time. It wasn't until we heard the nurse come in that we separated from each other. But the separation was only for a short time.

We were married the day after I left the hospital. Art's children are my own now. The terrible past is behind us. What concerns us is the future—because we've dedicated our lives to it. THE END

MY HUSBAND'S LOVE POTION FROM VIETNAM

He thought it was the only thing that would
make him a man again

American soldiers returning from Vietnam often faced profound emotional struggles, not only because of what they had experienced overseas, but also because of the way they were treated by opponents of the war back in the States. The wives and girlfriends of these soldiers would often share the burden, not understanding why their loved ones had changed, but hoping they could help make things right again.

This could be dark territory for True Love and True Romance, especially if the soldier had gotten hooked on drugs during his tour of duty. "My Husband's Love Potion from Vietnam!" is lighthearted by comparison; here, Dean's troubles are strictly psychosomatic. "He thought he had to drink some stupid white tasteless powder before he could make love to me, his wife!" the narrator exclaims. Luckily for this couple, she's able to snap him out of it pretty quickly.

I was helping Dean unpack. Actually, I didn't want to let him out of my sight. When he'd called from McCord Air Base and said he was home from Vietnam I'd gone through the ceiling. I hadn't expected him home before January first, and here he was, home three weeks

53

before Christmas.

"What's this?" I held up a long piece of what looked to be silk cloth.

"That's a yuki cloth," he laughed.

"What's a yuki cloth?" I asked.

"You put it around your head and yuki," he grabbed me and whirled me around the room. "Boy, are you gullible? That's just a piece of silk that I thought was pretty so I got it for you. I guess you could use it as a scarf."

"Or a G-string," I said boldly.

"Pretty bold, huh?" he kissed me, a long, hard kiss that made my toes tingle. "You been a good girl?"

"I have, have you?" I countered.

"You know better than to ask," he said. "Hell, I was stuck way the hell out on the base all the time."

"But what about R and R leave?" I asked him.

"Sydney, Australia, I'll take you there some day, honey," he said. "What a swinging place. No kidding, it was great!"

"Tell me about it, I mean the war, was it bad?"

He pulled me down beside him on the bed. "Who wants to talk war when we can talk about love?"

He pressed me back on the bed and his hands went over me lightly, as though remembering each curve. We hadn't had much time together before he had had to go to Vietnam. Dean had enlisted in the air force for three years and even though I'd known him before he'd gone into service it wasn't until he was home on leave that we really began to get serious about each other. It happens that way sometimes, a person goes away and comes back a different human being.

Dean had changed from a high school kid to a man by the time he'd been away six months. He had even grown taller if that were possible and certainly he looked handsomer with the clean cut look his uniform gave him.

"I know, you like to go out with a handsome uniform," he teased me after our first date. "It has nothing to do with me."

"Right. I'm being patriotic, I feel sorry for you."

"Show me how sorry you feel," he urged.

Dean and I did a lot of things we shouldn't have before he asked me to marry him. I mean we weren't kids and I knew I loved him and holding out and being coy wasn't in my book. Dean knew how I felt. His big drawback was knowing he would be in the service another two and a half years and he didn't want to get himself a wife until he was free.

After he went away we wrote a lot of letters and spent more money on phone calls than either one of us could afford. I was working as a waitress in a diner at the time and although the tips were good they weren't that fancy that I could spend my money supporting the telephone company. If I hadn't been living at home I'd have never made it moneywise.

One day Dean showed up on a weekend pass He said let's get married, this is driving me bugs. I quit my job and followed him to the air base where we made arrangements to be married. For a while I lived alone in town and Dean became a commuting husband. I got a job to keep myself and in a way it was lots of fun. Until Dean got the news he'd be going to Vietnam. That was during the time when a lot of servicemen were called up and regulars were sent right out to Vietnam.

Up to then our life hadn't been ideal but we'd been together. The last night we were together I clung to my husband with a kind of dread. I had a feeling I was going to lose him and I didn't know what to do.

"Be good," Dean kept murmuring in my ear. "Don't go out with other guys or I'll wipe you out."

"As if I would."

"I love you! You think it'll be like this when I get back? Nothing changed?"

"What can change?" I held him close. "The way we love each other it'll be better."

"I don't know. . . ." he seemed concerned. "People change—maybe something will happen to me."

"Stop that," I urged him. "Nothing will happen. I'll put a double whammy good luck on you before you go."

"Okay, double whammy me," he buried his face in my neck. I

wasn't at all sure he wasn't crying a little bit. I know I cried a lot when I returned home. I was married and I wasn't. I had a husband and I didn't. All I had were letters, thin pieces of paper telling me my whole life and heart were out there in some lousy jungle. Now I read papers and watched late news on television and worried. If it hadn't been for my job I'd have really cracked up.

Then suddenly it was over. I hadn't expected him for three weeks when the phone rang and he asked if I'd like to meet him at the airport at ten o'clock that night. Meet him? I went out there at seven to make sure I got a parking place and just to be there. When he came striding toward me my knees nearly buckled and I just stood there, I couldn't even run to meet him. He looked different. He was tanned, of course, and he had a small mustache, but he looked so much older somehow.

I had a surprise for him. Two months before, in anticipation of his coming home, I'd rented a small apartment for us. The furniture was stuff I'd picked up in secondhand stores and it needed a good coat of paint, but we'd be alone, that was what mattered to me. When Dean saw it he said it was a great place and by the time he got through fixing it the landlord would raise the rent one hundred percent.

Unpacking for him now I asked him what he thought of the car I'd picked up for a reasonable price.

"Great," he said. "You're a pretty good manager, I just might keep you on if you prove yourself."

"Prove myself?"

He laughed and grabbed me. "I've waited a long time for this," his voice was a little shaky. "Did you miss me this way?"

"You know I did," I felt like a virgin bride in my husband's arms.

"I dreamed about us like this," he whispered.

"There were girls there."

"You can have them," he said. "Some of the guys came back with stories but I won't go into that. I didn't want to be with anyone but you...."

"Wait, let me take this off," I whispered.

Dean turned and pushed the luggage off the bed. Then he leaned over and took something out of the small duffel bag on the floor. It was a small canister with weird writing on it.

"What's that?" I asked, curious.

Dean grinned. "Wait and see," he went toward the bathroom. I heard him running the water a second, then he was back, the bathroom plastic glass in his hands. "Here, take a sip."

"But what is it?" I peered into colorless water.

"A love potion," Dean looked a little embarrassed.

"Love potion? Where did you get junk like that?"

"In Vietnam."

"You've got to be kidding," I laughed then. "You don't believe things like that, do you, honey?"

"Listen, don't knock it. I mean just because we don't understand a thing doesn't mean it isn't so."

"You actually believe that junk can. . . ."

"Up the libido, make you sexy as all hell," he said. "I've seen it happen, no kidding. Guys were getting it when they could, it's really hard to come by. I guess it's one of those native secrets."

"But, listen, what's it supposed to do?"

"Heighten your senses, make you sexier, more aware," he said. "Dean, what if it's bad for us?"

"Hell, no, I've seen guys take it and go out. . . ."

"I don't like it," I shook my head.

"Come on, honey, don't be an ugly American, try it. The world's a pretty big place, you know, there're lots of things we don't know about but which are pretty positive proof that every culture has something good to offer."

"Boy, you sound like our old history teacher."

"Don't I?" he laughed with me. "Okay, I'll go first."

He took a sip of the colorless liquid. I watched him. Nothing happened. He handed me the glass. I sipped it carefully. It tasted like plain water.

"I think someone sold you a phony love potion," I told my husband. "That tastes like water."

"Sure, it's supposed to, what do you think it'd taste like, some exotic herb?"

"At the very least," I put my hands on my husband's flat stomach. "I'm glad you're not fat," I said. "I'd hate it if you were fat."

"And I'm glad you are what you are," his hands went over me, remembering. I was remembering, too. Together we explored and touched and remembered and it was so wild and fantastic that when we were through making love I turned to my husband and said: "Again, Dean, I can't get enough of you yet. . . ."

"I can't either," he said. "It's like we can stay here like this the rest of our lives."

"And starve," I giggled. "Two starving corpses still making love."

We made love again and then we got up and ate and time meant nothing to us for a few days. Dean continued the ritual of the love potion. We did a little routine with it now. We pretended to speak magic words over it and we sipped it slowly, exchanging the cup and taking turns. It was foolish and wild and right for that time. What else did we have to do but return to the sanity of everyday living after what Dean had been through and the separation we'd had to endure?

Finally it was time to think of the outside world. I told Dean I had to go to work or my boss would think I was dead and he'd pay insurance benefits.

"Good. Then we could live like this for another three months," Dean said.

He didn't mean it. Dean had things to stir him, too. He wanted to go to a trade school on the GI Bill and he arranged for an interview. We saw my family and had a big celebration dinner with them. Then we visited with Dean's father; his mother had died when he was fourteen. Always we returned to our small apartment and our love potion and the silly game we played.

Dean and I both agreed that we wouldn't have children for a while, not until he finished trade school and was able to support me and a baby. I wasn't particularly anxious to work anyway. I didn't mind doing my share now, but I preferred a family to being a working wife.

One night I asked some old friends over for some drinks and a buffet supper. Olive and her husband Bill had been school friends of ours, and they were interested in hearing all about Vietnam. The other couple were older and had small children. They lived in the building and we'd become friendly.

I can't remember what brought up the subject of Vietnamese habits but suddenly I heard Dean telling our guests about his love potion.

"Come off it, Dean," Bill hooted. "You really get sold on that stuff?"

"Ask my wife," Dean beamed. "Does she or does she not look satisfied?"

"Dean!" I was embarrassed. "I'm sure our guests don't want to hear about our love life."

"I'm just asking for a testimonial, honey," Dean said. "Like I was saying. You get away from home and you find out there're lots out there we don't even begin to know about. Like talking to the dead and raising the dead. . . ."

"Dean, you're getting morbid," I felt irritated with him. "Let's talk about something interesting, like Olive's baby...."

"How did you guess?" she shrieked.

"You told me, idiot," I said good naturedly "I'm glad."

"I'm not. 'Somebody else is taking my place,' " Bill sang.

From then on it was a fun evening. We talked about babies and Bill did his silly imitations. They all left around midnight.

"Phoo, I'm tired," I said to Dean. "Let's just leave all this and do it in the morning."

"Okay by me," Dean said, checking to see that the door was locked and lights off. "I'll be right with you, hon."

He went into the bathroom then came out quickly. "Hey, what happened?" He was holding the small canister of his old love potion. He was shaking it upside down.

"Oh, that," I felt nervous for no real reason. "I was cleaning in there and the stupid thing fell and the top came off and it all spilled. Well, not all, I mean there wasn't much left in there anyway."

"Oh, no," Dean said.

"Honey, what's the difference?" I said. "It was fun while it lasted but we don't need that junk."

He didn't answer me. I heard him brushing his teeth and then he came into the bedroom looking awfully sober. I kissed him and said,

"Don't look like you lost your best friend, I'm here." I thought it was all kind of silly really. So he'd lost his love potion, so it would have been used up in time anyway and I was getting tired of the silly game now that we were back in a married routine.

I got into bed and waited for my husband. He went out into the kitchen again and I heard the water running.

I was almost asleep by the time he came back. He leaned over and kissed me, said good night and turned on his side. I wasn't unhappy. I was tired from preparing for guests and I went off to sleep happily.

I awoke late the next morning. The first thing I noticed was that Dean was out of bed. He was puttering around in the kitchen again. I yawned, went into the bathroom to brush my teeth and then joined him in the kitchen.

"Caught you with another woman," I teased as I poured myself some coffee. "What's the big idea of deserting me and my warm bed, sir?"

"Oh, I didn't want to wake you," he sipped his coffee. "I think I'll go out and get some papers."

"Mind if I just go back to bed?" I glanced at the clock. "It's only nine o'clock! Are you feeling okay?"

"Sure! I had a little too much to drink last night. I'll wake up and get the papers, clear my head."

"Then when it's cleared come back and unfuzz mine," I said.

Dean didn't answer me. I went back to bed and fell asleep. When I woke up it was nearly eleven. Dean wasn't in the apartment. He hadn't even left a note. That wasn't like him unless he was having trouble with the car. I got up and dressed and began to straighten out the apartment. I even felt a little miffed that he hadn't stayed around to help me.

Dean came in shortly after noon. He brought a lemon chiffon pie and some rolls from my favorite bakery. He seemed his old self again. I told myself I'd been foolish to imagine something was wrong, it was what he said, he'd had too much to drink and he was tired.

But it was more than that. Dean stayed up until nearly one o'clock that night watching a late movie on television. When I reminded him he had to go to school in the morning and I had to go to work he told me not to worry but go ahead and get my sleep. I did. That night and for the next half dozen nights because Dean didn't come near me.

Finally, on a warm spring Friday night after we'd come back from a movie, I moved in on my husband. I pretended to go to sleep but I waited for him to crawl into bed beside me then I turned and put my arms around him.

"Hey, what's wrong? You fall in love with a book or something?"

"That's funny," he didn't sound like it was funny. "Nothing's wrong. I've got lots on my mind. I'm not sure I want to continue in this damned school, I'd rather get a job."

"Honey, we talked about that," I said. "This is the hardest way but the best in the long run. It won't be long now, you'll be in a job before you know it. Besides, we're not starving, we're doing all right."

"With you working," he said darkly.

"You, too. I saved all that GI pay," I said. "Come on, let's forget money now. I love you and I've missed you..."

I was making advances to my husband as my mother would say. I was running my hands up and down his warm flesh and kissing him with tiny butterfly kisses all over his face and into his ear. Other times this had aroused him immediately—now he lay tense beside me. Suddenly he jumped up out of bed nearly knocking me over.

"Stop it, stop it," he yelled.

"Dean, what is it, what's wrong?" I became frightened. "What did I do?"

"You know damned well what you did," he screamed at me.

"I don't, I don't," I screamed right back.

"You deliberately threw away that love potion! You know I can't ... you know I need it in order to . . . you know I have to have it before..."

Dean was babbling, but I got the picture. Dear God, he thought he had to drink some stupid white tasteless powder before he could make love to me, his wife! I couldn't believe it! Dean wasn't a stupid man, he was an intelligent young man who should know better than to believe a silly superstition! And hadn't he guessed I'd gone along with it as mere love play? That drinking a love potion hadn't meant a thing to me. I loved my husband and sex and passion came as easily as taking a drink of water.

"Dean, you're acting like a child," I said. "You can't believe seriously that we were drinking something potent."

"That's your small mind talking again," he said. "Just because something isn't part of your life you won't accept it. Well, I know better. I've been there and back! I know it works!"

"It works because you're young and virile and we love each other," I screamed at him. "Come here and let me show you you've nothing to worry about!"

"You'd like that, wouldn't you?" he sneered at me. "Put me down, make me out to be a nut!"

"Dean, you're wrong. I'm really being sensible about this," I said quietly. "All right, we won't make love, just come to bed."

He came to bed like a willful little boy. I couldn't believe it even then. I turned to kiss him good night. I edged closer to him. He didn't resist me. But a chill ran over me when I realized I was also doing nothing to him or for him. Every bit of common sense in me told me I was wrong, that Dean just imagined that silly love potion made him virile but here was proof positive. He held me quietly but didn't make a move to take me, make love to me or even talk to me. He went to sleep holding me in his arms.

I had to go to work the next morning so was out of bed and dressed by the time Dean woke up. I put on some coffee and wondered if I dared talk to Dean about last night when he popped into the shower. By the time he was ready to drop me off at work it was too late to do much talking.

I can't remember waiting on customers that day. I was in a fog most of the time. On the one hand I told myself to take it easy, guys who had been in Vietnam came back with odd notions, a thing like that was bound to change a man. On the other hand I was sure that Dean was using that love potion stuff as a crutch of some kind. But why? I loved him, I was his wife, we'd been beautifully compatible before. Why did he feel he needed a love potion now in order to make love to me?

The awful part about this was that I couldn't go to anyone and talk about it. I mean what would I say? "Do you know where I could purchase some love potion for my husband and myself?"

Great! They'd haul me away somewhere with a question like that.

I was taking a coffee break when Olive walked in. Olive had grown big with child as they say and she was wallowing in it, I mean she's the kind of woman who loves everything about being pregnant. I got her some coffee and joined her in one of the booths.

"What does the doctor say today?" I asked her. She always stopped to see me when she visited her doctor since he was just a block away.

"The heartbeat is strong," she beamed. "This is going to be a big baby!"

"What do you feed it?"

"It's not me, it's Bill!" she shook her head. "That man is driving me crazy! I think he wants to carry this baby for me! Do you know what he thought he wanted last night? Eggnog ice cream!"

"Yuk," I made a face.

"Well, don't laugh! At first I laughed, too, but Bill got hurt and it is his baby as much as mine."

"So what do you do?"

"I bought eggnog this morning and I put it in the ice cube trays and tonight I'll give him eggnog sherbet, what else?"

I laughed and laughed. "My God, I can't believe it! Bill's such a big baby!"

"All of them are," Olive shook her head. "Take my word for it, a man never grows up, he just moves from his mother's house to his wife's house."

"I think that's just about it," I said casually. And then not so casually I began to feel a tremor of excitement. Olive had spoken more than just a platitude, she had spoken the magic words for me and Dean. If Olive could give Bill mushy eggnog and make him think it was eggnog ice cream why couldn't I give Dean phony love potion and make him think it was the real thing? So okay, the idea was wild, he had a real hangup, but until he got over it himself why not go along with it? Later on, when we had a baby ourselves, when he finished school and got a job and Vietnam was just a fading nightmare, he'd forget all about this love potion stuff, too.

Meanwhile for his health and mine, this was the best solution. We've got an oddball shop in our town, this old man sells all kinds of things like lizard oil and rattlesnake steak, things like that. I don't know how he earns a living but he must because he's been here a long time. I left work a little early that day and went to this shop. I wasn't about to ask for a love potion but I was going to get something as nearly like it as I could. I found it, powdered coca leaves, a yellowish, tasteless substance that was supposed to provide a necessary vitamin to the diet. Well, it was going to provide a different kind of ingredient to my marriage for a while. That night I waited until Dean and I were getting ready for bed before I mentioned the new love potion.

"Oh, listen, you'll never guess what I ran across today! I was in this shop with Olive, she came down to visit her doctor and stopped in to see me, anyway I went to this shop with her and look at what he had!"

"What?" Dean didn't seem too interested. "Like what you brought from Vietnam!" I showed him the powder. I couldn't pretend it was the same thing, this was a different color and had a faint bitter taste.

"Come on, who said?" Dean asked me.

"The man who sold it to me," I said. "Olive and I were browsing around and you know how outspoken she is, she picked this up and said what kind of powder is this and the man told us the natives used it as an aphrodisiac. Olive said she was coming around in about four months and the man laughed and said don't knock it, it's the native's version of Vitamin E, the sex vitamin."

Dean wasn't laughing. He was looking at the container with the powder very carefully. He smelled it, sniffed it, touched it and then put it aside. I didn't bother him about it that night. I got ready and slipped into bed and yawned and said good night. Dean got in beside me and turned off the light. I knew he was awake beside me. I closed my eyes and pretended to go to sleep. I heard Dean get up and go into the bathroom. I heard the water running and then he was coming back to me. This time when he got into bed beside me he put an arm under me and pulled me in close to him. I trembled as his hands went over me, his mouth pressed down on mine. I didn't know whether to be happy or sad. He'd taken that stupid love potion and in his mind he was potent again. I knew it was all wrong but I would rather have this than the other. I pressed closer and closer to my husband.

"I love you," I cried into his shoulder. "I love you like this, I need you like this. Don't shut me out, don't."

"I won't," he whispered and he seemed to be chuckling.

I didn't care whether he laughed or cried or didn't speak to me. It was so good to be loved like this again, to be wanted and held by my husband. I stayed in his arms a long time afterward. I was afraid to break my own spell. Okay, so I'd fooled him, so what? This was better than nothing! I didn't feel like a cheat, I felt like a very smart wife indeed!

Finally Dean spoke. "Happy?"

"Ummm, yes," I murmured. "You?"

"Great, it was better than ever," he tweaked my nose "I forgot to tell you that I love you, too."

"Tell me."

"And that you're a big phony," he said casually.

"Phony?" I shot up in bed, reached for the bedside lamp. "What do you mean, phony?"

"That love potion in there," he was leaning back in bed, naked chest glistening from our lovemaking. "it was packaged in Brooklyn."

"Oh!" my hand shot to my mouth.

Dean began to laugh then, he laughed so hard he nearly tumbled off the bed. I laughed with him even though I wasn't at all sure why. Finally he was able to quit laughing long enough to tell me all about it.

"You see, I definitely was hooked on that stuff. In my mind. While I was over there the guys started talking about us not being able to make it with our wives when we got home; our libido got loused up and so forth. So someone came up with this stuff and we bought the idea. I mean why not? We're in an Asian country and they're supposed to know a lot about this kind of thing. But it was all in here," Dean tapped his head. "I let it get too strong a hold on me. I wanted to please you...."

"You did, you do," I cried out.

"So when you spilled the stuff I actually thought . . . well, never mind. Boy, what a nut! Then tonight I went in there and began to take that mess you bought, when I happened to look at the outside of the can. Did I get a laugh out of that! It was like a shot in the head! I was really going section eight!"

"I know what section eight is, you were going nutsy," I laughed and leaned over to kiss him. "You think I'd let you do that? I need you. I want to be like Olive, fat and pregnant and feeding you eggnog mush!" I had to explain that last bit then. Dean kept shaking his head.

"The things a person's mind will make him do," he kept saying.

"I'm glad that's all that happened to you over there," I said to my husband. "You're right, I can't imagine what it was like or how those people think or feel. Your problem was that you had to adjust to this world again and that takes time."

"I'm here," Dean said quietly. "Let's forget it."

Maybe it wasn't a serious problem but it could have become one. Who knows what makes or breaks a marriage? It takes an awful lot of understanding on the part of both husband and wife to accept change in either one. I hope Dean and I have weathered this storm for all time but I'm not kidding myself there won't be others. We'll just have to take them as they come, one at a time. THE END

SOMEONE IS MAKING OBSCENE PHONE CALLS TO MY WIFE

Is it our son?

This is another one of those stories I plucked from the True Love archives based strictly on the title, because it just screamed "1970s." But it turned out to be even more remarkable than I thought it would.

For one thing, it's narrated by a man—something you didn't see a lot of in these stories—and Sam's a widower whose wife died of cancer when she was 28, leaving him with a young son who doesn't want a new mother: "Just you and me, Pop, right? Just you and me forever and ever, promise?" Fast forward a few years, and Sam's finally fallen in love with another woman, which the boy doesn't take well at all.

The other amazing thing about "Someone Is Making Obscene Phone Calls to My Wife" is the ending. Most of the time, even when a story is filled with hardship, there's a ray of hope at the end. Spoiler alert: That doesn't happen here. This story is actually kind of... depressing. But still so lurid and melodramatic that you can't help but be impressed.

I suppose I should go all the way back to the beginning and tell you everything. But I'm not that kind of a guy. I don't like to live in the past, so I'll just tell you fast and get it over with: my first wife Betty died of cancer when she was only twenty-eight, after we'd been married for nine years.

There's a lot I could tell you about Betty and me. How happy we were and how much we loved each other, but as I said at the start, I don't like to talk too much about what happened. It happened, and all the talking isn't going to change it, so why go on about it?

Not that I've forgotten. You can never do that. Sometimes I hear an old song or see a girl walk down a street in a certain way, and I think, "Betty." But I don't talk about those things, and because I don't talk about those things, and because I don't, people think that I have forgotten—and by people I mean Betty's parents . . . and my son Alex.

Alex was eight when his mother died, and the next few years were tough for both of us. First of all, everybody kept offering me a home for Alex, as though he were a puppy I had bought and gotten tired of. Betty's parents were crazy to have Alex live with them, and my mother wanted Alex to come stay with her. What made it even more complicated was that Betty and I had moved to Florida shortly before she had gotten sick, and our parents lived in New Jersey—hers and mine.

"You've got a good job here," was what Betty's father said when he and my mother-in-law visited us after Betty died. "It'd be a shame to give it up. Why don't you let Mom and me take Alex back to Jersey? We could give him a real home."

My mother, who was there at the time, had something to say about that. "Alex can come live with me. After all, Sam's my son."

"Yes, but Betty was our daughter. Alex is all we have left."

"Alex is all I have left," I corrected Betty's mother.

I heard a big sigh of relief. The kind of sigh an eight-year-old would make, and I turned and saw Alex huddled behind the back of the couch.

"Come here, son," I said.

Alex came around to the front of the couch, and he leaned against my knees while I put my arm around his shoulders.

"Alex and I are a team," I said to his assorted grandparents. Even though the words were said to them, they were really meant for my son. "Nothing's going to break us up—not ever."

I could feel Alex's body relax, and my in-laws and my mother kind of nodded and gave in. My mother did more than give in. She closed her house and stayed with Alex and me until I could find a job up north again.

I work in electronics, and even though there were jobs available in those days, I also had to see about selling my house. That all took time, and my mother was chief cook and bottle-washer through the whole thing. That was nice, and I was grateful, but it's kind of tough for a grown man with an eight-year-old son to live with his mother again. My mother tried not to: get in the way, ask me too many questions, cook food that I hated. And I tried to: play cards with her in the evening, talk about my work when I came home, not raise my voice. Alex had his tries, too: to be respectful, let his grandmother know where he was going, keep his room neat.

As you can imagine, all that trying didn't make life easier for any one of us.

"You gotta get married again," one of the guys I worked with said at every lunch time and coffee break. "The way you're living—it's not normal."

"I'd like you to meet a friend of mine," one of my neighbors said whenever she invited me over to a Saturday night dinner. "She's such a wonderful girl. Loves kids."

As subtle as a ten-ton truck, all of them. And all the time I was thinking, Me get married again? Not ever. Alex is no dumb kid, and even at eight he was pretty bright. He understood the hints, the remarks, the not-so-veiled comments of my mother's about, "Someday you'll meet a nice girl, Sam. You'll see."

It was that last one that really bugged Alex, and one Sunday when we were walking through a grapefruit orchard near our house, picking up windfalls, he asked me about it.

"You going to get married again, Pop?"

"Why?" I asked him. "Would you like me to?"

"No." His voice was shrill. "No. If I can't have Mom, I don't want any other mother."

"First of all," I said, "even if I did get married, she wouldn't take the place of your real mother. You've only got one real mother, and that's that. And second of all, no, I'm not going to get married again."

"Not ever, Pop?" Alex persisted. "Not ever?"

What harm would it do to reassure Alex? Betty had been dead for only ten months, and 1 certainly wasn't planning to remarry. It was easy enough to say, "Not ever, Alex."

Alex dropped the grapefruit sack and ran over to hug me.

"Just you and me, Pop, right? Just you and me, forever and ever, promise?"

I had to laugh, he was so intense. "Sure, I promise, you and me. Until you decide to go off and get married and leave me alone."

"I wouldn't do that, Pop," and you've never seen a kid as solemn as Alex at that moment. "Cross my heart and hope to die, I'll never leave you. Never! Besides, girls~yuck. Who needs them?"

I laughed again. Alex was the only one who could make me laugh in those days, and the two of us went back to collecting our grapefruit. I still remember that when we lugged our haul into the kitchen of our house, my mother went crazy over all that fruit. All her life she'd been buying grapefruit at two-for something, and now here were piles of the stuff free. We had grapefruit for breakfast, grapefruit marmalade on toast, and candied grapefruit rind for dessert.

There were still jars of the stuff in the house months later when I sold my house and packed up for the move back to New Jersey. I had a job waiting for me, and I was going to stay at my mother's place until I found a house for Alex and me. Betty's parents wrote long letters about how glad they were that I had decided to move up north, and I figured that life would be a little less lonely with the family around. Especially for Alex.

Of course, after we got to Jersey my mother gave me long speeches about why did I have to find a house of my own? And why couldn't Alex and I keep on staying with her? But I went ahead and found a two-bedroom apartment, and Alex and I managed fine—just the two of us.

I'd get up early and fix breakfast and see Alex off to school. At three-thirty Alex would go over to my mother's house or Betty's parents' house and have some milk and cookies and go off to play with his friends. I'd pick him up after work, and I'd fix us dinner. Sometimes those TV things which we'd eat in the living room watching TV, or sometimes if I got ambitious, I'd throw a steak on the griddle and fry it up with some potatoes. And if the steak was burned on the outside and purple on the inside, so what? My son always said it was delicious.

There were nights when I played poker with some of the guys I worked with or stopped to have a few beers. Sometimes I'd be asked over to someone's house for supper, and I went out with quite a few different girls during those years. Some of them could cook, some of them were good in bed, some of them were sweet, some of them were all those things. But if any of them ever felt serious about me, I didn't feel anything about them. And all I had to hear was one of them say, "I'd love to meet your little boy. Why don't you bring him over for Sunday dinner?" Or a picnic. Or a movie. Or a day at the beach. That's all I needed, and I'd stop seeing the girl. Because Alex and I, we were something special. He was my boy—the only person I loved after Betty died.

I really thought I'd go on that way forever. I used to picture Alex grown up and married with kids of his own . . . my grandchildren. That's what I figured life had in store for me. And that's all. Betty's death had left me cold as ice inside, and I didn't even know it. Had I ever been any different? I couldn't remember it.

Okay, so you're going to say that even ice melts. And I'll say yes to that—even the ice that coats your insides—if you've got the right kind of heat. It was years before that heat got to me. Years, partly because I wasn't looking and partly because I had really loved Betty very much; it took someone pretty special to get me interested.

Who was all that special? First, let me tell you who she wasn't. She wasn't any of the girls my mother tried to fix me up with. She wasn't any of the eager girls I met at work or any of the others that were introduced to me at those dull Saturday night suppers I was always being asked to. And she certainly wasn't any of the girls I picked up in the swinging singles bars. She was Alex's grade advisor, and I got to meet her because Alex brought a note home saying she'd like to see me, please, at my earliest convenience, and it was important. The word *important* was underlined, just the way I'm doing it here.

I showed Alex the note, and asked him what it was all about.

"You in some kind of trouble, son?"

No, he assured me, he wasn't in any kind of trouble.

"Is it your arithmetic? Is that it?"

"It's called New Math," he said with all the superiority of an eleven-year-old dealing with his old, old man, "and I'm okay in that."

"Well, then, what aren't you okay in?"

Alex shrugged, and just stood there kind of silent, and I 'got scared. *Drugs,* I thought. *You hear a lot these days about even little kids and drugs. Maybe Alex...*

"Listen, Alex." I tried to pull him over to me, but he resisted. "Look, if you're in any kind of trouble, you just tell me. Tell the old man. There's nothing we can't fix. You know that, don't you?"

Alex pulled away from me, "I'm not in any trouble," he said kind of angry. "It's that dumb Miss Selis."

"Who's Miss Selis?"

"She wrote you that note. She's always asking a million questions. Always poking around."

"Poking around? About what?"

"I don't know," Alex squirmed. "just about things."

That told me everything I needed to know about Miss Selis. Some dried-up old lady who asked my boy all kinds of questions about things that were none of her business. After that, I got over to the school pretty fast. I explained to my supervisor that I had to take some time off one morning, and off I went.

I waited outside one of those doors with the half-frosted glass, and the little black and white sign that said "Amy Selis." Amy. She had to be ninety. Who's named Amy anymore? I saw this girl come to the door after awhile, saying goodbye to a woman who was obviously a parent. You could tell by the worried look. And I could tell that the girl was Miss Selis' secretary. Poor thing. Imagine working for an old witch like that.

"I'm Sam Washburn," I told her, "I'm here to see Miss Selis."

"I'm Miss Selis," the girl I thought was Miss Selis' secretary said.

That made the whole thing even funnier. She was so young. And pretty. What was she doing, writing me a dumb note about Alex? She was probably just out of school herself. After I stopped thinking it was funny—and that took about a minute—I began to get mad. I had taken off an hour from my job to talk to this kid?

"Look," I said, "I'm Alex Washburn's father."

"Oh, I know," she said, "Won't you come into my office?"

Come into my office. I had been working for around twelve years, and I didn't have an office. And the way she had said *I know.* What could she know?

Turned out, she knew plenty. Anyway, she knew more about me and Alex than I thought anyone could know. And I can tell you that I didn't like the meanings she put into the things she knew.

"You and Alex are devoted to each other." So what's so wrong about that? "And, of course, that's fine in its own way." Well, thanks a lot, lady.

"But it's not enough." Oh, yeah, says who? "Your extreme involvement with your son and his involvement with you has not allowed him to have normal, healthy relationships with anyone else." So, who else does he need?

"He has no friends."

That's when I started to speak up. "He sees his friends every afternoon," I told her. "He goes home or he goes to one of his grand-mother's, and then he plays with his friends."

"No. He goes home, or to his grandmother's and that's where he stays."

"But he always tells me that he plays with his friends."

"Do you ever ask him who his friends are? Have you ever met any of them? Did Alex tell you that last weekend he, along with the rest of his class, was invited to a sleep-over Halloween party at a classmate's house?"

"Alex didn't tell me! I wish he had. I would've been happy to let him go. I want him to have fun—a good time."

Miss Selis nodded. "He said he couldn't go. Something about not leaving you alone—something about promising never to leave you."

I stared at her. At first, I wanted to tell her she was crazy. But then I remembered that whole mixed-up time after Betty had died. And I especially remembered that day in the grapefruit orchard. Oh, those words. They were just words, weren't they? But, maybe if an eight-year-old kid says them, he thinks they're an oath like cross my heart and hope to die, I'll never leave you.

For the first time in a very long while I thought of my wife. Oh, Betty, what do I do now?

"I didn't know," I said to Amy Selis. "I really didn't know. I want Alex to have a normal life, to have friends, go places, see other people besides me."

Miss Selis smiled a little. Her first smile I'd seen, and it was something of a relief for me. "I'm glad to hear you say that. So many parents in your situation just cling to their children. They don't let them live, don't let them breathe."

"Me?" I said. "Me?"

"No, Mr. Washburn, I certainly didn't mean you."

She had me believing her, and that's why I asked, "What should I do?"

And then she let me have it. Right then and there with the same sweet smile. "Maybe if you lived a more normal life, Mr. Washburn, then Alex could live a more normal life, too."

"Normal?" And I bet they could hear me through that whole school. "What do you mean normal?"

"I mean do you and Alex have to spend every hour of every weekend together? Don't you have anyone else you could spend some time with so that Alex could be with other children?"

"But I'm devoted to my son. I didn't want him to feel neglected after his mother died, so so—"

"So you swamped him," she said, "with love, with affection, with all the good will in the world. You haven't let him develop a life of his own."

"He's only eleven!"

"It'll be too late when he's twenty!"

"Yeah," I said, "yeah." And I knew she was right. Because when I was eleven I had wanted to be with my friends. Maybe I went to an occasional ball game with my father, maybe I let my mother take care of me when I had a cold, but I was already moving out, away from my family. Even at eleven I had had a life of my own ... the life that I wasn't allowing Alex to have. After Betty died, I crawled into a shell and I took Alex with me.

"What do I do?" I asked her. "What do I do now?"

"See some of your own friends," she suggested, "and encourage Alex to see some of his. He's a likable boy, and I know he could be part of a group of boys if only you would let him."

I nodded my head, and left her office in sort of a daze. What she was advising me was easier said than done. Sure, next Saturday I told Alex to go find his friends and play ball with them. But he said, "I'd rather be with you, Pop."

And as for me, I'd been saying "no thanks" to invitations for years. For so long that people had practically stopped inviting me. Remember that picture I'd had in my mind of Alex married and me sitting around with my grandchildren at my knee? Well, at the rate we were going that picture would only include two men: one oldish-young man who had never married taking care of his father and one old man who had given up on life a long time before. That's when I got that idea of calling that know-it-all Amy Selis. Maybe it wasn't so smart, I mean the way I asked her out. "For Alex's sake," was what I said.

"No," she said. "No, thanks."

I coughed and swallowed and choked, but finally I got the words out. "For my sake."

"Yes," she said, "thank you, I'd like to very much."

It started with a Saturday night dinner and a movie. From the first, I told Alex where I was going and with whom I was going.

"Miss Selis? Miss Selis!" He was stunned. "Why Miss Selis?"

"She's nice," was all I said. "You want to sleep over at a friend's house, Alex, or go over to one of your grandmother's?"

"I'll stay here," he sulked. "I'll be fine here."

That meant that I couldn't stay out too late because I didn't like to leave Alex alone in the house, but I figured that was okay, too. Let him get used to the idea, and soon he'd be making friends with the other kids in his school.

It was almost funny—that scene between Alex and me when I came home that Saturday night. "It's late," he said. "Where've you been? How come you're coming home so late, Pop?"

It was hearing him say Pop that started me laughing. This was my son, and he was questioning me as though I was his child.

"Go to bed, Alex," I said, "just go to bed."

Alex kind of slumped to his room, and he never questioned me quite that way again No, his questions became more intense, because, you see, I kept going out with Amy, and it had stopped being for Alex's sake on my part too. I went out with her because for the first time in three years I actually felt something about a woman.

"Are you having an affair with her?" Alex asked me one Sunday morning over breakfast. "Are you having an affair with Miss Selis?"

I had never hit my kid, but I could feel my palm itching. ; Affair. What did Alex know of that word? I couldn't believe that he actually knew its meaning.

I kept my voice calm. "What's an affair, Alex?"

"It's when two people have intercourse without being married," he answered promptly.

Intercourse. Alex certainly knew all the book words. I was just hoping that he didn't know the others. But maybe knowing the others—the words boys whisper to each other when they're too young to shout them—would be normal. Here was my eleven-year-old son asking me these cold, clinical questions, and I didn't know how to handle him. That's why I made a joke of it.

"You been sneaking into those R-rated movies, son?" I asked him. He looked at me the way he had when I had called the New Math "arithmetic."

"Nobody has to sneak in anymore," he said. "You just go with somebody's brother or sister who's over 18."

"Oh, fine." But at least he had stopped asking me about Amy Selis. What could I do about Alex? He needed me more than ever. Not as a friend or a buddy but as a strong father. And more than that he needed a normal, family life. A mother and maybe some younger brothers and sisters.

"Is that why you're asking me to marry you?" Amy wanted to know. "For Alex?"

I looked at this girl who had thawed the ice. The girl who had made me into a feeling human being again, the girl who had turned me into a real man, not just someone going through the motions, and when I answered her I spoke the truth. I only hoped that she'd believe me.

"For me," I said. "Because I love you, Amy. Really love you."

She nodded, and she was warm and melting in my arms. "And I love you, too, Sam. And we'll have a good life and make a good life for Alex because of that love."

I held her close, and I didn't say the words I was thinking, I hope so, I pray so. But when I told Alex he quivered with rage. "You promised," he shouted, "that time in Florida. You promised."

"Alex, Alex." I tried to take him in my arms. "That was such a long time ago."

"I just can't get it into my head," he said, "I just can't believe it."

"You'll like her," I pleaded with my boy. "You'll see. We'll have a real home. Alex, we need her."

"I don't need her," and I could see that his eyes were filled with tears, "I only need you. And I thought you only needed me."

"I do need you," I tried to explain, "and I love you. This has nothing to do with us. You're my son, Alex. And I love you. I'll never love anyone more than you."

"Until you have more kids with her. You and her. I know what you'll do. You'll—"

Okay, so he used the dirty word for making love. It came out of my son's mouth, and he was saying it about me and the girl I was planning to marry, and I hit him for talking that way. I hit him hard.

"Alex," and then he was running out of the house. Running, running, away from me. "Alex, you get back here!"

But Alex had stopped listening to me, and for a moment I was sorry that Amy Selis had ever melted the ice around my heart, because not since Betty had died had I ever felt so bad. And what about Amy? With Alex acting that way, I began to worry about her. What would it be like for Amy moving into a house with a ready-made family? How did she feel about it?

"I'll love it," Amy assured me. "It'll take a while, but I know we'll get along just fine. Are you worried about me turning into a wicked stepmother, Sam? Not a chance. I want to be a real mother to Alex. He's not going to be my stepson. He's going to be our son."

Maybe I should have told her then about what I had said to Alex that time in Florida. I mean about nobody ever having more than one mother. But Amy seemed so happy, so eager to take on the job of mothering Alex, that I didn't have the heart to tell her to forget it. Besides, I kept hoping that it would really work out that way. That Alex and Amy and I would be one happy family. Just like you see it on TV.

The only trouble is that life's not like TV. My life isn't anyway. And I bet yours isn't either. Amy and I got married, and right from the beginning Alex hated her. He treated her like a housekeeper rather than my wife. If Amy cooked his favorite meatballs and spaghetti he would turn to me after eating a heaping plateful and say, "Can I have some more, Dad?"

It was Amy who went into the kitchen to bring Alex some more, but he never thanked her.

Amy had received an old, green-quartz lamp from a favorite aunt, and Alex delighted in playing with it. He played and pushed and tugged until he managed to break it.

"It was an accident," Alex said.

All little things, you say. But little things that happened every day, day after day. It was Amy who said, "Be patient." It was Amy who said, "He'll change, give him time."

But even Amy was shook one Saturday morning when she walked out of our bedroom to find Alex crouching by our door.

"Alex!" And for the first time, Amy shouted at him. "Alex, what are you doing?"

"Nothing," he said, "just—just nothing." And he moved away from

Amy.

"Alex, you come back here," I heard Amy say. "I want to talk to you."

"But I don't want to talk to you!" Alex shouted back, and he ran out of the house.

I remembered those brave words of Amy's before we were married: "Alex isn't going to be my stepson. He's going to be our son."

Amy had gotten herself some son: an eleven year-old who looked at her with cold eyes of hate whenever she so much as put her hand on my arm.

It was soon after that Saturday morning that the phone calls started. At first Amy didn't tell me about them. But one evening I came home from work and walked into the kitchen where Amy was fixing supper. I guess she hadn't heard me walk in, because when I put my arm around her and kissed the back of her neck she pulled away, and let out a terrible scream.

"Amy honey!"

"Oh, Sam." Her words were somewhere between a sob and a laugh. "It's you."

I pretended to be mad. "Who'd you expect? The iceman?"

I meant it as a joke, and I was shook up when Amy started to cry. "Honey, I was just kidding."

"I know," she sobbed. "I know, it isn't that. It isn't you."

I took her in my arms. "What is it, Amy? What's wrong?"

That's when she told me about the calls, the telephone calls that started every afternoon when she came home from her job at school.

"They're awful, Sam. This man—he says the most terrible things to me."

I made her come into the living room and sit down with me.

"What things, Amy? What does he say?"

At first, she wouldn't tell me. And when she finally did, I could understand why she had trouble getting the words out. The person who was making the obscene calls was threatening my wife. He told her that he would find her alone someday, and when he did, there were things he would do to her—and things he would force her to do to him.

I felt sick when she finished and frightened for my Amy that there was a man somewhere like that on the loose.

"What does he sound like?" I asked Amy. "Young, old?"

She shook her head, "I can't tell. All those things he says—he says them in a whisper—a terrible, shivery whisper. It could be almost anyone disguising his voice. A friend, a neighbor, maybe even another teacher at school. . . ."

It was just at that moment that Alex walked into the house. Amy and I looked at each other. Alex was now twelve and big for his age. I knew that my son was familiar with most of the words that Amy had heard on the phone. Most kids are.

Could it be? Could Alex—the boy that Amy insisted on thinking of as our son—be making obscene calls to my wife? It was because I was suddenly so sure that it was Alex that I started to shout at him.

"Alex, come here! Where've you been? What've you been doing all afternoon?"

Alex looked frightened. I had never talked to him that way before. He was so frightened that his words came out in a stutter. A sign of his guilt, I was sure.

"I—I was at Grandma's."

"All afternoon?"

"N—no. Then I—I went to the library."

"And how long were you at the library?"

"I—I'm not sure."

"Why aren't you sure? There are clocks in the library, aren't there?"

"Yeah, but I didn't look at them."

"All right. Where'd you go after that?"

It was Amy who made me stop. "Sam, don't! Don't do this. You sound—you sound—,"she searched for the word, and then finally said, "you sound terrible."

But I sounded more than terrible, and I knew it. At that moment I sounded as though I truly believed that when Alex wasn't home he was sneaking from one phone booth to another making obscene calls to my wife.

I put my head in my hands, and Alex asked, "What is it? What have

I done now?"

I looked at him. "Go to your room. I'll come in a few minutes, and we'll talk about it."

Alex slumped out of the living room, and before I followed him, Amy said, "Sam, it can't he. It just can't be Alex."

I wasn't so sure, and when I went into Alex's room, I started questioning him, not about the phone calls, but about his feelings for Amy.

"Son," I sat down on the bed next to him, "are you still unhappy that I married Amy?"

He stared at me. "What did she have to come here for?" he said finally. "We were doing great by ourselves."

I nodded. "We were. But don't you see, I think that with Amy we can do even better. I think we can be a real family."

"We were a real family before," he burst out, "a real great family, just you and me. I hate her! I hate her for coming along and messing everything up!"

That got me really mad. "You hate her." I said. "Just how much do you hate her? Do you hate her enough to call her on the phone and say this, and this, and this?"

Alex recoiled from me as though I had hit him. "I'd never do anything like that. That's crazy stuff."

"Exactly. And when you hate someone as much as you hate Amy you're liable to do crazy things."

"I didn't," Alex said, sullenly. "I just didn't."

I didn't believe him, and because I was so sure that it was Alex, I didn't report the obscene calls to the police or the phone company. The next few weeks were terrible, grim weeks in our house. Alex and I hardly spoke to each other. Amy jumped whenever the phone rang. Betty's mother called me to ask what was the matter with Alex. My mother called me to ask what was the matter with Alex. And Alex ignored the fact that Amy was even in the house. And all the time, Amy kept receiving those dirty, frightening phone calls.

Finally, the calls stopped. But still, there was no peace in our house, because I knew that Alex had made them. And then a few days after the last of the phone calls, I read a small item in our local paper. It was about a man who had been arrested for making obscene calls to the women in our neighborhood. Someone else had reported the calls to the police, and working with the phone company, they had been able to trap that sick, crazy man.

I passed the paper to Amy, and she breathed a sigh of relief. Then without a word she showed the paper to Alex. My son read the four paragraphs and looked up at me.

"I'm sorry, son," I said.

But it was too late. Because now Alex was looking at me with those cold eyes of hate. And then he said it. "I hate you. I'll hate you always. I'll never forgive you."

Alex meant it. In that terribly clear way that children have of saying things, he meant it.

Today, my son is living with Betty's parents. He visits me and Amy once a week, but they are bitter, cold visits.

Will Alex ever be our son, mine and Amy's? No, I have no hope of that. The most I can wish for is that he returns to being my son.

My boy truly feels that I betrayed him by marrying again. He still remembers the promise I made to him when he was eight years old, and now I'm paying the price of the too-intense relationship that went on until he was eleven.

Forgive me, Alex, for not letting you grow away from me during the years of your young boyhood. Forgive me, and come back to me. THE END

WE JOINED OUR TEENAGE DAUGHTER AT A
Free-Love Farm

In the pages of True Love *and* True Romance, *at least in the early 1970s, hippies were nearly always drug addicts who hung out at filthy communes and "rock festivals" looking for their next fix, luring young women into their cesspits of depravity. (Fortunately, these women inevitably found their way back to civilization by story's end, a bit worse for wear but humbled by their experience.) "Free-Love Farm" breaks away from all that. Okay, it starts out with a teenage girl mixed up with nasty bikers, but this time around the story gets told from the mother's point of view.*

Shirley and her husband Norm are trying to track down their daughter after she's run away from home, and they wind up being so intrigued by the first commune they visit that they decide to move in. (Well, Norm decides, anyway.) Sure, conditions are "primitive," but ultimately it's not much different than a small rural farm, and the men and women who live there are portrayed sympathetically—ordinary folks who want to live off the grid. Ultimately, it becomes a story about reigniting the spark in Shirley and Norm's marriage, the real first step towards healing their family.

We heard the roar of the motorcycles even over the television program we were watching, and Norm glanced at me questioningly. "What the heck is that?" he growled I got up, went to the window and pulled back the drapes. In the street light they were a frightening looking sight—right in front of our house gleamed four ugly black cycles, their riders standing astride them cockily. They were boys with long, matted hair, beards, and wearing fringed leather vests over bare chests. Two words leaped into my mind: Hell's Angels!

I started to shout to Norm, "Go call the police—" when I noticed the girl sitting on the jump seat of one of the cycles. It was our fifteen-year-old daughter, Debbie! I was too frozen with shock to say a word.

Norm came up behind me, took in the scene, and yelled, "Well! This beats all!"

With a set expression on his face, he started for the door, but I grabbed his arm. "Oh honey, be careful! Please don't go out there and get rough with them. You—you've heard the stories—"

"Well, what do you want me to do? Our little girl happens to be out there, Shirl!"

Before I could say anything else, the phone rang. I went to answer it while Norm barged out the door. It was one of our close neighbors calling. "Will you please ask your daughter to take her Hell's Angel friends elsewhere?" she shouted. "They're disturbing the whole neighborhood! This used to be a peaceful place until you people came here. Really! It's a disgrace—"

I slammed the phone down when I heard yelling in the street. Norm! He shouldn't be out there facing these young toughs alone. It wasn't as if he was a big man, or even that young. And there were four of them!

I found my husband on the sidewalk waving his arms about. It was Norm who was doing the shouting. "—right in this house!" I heard him tell Debbie. "And you're grounded for a month!" He looked at the fellows standing around. "Beat it! Don't come back here again or I'll call the police."

They didn't move, just exchanged amused looks. "Cool it, Daddy," one of them told Norm. "You're putting out bad vibes. Dig? So don't hassle us, you little plastic man. We were just rapping with your daughter."

Norm shook his fists at them. "I'm warning you—"

Suddenly one of them got off his cycle and started for my husband. "You're bumming my trip, Dad—"

I screamed then, and ran down the path. "Don't you dare lay a hand on my husband! Just don't dare!"

"Mom! Dad!" Debbie wailed. "Please—"

From somewhere nearby, maybe a couple of blocks away, we heard the howl of a police siren. All up and down the street, windows had opened. Somebody had called the police.

The cyclists knew it too. They glared at us, then kicked their cycles to life. But before they roared off, one of them shouted to Debbie, "Keep believin', doll! We'll be groovin'!" And they tore off down the street.

I was so frightened and angry that I turned right around and slapped Debbie's face. "Now get in the house!" I said, my voice breaking. "I think it's time we had a serious talk."

We hadn't been in the house two minutes when a police officer appeared at the door. Norm went to answer it, while Deb and I stood in the living room, listening. We heard the officer's gruff voice say, "We've had several complaints from your neighbors about motorcycle hoods disturbing the peace."

I glared at Debbie while Norm tried to smooth things over, and I hissed, "Now see what you've done!"

Her pretty face was tear-streaked, but stubborn. "Well, this neighborhood is full of nothing but uptight creeps. What do you expect?"

"Debbie!"

Finally Norm came back. His face was pale and set and I could see he had been badly shaken. For a minute he just looked at Debbie, then went and sank down in a chair. I was alarmed! After all, Norm isn't a very young man anymore. He's thirty-nine, going on forty years old! And it isn't unheard of for a man his age to have a heart attack!

"Honey," I put my arm around his shoulders, "can I get you something? Maybe a glass of water—"

"A drink," he muttered. "I think I could use a drink."

I hurried past Debbie, who stood there white-faced, and on into the kitchen. While I was pouring a little whiskey into a glass, I heard her say, "Dad, why did you have to kick up such a fuss? I mean, those fellows were okay. They didn't do anything—"

"Shut up, Deb!" Norm cut in. "Just—just don't say anything."

I carried the drink back and gave it to him, watching anxiously as he drank it. Oh, I was so angry at Debbie for worrying her father! For worrying both of us! Was she trying to land us in the local mental hospital? Only three months before, she had run away overnight. Then, shortly after that, I found the joint in her pocket. That time she pleaded with me to believe her. "I only tried it to see what it was like," she cried. "But I hate it, Mom! I'll never smoke those things!"

I believed her and thought our troubles were over. But a month hadn't gone by when she ran away again—this time to a commune downstate! She was gone four days, and we had to call out the police to find her and bring her home. We lectured her and the police gave her a stern warning and she vowed it would never happen again. But now this! I turned to her, crying, "Doesn't it bother you to have trash like that call your father names?"

She blinked. "They— they didn't—"

"Oh yes they did, my girl!"

Norm got up and put his hand on my arm. "I'll handle this, Shirley," he said in a quietly controlled voice. He made Debbie sit down. "You know I lost my job a couple of months ago?"

She nodded. "You realize I haven't been able to find another; that things haven't been easy for us. Right?" She nodded, head down. "We'd be better off living in an apartment instead of renting this house?" Debbie stared at him.

"Why do you think we rent this house?" She shrugged. "For you, that's why!" Norm roared. "So you can have a real home! So you can have all the things your older brother and sister had. Sure I can't afford to rent this place now. I have no job! And business being what it is today, I might not have a job for some time. But your mother and I are struggling along, trying to keep things nice for you anyway."

"I didn't ask you to—"

"That's not the point! We wanted to! And why? Because we love you, Debbie! We want you to have a nice home and all the good things in life. Yet you don't appreciate one thing. Nothing! Never have I seen such an ungrateful brat!"

For a minute there was a tense silence. Debbie looked at her father, then down at her hands. After awhile, she said. "You don't understand, do you? You don't know how things really are today. You and Mom— you're living in the past. You think that because you gave me a home and clothes and food I've got to repay you by living the way you do. You think—"

"I'll tell you what I think!" Norm cut in. "I think I've heard enough! I think I know a little more about life than a fifteen-year-old girl! So I tell you what: We'll just say that as long as you live in my home, you'll obey my rules. Okay? When you're grown up and in a place of your own, you can do what you like."

She got up and headed for the stairs, tossing her hair angrily.

"And you're grounded for a month!" Norm called after her. "It will give you a chance to think things over."

Debbie didn't say anything, just went on upstairs.

Norm and I were exhausted. We went up to bed, too, but not to sleep. We lay awake for a long time asking ourselves where we went wrong. How could Debbie be so different from her older brother and sister, who had never given us any trouble? It didn't seem possible that all three were from the same family!

Our son Norrie is twenty now, stationed in Germany with the army. A quiet, easy-going boy who was always such a joy to us. Beth, our nineteen-year-old is married, and the mother of a six-month-old baby boy. Bethie, with her bright and bubbly ways, was an easy child to raise. But to be honest, Debbie has always been difficult. You could say it began right at birth! I was in labor for eighteen rough hours with her.

Debbie had everything, was colicky as an infant, had severe teething problems. Later, she was a sensitive child, the type that was easily upset. Easily frustrated. Norrie and Beth would spend hours trying to amuse their baby sister. But the minute they ran away to ride their bikes, or play with their friends. Debbie would trail after them, screaming.

I'm not saying she was all bad. She could be sweet and loving too. I always tried to give her lots of loving because I sensed she needed it. She ended up being spoiled by all of us, getting more than her sister and brother ever had, but still we failed, somehow.

That night I lay awake almost until dawn, trying to figure out where we went wrong and what we could do about it. We had other worries too, like Norm losing his job after working with the same company for sixteen years! Things hadn't been easy for us. I know lots of people have had it hard, so I try not to complain in front of Debbie. But with our lease on the house coming up for renewal at the end of the month, I don't know how we are going to swing it. We have gone through a lot of our savings, and Norm's unemployment check doesn't come near covering everything.

These were the thoughts going through my mind as dawn began to turn the room light. I debated whether I should go to sleep, or maybe get up and fix some coffee and get a head start on my ironing. Later, I was to wish fervently that I'd gotten up! But I didn't. I snuggled close to Norm and put my arms around him and told him silently that somehow we'd work things out. That he shouldn't worry.

The next thing I knew it was nine o'clock! Norm lay on his back, one arm thrown out of the bed, snoring softly. Smiling, I stooped to kiss him, lifted his arm back in bed and decided to let him sleep. He'd had a hard night. He'd had a lot of hard nights lately, what with worrying about getting a job. So a long sleep would refresh him. I would fix breakfast and bring it up on a tray. It would give me a chance to have a few words alone with Debbie too; I'd try to get her to understand how worried her father was right now.

The house was very quiet. Debbie must be sleeping late too. I drew on a robe, fastened it around me while I stuck my feet into old slippers, and started down the stairs. I could tell Debbie wasn't up. There wasn't a sound.

The minute I walked into the kitchen and saw the note propped up against the toaster, my heart froze over. I stood there at the door, unable to move. I didn't know what was on that note, yet I did too. I sensed what it was even before I opened it and read, *Dear Mom and Dad, I'm sorry I've caused you so much trouble. But you are living in a dying world. You just don't dig how things really are today. I've decided to move to a commune for awhile. It's the only way to live. Don't send the police out looking for me because if you bring me home, I'll just run away again. Don't worry, I'll be okay. I'll write once in awhile. Love, Debbie.*

I let the note drop and put my head in my hands and cried. If only I'd gotten up at dawn, I might have prevented this! But if I'd stopped her running away today, what about tomorrow? I realized I couldn't hang over her all the day long. Oh Debbie, I sobbed, why have we drifted so far apart? We love you. We want to understand you!

Footsteps on the stairs made me glance up. Norm appeared in the doorway, dressed in crumpled pajamas, hair standing on end. "Where's Deb?" he asked, rubbing sleep from his eyes. Then, "Hey, isn't the coffee ready yet?" Then he saw the expression on my face.

Wordlessly, I handed him the note, which he read in tight-faced silence. "This is it!" he bellowed, his face flushing an angry red. "I've had it with that girl! Finished understand, Shirl?" And he glared at me as if challenging me to contradict him. But I was too weary to say a word: too depressed.

"Do we call the p-police again, Norm? "

"Darn right we do! Let them find her! Let them throw the book at her—I've done all I can."

He was bristling with anger. We had already gone through all this twice before. No wonder he was teed off. But then, after a minute, the fury went out of him and he sank into a chair and put his head in his hands. "No," he said, "we don't call the cops. Not this time, Shirl. Because this time it would go hard on her."

Relief washed over me. "Norm, there are at least three new communes within driving distance of here. And it's Saturday! You don't have to go job hunting today. Why don't we get dressed and go after her ourselves?"

When we were dressed and I was combing my hair, Norm came up to stand behind me. I looked at us through the dresser mirror. For a couple in their late thirties, we weren't too bad. Not middle-aged yet, by God! Sure, Norm isn't too tall, and he's put on a little weight and over the years he's developed a bald spot, which he conceals by combing a flap of longer hair over it. But he still has great eyes and a nice smile!

One of these days soon, I'm going to get rid of my extra ten pounds. Well okay - fifteen! And I'll he more faithful about touching up the grey in my brown hair. But my features are still good and my skin is firm.

Norm's arm came around me and he put his lips against the back of my neck. "You're still a good-looking woman, Shirl. You know that? Still a lot of woman."

I turned in his arms and kissed him—hard! "And you're still a lot of man!"

And at that moment, it no longer mattered that delivery boys had stopped whistling at me, or construction workers barely glanced up when I passed, except to shout, "Watch it, you dumb broad! Can't you see that manhole?"

It was a three-hour drive to the nearest commune, which was called, Azure Farm, and was a few miles outside the town of Bridgemore. We passed through the town, after asking directions to the commune, found the dirt road leading to it and drove down for about two miles. Then we came out into a clearing. Hairy, bearded people stood or sat aimlessly. Rickety buildings were all around and a few puny chickens pecked in the dust.

The people stared at us but nobody moved or spoke a word. Norm sat in the car for a minute, before getting out. I put my hand on his arm. "Honey, maybe this wasn't such a good idea -"

Norm straightened and reached for the door handle. "You wait in the car," he muttered, and got out.

A tall, bearded hippie with love beads dangling around his neck, came forward. To my relief, he held out his hand and Norm took it. "I'm Tor," the hippie said. "I'm the guru around here. You looking for something, Daddy?"

Norm confessed that we were looking for our daughter, and gave Tor a description of Debbie. The big man shook his head. "Nobody like that around here. We don't take in real young ones. They mean trouble with the fuzz. We don't want trouble."

I saw, with a start of surprise, that Tor was about as old as we were! Some of the others weren't exactly spring chickens either!

Tor came over to the car and stuck his hand through the window to shake mine. He was quite a handsome man, very big, bronzed, virile looking. And when he smiled, his teeth flashed out white and strong. "Come out and have a glass of wine with us, now that you're here," he invited. "And maybe we can rap about your daughter. I might be able to help."

Very reluctantly, I got out of the car and, after a minute, we squatted on the grass with Tor and some of the others. A woman came out of a bar with an old-fashioned stone jug in her hands and poured wine into chipped cups. I stared into my cup dubiously. There were flecks of dust floating in the wine. But when Tor said, "Here's to good vibes!" I raised my cup to my lips and closed my eyes and hoped for the best as I drank the stuff.

"When did your daughter split?" asked Tor.

Norm told him then, to my surprise and embarrassment, added that it wasn't the first time she'd run away.

"Let her go, Daddy," was Tor's advice. "If you bring her home against her will, she'll just take off again. So let her go. Maybe she likes the idea of keeping you chasing after her. Have you ever thought of that?"

Well, we hadn't. "Anything could happen to her," I said.

"She can't do anything worse in a commune that she can do right around home," Tor came back at me.

Norm and I exchanged a look. "That makes sense," my husband said.

"Sure it does. Right on!"

Then Norm said something that completely took me aback. "To make things worse, I recently lost my job."

"Congratulations!" Tor beamed. "Now you're a free man!"

Norm's mouth sagged open. "How's that?"

Tor went on to explain that he too used to be a member of the "establishment," as he put it. He'd been a big executive with a fancy house, two cars, a beautiful wife. Also ulcers, insomnia, and a load of debts! Finally his wife divorced him and he had a nervous breakdown. It was while he was in the sanitarium that he remembered the piece of land his grandfather had left him.

"I walked right out of that hospital and came here, " he continued, "I've been here ever since, grooving to nature. My ulcers cleared up. I sleep like a baby. And every morning I wake up to clean fresh air, knowing I don't have to prove anything to anybody. I'm happy for the first time in my life!"

"That a fact?" Norm said, impressed. "What do you do for money?"

"Don't need much here, Daddy. We grow our own food, raise chickens, make arts and crafts to sell in the city. We get by."

"Righteous! Wo-oow!" the others agreed enthusiastically.

I was shocked to see that some of the women wore nothing except tattered skirts or shorts. The few children playing around were naked.

Suddenly Tor slapped Norm on the back, making him cough. "You ought to try it, Daddy. Far out! You look like you could use some real living. You're too pasty and flabby. How old are you anyway? Fifty?"

"Thirty-nine," Norm whispered, shame-faced.

"Wo-ow! I mean, you're kidding!" Tor slapped Norm in the stomach, making him turn blue.

"Thirty-nine? You look fifty, Daddy."

I put down my cup, not about to sit with these—these creeps and be insulted. "We have to go," I said coldly.

"Relax, Mama. Don't buck it." Tor stared at me, looked me up and down until I turned red. "You and your old man come back here and stay awhile; I'll make you both look and feel ten years younger."

"Righteous!" the others agreed, nodding.

I looked at Norm pointedly, angry that he seemed in no hurry to leave. "No thanks," I said. "We have to go."

Finally my husband got the message and he rose too. "Thanks for the wine," Norm said, then, "Boy! Smell the air up here! It's clean!"

Tor walked with us to the car. He hung in the window for a moment. "You two come back," he said. "This is where it's at. C'mon. We'll be glad to have you."

Norm was quiet and thoughtful all the way to the second commune. We got there at eight o'clock that night. It was a scruffy place, full of young kids, not anything like Tor's "farm." Norm took out a picture of Debbie and showed it around. Nobody had seen anyone answering her description. Half the kids were glassy-eyed anyway and wouldn't have known the difference.

Wearily, we turned the car for home, planning to start out again the following day. But when we were getting ready for bed, Norm suddenly burst out, "Maybe Tor's right. It doesn't make sense chasing after Debbie. If we bring her home, she'll just run away again."

"But- but we can't just sit here doing nothing! I'd go crazy, Norm!"

"We aren't going to sit here going crazy," he said, a grim expression on his face. "We've waited around for that girl too often in the past. You know Deb, she never stays away long. Pretty soon she'll get to thinking of her creature comforts and she'll hightail it home. Only this time we won't be here!"

"Where will we be?" I asked faintly, but I think I already knew.

"Now it's our turn to run away!" Norm announced triumphantly. "To a commune!"

"Are you out of your mind? If you think for one minute~"

"Look at it realistically, Shirl," he interrupted. "I'm out of a job and can't find another. Our savings are running low. Our friends give me pitying looks. It gets me down. I could use a break, a change. And who knows, maybe we'd learn something. Maybe Debbie is right. Could be we are behind the times."

I could see his mind was made up. No matter what I said, he had an answer for me-a reason why it would be good to try life at Azure Farm! In a way, I could understand how he felt. It had been rough for Norm, chasing around after a nonexistent job. A break might be good for him.

It was crazy, but I reluctantly agreed to give it a try. The lease was almost up on our house anyway. But we decided not to say anything to our family and friends. We just told them we were going out to the coast for awhile, to look over job prospects. Only our daughter, Beth, knew the truth—and she thought we were out of our minds!

If Debbie returned to find our home closed up, we knew she would go to Beth's apartment. So after our furniture was stored in my sister's basement, we packed a few things into a suitcase, got into our five-year-old car, and headed west. "I must be mad!" I giggled as we started out. "And at our age!"

Norm laughed back. "I feel ten years younger already! It's like a big adventure; like being back in the Boy Scouts!"

Tor and his "disciples" gave us an enthusiastic welcome back. "Hey, righteous! Far out! It's going to be a beautiful scene."

He asked a girl called Callie to show us to Sunset Lodge. Callie, in her mid-twenties, was tall and shapely and bare-breasted. Norm followed after her like a puppy after a bone. Sunset Lodge turned out to be a broken-down shack which was little more than one room with a blanket curtain dividing it in two. Callie waved a hand to one side, where a dirty mattress lay on the floor. "This is your pad, dig?"

Norm hadn't taken his eyes off her. I grabbed his arm. Hard! "Honey," I said. sweetly, "we didn't bring any bed linen."

Callie smiled. "Nobody uses any here, Mother. We don't hold with unnecessary frills."

Norm was quick to agree. "All the less to wash!"

"You catch on fast, Daddy." Callie beamed.

I caught Norm's arm again, digging my nails in until he yelped, "Hey! For God's sake, Shirl!"

"You're supposed to feel like a Boy Scout, remember? A Boy Scout not a grown wolf!"

We set down our things and went back out to the clearing, where Tor pointed to our car. "Take that into town on Saturday and sell it. We'll pool the money for the whole family. We got the truck here. We don't need your car."

"But what if I want to go into town?" I protested.

"You ride in the back of the truck."

In the back of a truck! Like an animal on its way to market. I looked at Norm, waiting for him to refuse, but he didn't say anything.

Tor stared me up and down. "What kind of freak are you supposed to be anyway?"

My mouth fell open. "Freak! You have the nerve—"

"Your clothes. You can't go around here dressed in a suit, nylons, high-heeled shoes. I'll bet you even wear a bra."

"Maybe you think it would be better if I went around looking like that!" And I pointed to a girl who was sitting nearby, dressed in nothing except the lower half of a bathing suit.

A broad grin spread over the men's faces. "Yeah!" Norm breathed. And Tor added, "Right on!"

Oh, I wanted to slap both of them! But I went back to Sunset Lodge—all the shacks had fancy names—and changed into a pair of denim shorts and a blouse. On an impulse, I left my feet bare. But that's all I intended to leave bare.

When darkness fell, a huge fire was lit in the clearing and everybody gathered for meditation hour. The trick was to fasten your eyes on a flame, let it go inside you, and see what it illuminated. As Tor explained it, "Groove on that flame and ask yourself, 'Who am I?' "

The minute Tor moved away, Norm chuckled, "While the others groove on the flames, I think I'll just groove on the flower children." And his eyes roved eagerly over the half-naked girls. I was beginning to regret I'd let him talk me into coming here!

Callie, who was sitting on my left, stuck a cigarette in my face. "Want to fly, Mother?"

"Fly?"

"Get high. You know, grass!"

I stared at her in horror. "No!"

"Well, don't get uptight about it," she laughed. "Relax. None of us are on the hard stuff here. Tor won't even allow acid. He feels we can get our highs without it. Dig?" And she gave me a wicked wink.

I felt more uncertain than ever. What did that mean?

After meditation, Tor got out his guitar and we had a rollicking sing-along. At the end of each song, the group would yell, "Righteous! Right on!" until I thought my ears would burst.

My head was reeling by the time we went to our shack to sleep, but we hadn't been there five minutes when a young couple arrived to take over the other side of the blanket curtain. And after a minute there was no mistaking what they were doing.

Oh, I was mortified! I tried to cover my ears, but it was impossible. The thin blanket curtain hid nothing. And I mean nothing! I sank down on the mattress whimpering, "We should never have c-come here, Norm. This is not for us."

He tried to comfort me. "Maybe we're just too uptight, Shirl. Have you ever thought of that? Maybe that's why Debbie, well~ got tired of us. Look at it this way—people do make love. Right? So why hide it, make out like it's something shameful and dirty?"

I couldn't believe it. This wasn't my Norm talking. "I-I feel like you're suddenly a stranger," I breathed.

To my amazement, his arms crushed me to him in an unexpected— for Norm—bear hug. "Maybe tonight I will be a stranger!" he growled seductively. "A nice, sexy stranger. Shirl, I think all this fresh air is getting to me already!"

He might have brought it off too—except I happened to run my fingers through his hair. My hand touched the bald spot on top of his head, encountered the long flap of hair that usually covered it, hanging loose. And suddenly it was too much.

"Oh Norm, honey," I giggled. "Maybe, now that we're going natural, you should cut off this flap of hair."

"What?" He drew away from me, shocked. "Never!"

Suddenly, from the other side of the blanket curtain, a male voice said, "I think you should, Daddy."

"No, he looks kind of cute with that flap blowing in the breeze," said his girl companion. "He reminds me of a pet rabbit I once had. It was always having babies—"

"Oh great!" Norm groaned, sinking back on the mattress. "Just-great!" In the semi-darkness, I saw him gesture to the curtain, and I knew what he meant.

"How come he reminds you of the rabbit?" the boy asked, continuing the conversation that we started. "What's his hair got to do with your rabbit?"

"Our rabbit had only one ear, stupid!" the girl replied. Norm groaned again. I hardly slept that night. The mattress was lumpy and smelled of dampness. The young couple was fantastically active. Finally, around dawn, I dropped off for awhile. A bugle woke us at five.

Norm sat bolt upright in bed. "God! The alarm! Gimme my rifle—"

"Relax, Dad," called the boy from over the curtain. "It's just Tor blowing work detail. You're not in the flipping army, you know."

After a dip in an icy river, we were assigned our chores. I had to help sew clothes on an old-fashioned, foot pedal sewing machine while Norm went with the men into the woods to chop down trees to build more shacks. Well, the sewing didn't bother me. I'd always made my own clothes. When the other girls saw this, they were impressed. One of them brought out a piece of print material she had been saving.

"Do you think you could sew me a granny gown?" Pat asked shyly.

I could have, but I had a better idea. "Why don't I teach you how to sew it?"

Her eyes widened. "Oh far out! I mean, groovy!"

After a lunch of scrambled eggs, Callie joined the group that had gathered to watch me teach Pat how to sew. She didn't say anything for a minute. "There's other work to be done," she finally pointed out. "I think this sewing lesson has gone on long enough."

The other girls protested, but she stood firm. I knew Callie was Tor's "woman." She was also the queen-type around the commune. As I stood up, her blue eyes narrowed. Suddenly I wondered if she could possibly be jealous of my little popularity with the other girls.

"You can help clean out the chicken coop, Shirley," she said. "Work with Pat."

"The—the chicken coop!" I was horrified.

"Sure, right on," she smiled sarcastically. "This is a working commune, you know. Everybody does chores. And since you've been sitting down all morning—"

"Come on, Shirl," Pat said, giving Callie a look. "You can continue my lesson tomorrow!"

After cleaning out the coop, I vowed I would never eat another egg. I was worn out by the time evening came and the men returned from the woods. Norm was one of the last to arrive, supported between two other men. I screamed when I saw him, sure he had been hurt, but he gave me a sheepish grin. "Easy, Shirl. I'm okay. I'm just not used to chopping down trees, that's all."

When he tried to straighten up, he gasped and reached around to rub his back. "Oh my God! I-I think I should be in traction!"

Later, in the shack, I whispered, "Let's go home, honey. This life isn't for us. Would you believe I cleaned out a chicken coop today? Honey, let's go home. I-I miss Beth and the baby and—and all our friends."

But Norm shook his head stubbornly. "Look, Shirley, we have to give this thing a real try, for Debbie's sake if for nothing else! And—and I like it!" he added staunchly, still rubbing his back. "I love the fresh air, the singing around the fire, the lack of tension. It's a-a great life!"

I lay down beside him, sure I wouldn't go to sleep. But I hadn't counted on all that fresh air, hard work, and rising at dawn. We were both asleep by nine-thirty! After awhile, things fell into a routine. Every morning I gave the girls a sewing lesson. Every afternoon I worked in the vegetable garden, or cleaned the shacks, or some other chore. Everything was so primitive. Clothes were washed in the river, dried in the sun. Cooking and baking were done the old-fashioned way, right from scratch. When they discovered I knew how to make orange and date bread, they kept at me until I taught them. Somehow, the days passed quickly.

Norm stopped shaving and soon grew a beard. And, after taking a poll on it, most of the group decided he should clip off his flap. When he grabbed a pair of scissors and did it in front of everybody, I knew he had really gone all the way over. Well, I thought, if he could, I could too! I got so I went around in brief shorts and an even briefer halter top. Soon our skin was bronzed by the wind and sun, and both of us dropped a lot of extra weight.

A few weeks later, we went into town to sell the wooden figures that we carved, together with the baskets and aprons and other knickknacks. Pat and I set up a small table on the sidewalk and set out our wares. People drifted by, staring at us--staring at the things. A lot of them tut-tutted and shook their heads. "Filthy hippies," we heard them mutter. "And did you see the old one?"

That made me feel bad! I felt like crawling under the table and hiding. When Norm and I were alone later, I said, "Well, we've given this thing a good try now, honey, so how about going home?"

He was stunned. "Home? Why? What could be better than this clean, healthy outdoors life? The trouble with you, Shirl, is that you haven't committed yourself to this."

I thought about that a lot over the next few days. And I realized it was the truth. I hadn't committed myself! As far as I was concerned, once we'd asked around and let everybody see Debbie's picture and determined that she wasn't anywhere around here, I was ready to go home. Yet if we were to get anything out of it, if we were to try to understand this kind of life, we had to commit ourselves to it. After that I made a more determined effort to get into the groove. At meditation hour, I really meditated. I threw myself wholeheartedly into the work around the commune.

One day Tor stopped me. "Hey, Shirl, you're really digging in here," he said, his blue eyes roving over me. "You really make this commune groove, teaching the girls to sew, bake sweet bread, and stuff like that."

"Thanks," I said. "I enjoy it."

"You look lots better too than when you first came. You look like— wo-oow!"

I blushed, but felt pleased. It was a real compliment. "Walk with me to the river," he invited. "Let's rap."

Norm, exhausted, had gone right to the shack after supper. The clear, evening sky was washed with pink. It was a beautiful night for a walk to the river, but as we got up, I saw Callie's lips tighten and felt her following us with her eyes.

After a little while, Tor put his arm around my waist. It was a hard, muscular arm. Everything about Tor was hard and muscular, except for his eyes. They were full of fire. Suddenly, feeling the heat of his body close to mine, I felt a well of longing fill me. How long had it been since Norm and I made love? What with having the couple on the other side of the blanket, and Norm being so pooped out after his long day chopping down trees, he was in no condition for lovemaking.

Only I was! Never had I felt so healthy and vibrantly alive, so eager for love!

With a shiver, I tried to force such thoughts from my mind as Tor and I sat down on the bank of the stream. For a few minutes we rapped about spiritual things, and the kind of stuff we thought of while meditating. I didn't plan to, but I found myself spilling out a lot of secret things I never usually told anybody—not even Norm!

"Hey!" Tor said, impressed. "You really dig it! I mean, far out! You're right into the scene. Beautiful!" He took my hands and turned me to face him. "Shirl," he said, "I think you're finally ready for Tantra." I gaped at him. "Tantra'?"

"Far out! It's a kind of yoga. It's the choicest. Wo-oow!"

"Oh." I felt vaguely alarmed.

"Sit yoga style and face me," he instructed. "Put your hands on my thighs. Go on! I won't bite! Concentrate." he muttered. "Concentrate. In a minute. I'll tell you what you're thinking."

There was a brief span of silence. It was all I could do to stop shaking.

"Sex!" he exclaimed. "You're thinking of sex!"

Suddenly he reached over and, before I knew what was happening, he undid my halter top.

"No—"

"Groove on it, baby, Groove on it~~~"

His mouth fastened over mine and he lowered me to the grass, but hardly had we lain down when the bushes behind us parted and Callie and Norm stood there.

"There's your wife, Daddy!" Callie shouted triumphantly. "I told you she was making out behind your back!"

Norm's face was livid. His eyes bulged as he advanced on Tor. "Why, you double-crossing creep! You con-artist~"

Tor jumped to his feet. "Watch it, Daddy. Don't crowd me!"

But Norm was past listening. He lunged at Tor, who struck him across the shoulders, sending Norm flying into the river. The next minute I was screaming at Tor, slapping and scratching at him. He shoved me on the grass. "Go fish your old man out of the river, Mama. I think he might need help." And he strode off back to the commune.

Sobbing, I got up in time to see Norm drag himself out of the river. "Why did you do it, Shirl?" he asked.

"I-I don't know," I cried. "I don't love him. Norm. I love you! Only we never have any time together anymore!"

Without a word, he put his arm around me and led me back to the clearing. When we got there, I heard a girl's voice yell, "I know they're here!"

We walked into the clearing to find our daughter, Debbie standing there! She stared at us, speechless, her eyes wide as they went over her father, then fell on me. She opened her mouth, but nothing came out. The after a minute, she whispered, "When Beth told me I-I didn't believe it. I just didn't believe it! Now~"

I ran to her and put my arms around her. "Oh honey, you came home!"

"Yeah —to find the house closed up! Oh Mom, how could you?"

"Well, your mother and I decided to run away for a change," Norm said.

On the way back to the straight life, we did a lot of talking. Debbie realized she had been thoughtless and rebellious; we realized that people are still people, even in a commune! They are still subject to the same envy and jealousy, the same lust and greed.

Debbie confessed that she'd always felt less important than her older brother and sister. Everything she did or accomplished, they had already done.

"You'll never know how I felt when I got home to find the house closed up," she said, shaking her head.

I hugged her. "I think I do, honey. It must have felt something like the morning I came downstairs to find you'd run away."

We look at each other tenderly. It was a point of real understanding. A shared experience. And it was a fresh beginning for us as a family. THE END

Four in a bed

THE NIGHT MY HUSBAND
DEMANDED AN ORGY

Apartment complexes were great venues for sexual turmoil in pulp romance stories—especially when they explicitly refused to rent to families with children, which leads to a lot of horny adults with spare time on their hands. Time they can spend gossiping about each other's relationships or, as Becky discovers, putting the moves on each other's spouses.

Rob, Becky's husband, starts out as a "square," but get a few drinks in him and he's ready to start talking about "how a man can love one girl in one way and another in a different way and yet, he's really not unfaithful to his wife." Becky assumes Rob's looking for an orgy—it's right there in the title, after all—but it's possible he might actually have been suggesting a polyamorous arrangement and not just a one-night fling. Either way, it's not something that would fly in the pages of True Love.

As soon as I saw that apartment building, I wanted to live there. Ever since I'd lost the baby when I was three months pregnant, I'd had the weepies. Somehow, seeing that sign that said "Young Marrieds Only— No Children!" I decided I'd be happier there—this was the place for Rob and me to live. We'd rented a little house back home in Murphysville, and either his mother or my mother was nearly always coming over, trying to make me feel better about the baby, so I never got a chance to forget about it. Mom Anderson had had ten kids, though, so a miscarriage didn't seem very tragic to her. And my own parents didn't seem very concerned either. It was funny, but my mother seemed mostly worried about how my marriage was going, as if she was scared I might leave Rob and come back home.

I was the last of four daughters to marry, and when I did, I'd had an awfully hard time making up my mind about Rob. He was handsome, smart, and at home, he had lots of friends. He'd been a straight A student and captain of both our school's football and baseball teams.

My mother was crazy about him and my father respected him. There was just one catch—Rob was square. I don't mean I was one of those mod swingers who believed in free love and having babies when you aren't married, or making the true hippie scene—I just mean that there were times that my husband exasperated me beyond belief. Even in high school, when we were going steady, you could set your clock by him. He always came for me at exactly fourteen minutes before eight in the morning and on our date nights, Friday and Saturdays, he always came for me at five minutes before seven.

When we'd both been working a year, it was Rob's idea that we take so much out of our paychecks and save, so that we could buy furniture and not go deeply into debt. I never seemed to be able to put in my twenty percent—I was always goofing up, borrowing money at work, getting mixed up on my budget, but every week, Rob put in his share, and when we got married, we were able to buy nice furniture.

To tell the truth, there had been times when I'd wondered about how he'd be in bed. With three older, married sisters, I got plenty of teasing, so much so that I began to wonder if maybe Rob might not turn out to be a disappointment in bed. I wanted us to become lovers before we got married, but Rob didn't want to. He seemed to have weighed the good things against the bad and he decided we ought to wait.

I'd been wrong to worry—he was a wonderful, passionate lover, although he was shy at first—but so was I. After I lost the baby, Rob got shy all over again—like he was worried for fear he might hurt me, or get me pregnant again.

The doctor had told me to wait a year before trying for a baby, and that was the main reason I begged Rob to get me out of our home town. The girls I'd gone to school with and grown up with were all having babies; I couldn't walk down the street without seeing somebody I knew who'd just had a baby, or who was hugely pregnant. It depressed me and made me cry a lot, so Rob got a transfer to Chicago and we started looking for an apartment.

We moved into our new place on a Saturday. We could have moved out of the motel where we'd been staying into our apartment, a week before, but Rob had to do it methodically. He was renting a truck to haul our stuff up to Chicago, and he had to first look at the apartment and the rooms, and measure them and figure out what would fit in where. He said it would be easier that way, doing it first on paper.

Anyway, when we did finally get moved in, everybody was relieved. The last thing my oldest sister said was that a man like Rob would drive her out of her tree. Rob was at the hardware store, buying a new mop, when we got our first visitor. She didn't bother to knock, and for a moment, she startled me. She was a big girl, kind of fattish, with a pretty, round face and lots of eye makeup.

"I'm Joy Hastings," she said, and she smiled at me. "I saw the truck with your stuff on it —welcome to the Group!"

It was impossible not to like her, even though she was weird. For one thing, she didn't wear a bra, and she had on one of those see-through blouses. She didn't have especially pretty breasts, but all the same, it worried me to know that at any second, Rob would be coming home. He'd dislike her on sight, I felt sure. In the first place, he didn't go for the "kooks" as he called people who weren't like he was, and in the second place, he wouldn't want me associating with a girl who was this far-out. I suppose he knew I had a few kookie tendencies myself.

Things worked out pretty much as I expected. Rob came home with the mop, and the sight of him standing there in the doorway, that mop over his shoulder, staring at Joy as if she was some creature from outer space who was threatening his world—was something to see.

He griped about her all evening. "If that's the kind of creeps they've got in this building, we'd better forget about moving in here, Becky!"

I had visions of his carefully moving all our furniture back out, onto the truck, and drawing floor plans of some other apartment. I liked it here and I wanted to stay—and in spite of the fact that she didn't knock and went bra-less, I liked Joy.

Joy wasn't married, but most of the people out there were. It didn't take me long to discover that most of them were having problems, too. At home, kids that Rob and I had gone to school with had problems, got divorced, and got into various kinds of trouble, but nobody talked about it. I mean—people talked about it—they gossiped—but nobody sat around and discussed the fact that so and so didn't have an orgasm. It would have shocked even the wildest young marrieds in town.

But here, at least in our swinging apartment building, that's just what they did. I was grateful that Rob worked long hours and wasn't around during the day to hear the talk that went on by the swimming pool. Rob liked our apartment to be clean and neat, but since I didn't like "the housekeeping bit" as my new girlfriends called it, I'd usually wait until he left for work, then I'd hurry to Joy's or maybe Peggy's apartment and we'd have coffee and talk about Life. There were other girls who came sometimes, but most of the time it was Joy, wearing a see-through nightie or blouse, and Peggy, wearing the kind of clothes that automatically turned men off—like dumpy dresses and dark brown colors and baggy slacks that made her look kind of clown-like. Peggy was married, and she and Tom, her husband, were having problems. She liked to sit around and talk about how there had to be something deeper than sex in marriage, and about how Tom just never excited her because he didn't understand her.

"Her husband must hate her," I said to Joy one day. We were in my apartment, and I was hurriedly slapping together a meat loaf. I'd learned a little trick—if I got the table set, Rob would think I was busy with dinner, even though I hadn't started it.

The girls had laughed when I told them that he liked me to wax floors and cook a lot, and Joy had winked at one of the other girls, as if my husband was some kind of a big joke. Joy was doing her nails, painting them an ugly gold color.

"Her husband doesn't hate her." She looked at me, her eyes suddenly lonely. She'd only been divorced a few months and her ex-husband's stuff, some of it, like books, was still around in her apartment. "Tom's crazy about Peg. She turns him on with that bit where she doesn't want to make love when he does. She drives him crazy, covering up her body with all those ugly clothes. She couldn't excite that man any more if she was trying to. But the trouble is—she isn't trying to."

So there we were, a cozy, girly threesome—Joy, who flaunted her body and tried to seduce every man in the building, including mine, and Peggy, who had turned away from sex completely. I didn't really understand either of them, but at least I wasn't going around crying all day because I'd lost a baby and couldn't have another right away. I sometimes felt like somebody who'd been invited to a freak show, as I sat in the sun, or sat in somebody's apartment, or by the pool, and Joy would come on with her revealing clothes, shorts and a sheer blouse and no bra and Peggy would come around in her baggy, comic's pants and a cover-up shirt and no makeup, like she was deliberately trying to be Miss Ugly of the Year, or rather, Mrs. Ugly, although she didn't seem to me very married at all, since she was seldom with Tom.

We'd been living there about a month when Rob came home and found the apartment in an unholy mess, Joy on the couch doing her toenails, her narrow breasts plainly showing through her blouse, and Peggy sitting on the floor like a Yogi, wearing a turtle neck sweater and a pair of Tom's old fishing pants that smelled like minnows.

Rob took one look, then he went to the bedroom, slammed the door and stayed in there. The girls left right away, but Joy looked kind of amused.

"He's cute," she said, whispering. "That kind of man can really be great in bed if you can just get his straight-type thinking to go crooked. I guess he didn't think much of Peg and me, did he?"

I opened the bedroom door, after the girls had gone, and went cautiously in. Rob was lying on our bed, his hands behind his head. He didn't look mad, but I knew he was. He was controlled mad. He never let his emotions get the upper hand.

"You don't like them, do you, honey?" I sat gingerly on the edge of the bed.

His eyes, frosty blue, met mine. "I'm crazy about them. Especially the one with the boobs that flop around when she walks. But the one in the pants with the fishy smell on them—she's a doll, too."

"Don't," I said, tears behind my eyes. I reached for his hand. "If it hadn't been for those girls, I'd still be all torn up inside because we lost the baby. They might be strange, but they're good hearted. Honestly, honey—they've helped me over a big hurdle."

I saw his eyes soften. He put out his hand and traced the outline of my face, then he pulled me down next to him, there on the bed. "I'm sorry," he said quietly, "I guess I ought to be grateful to them, for getting you through a bad time. Look—I'll try to—play it more loose, okay?"

I couldn't help but smile. Rob was funny when he came on with hippie language. It was terribly out of character for him. But I knew he'd softened up about Joy and Peg—and I knew from now on, he'd be much more understanding about my spending time with them.

Tom—Peg's husband, and Allen, who was Joy's ex-husband, came around once in awhile, when Rob was home. I didn't really think he'd like those men, because I didn't think he'd want to be friendly with men who had picked such weird girls to marry, but surprisingly, the Saturday that both Tom and Allen appeared at the swimming pool, Rob spent most of the day with them. Rob didn't like to loaf around the pool, but that day, he did spend a few hours there, talking to Tom and Allen. Joy, Peg and I sat in deck chairs, soaking up the sun. Actually, I'd never seen Joy as covered up as she was that day—I guess she couldn't find a see-through bra bathing suit. Anyway, she told me her ex-husband had stopped by to pick up some of his things.

"He's sleeping with somebody," she said, her voice bitter. "Well— he'll have to look long and hard to find anybody as sexy as I am."

She stretched, and I realized that if a man liked plumpish girls, he might find Joy attractive. I wondered if my own husband had ever noticed her—but of course, he hadn't.

Rob had noticed her only in a way that had disgusted him and shocked his old-fashioned nature.

Peggy, wearing a pair of slacks and the usual ugly shirt, watched her husband, my husband and Joy's ex-husband as they went off the diving board, taking turns.

"Show-offs," she said. "That's what they are—trying to turn us on. They don't understand that a girl has to feel that a man wants her because he loves her soul, not just her body. My psychiatrist told me that the reason I feel I ought to hide my body is because I'm waiting for the right man, the man who'll be my friend, not just my lover."

I didn't say anything, but long before, I'd secretly decided that Peggy had to be crazy. No woman could keep her husband around if she didn't let him make love to her. I began counting—Rob and I had made love our usual four times this week, and that was fine. Four times a week should be enough to keep him from straying, not that he'd ever stray anyway.

I watched him as he went off the diving board. Joy's ex-husband was kind of out of shape, and Tom, Peg's husband, was pale and freckled, but my man looked like a young god on that diving board. Just before I went in, I noticed that both Joy and Peg were watching the diving board and the show-off on it. There was just one show-off now—Rob. Tom had gone in because too much sun made him burn, he said, and Allen had gotten tired because he was out of shape.

A brief, unreal feeling of jealousy went through me, so swift that I could hardly believe I'd felt it. How could I possibly be jealous of those two—silly Joy with her too-sexy clothes hanging on that too-heavy body, and silly Peggy with her weird ideas about how a man had to feel before she'd sleep with him?

All the same, when Rob and I were back in our apartment, and he came out of the shower, I went over to him and put my arms around him.

"Let's make love," I whispered, my face against his nice-smelling, still damp chest. "There's no rush to eat dinner, is there?"

I was conscious of an ever-so-brief pause, as if he didn't want to, but he didn't want to say he didn't want to. Rob—not want to? Why, he'd always been eager for sex!

"What's going on, Becky?" he asked teasingly. "Usually, it has to be after dinner, after dinner dishes, after your favorite TV show and then only if there's a full moon!" He grinned at me. "So why the big change in habit?"

That bit about the full moon was just plain nasty—and the other part, although it was mostly true, made me sound like some kind of dud in bed. I felt sudden resentment go through me and I turned around, making some light joke of it all. So we didn't make love right then, and after dinner, I realized the real reason. We had company— Joy, wearing a mini that made her look like a fat Venus, her ex- husband, slightly drunk, Peggy, wearing one of her weird, hippie- granny outfits, and her husband, also slightly drunk. Everybody talked a lot about everything, even my usually quiet, reserved husband got real carried away when the discussion about Doing Your Thing started. I remember being in the kitchen, putting some squeegy stuff on crackers, and thinking that all of a sudden, my husband didn't sound much like himself anymore. All of a sudden he didn't seem to dislike Joy and Peggy—in fact, he was talking more to them than he was to their men. And I guess you could still call Joy's ex her man, since he seemed to be around her a good deal of the time. They would have these bitter arguments where he told her she ought to cover herself up and not go around in see-through clothes like she did, and of course, she'd tell him—maybe rightfully—that what she did was no longer any of his concern.

But it was Tom I felt sorry for. He always looked pale and weary, and lonely, and when we were all sitting around that night, the night I served the snack with the squeezed-cheese and decided my own husband had changed, I realized that poor Tom was about at the end of his string. Still, it embarrassed me when Peg began talking about their problem in a loud, fretful voice.

"She hasn't slept with me for seven weeks, six days and thirteen hours," Tom said. "Plus about—let's see—twelve minutes."

"And I'm not going to either," Peg said. She sure didn't look very appealing—at least I didn't think she did—with her old Nehru jacket that came up to her chin and all her ugly, heavy hippie beads. "Sex is only one part of a relationship. A man has to understand the deep part of me. And you never did, Tom. You never did."

It wasn't long after that when Tom moved out. Peggy used to come up to our apartment every night to talk about it, still wearing her weird clothes, still looking ugly. At least I thought she did. Rob seemed to enjoy her company.

I'm not sure just when it was that I realized things had reversed themselves. In the beginning, I was the one who wanted to really get in with the in-crowd there at the apartment house. I was the one who wanted to find out about Doing Your Thing, Loving for Real, and Letting It All Hang Out—as Joy liked to say. But after a lot of times at the pool, a lot of cups of coffee and a lot of parties in different apartments, I had decided that for the most part, these people had nothing to offer. Sure, for a while, they'd taken my mind off the fact that I'd lost a baby and that I couldn't have anymore for a while. But now, I was bored with Joy's nudity, her flopping breasts, her desperate attempts to appear sensual in front of men. And Peg, with her stupid reasons for not letting her husband touch her—well, it seemed to me she deserved to lose him!

I was glad when the summer ended and they closed the pool. In fact, I began to look in the paper for another apartment, maybe even a house. After all, it wouldn't be too many months before Rob and I could try for a baby, and they didn't allow babies in this apartment building.

One night in September, Rob came home with a big grocery sack in his arms. He glanced at me, said hi, then he began taking out the stuff he'd bought.

"What's all that?" My voice sounded sharp, and I realized I was beginning to feel a kind of anger and dread. I guess I knew a party was on its way, and I was sick of parties, sick of Joy, Peggy, and Allen, who was around more and more.

"Well," Rob said, "this is wine, in case you hadn't noticed. And black candles, and—"

"Black candles!" My voice rose. "What for?"

He smiled at me, his eyes kind of secretive. "For the party, honey, for the party. It's our turn—round robin—remember?"

"You didn't get the stuff I told you to get at the grocery. Soap. Salt, two cans of baked beans—"

"Ah," he said, and he opened the wine and sniffed it. "But I got food for the soul!" His eyes met mine and passed me by, as if my anger wasn't important. "They'll be here early. Especially Peggy. She called today to tell me she wasn't going to come, but I talked her into it. Listen—that girl has the right idea! I mean, if a man doesn't really understand a woman, then he's got no business making love to her—because that isn't love. It's sex—and that's another ball game entirely, right?"

I didn't answer him. I didn't like any of it—the wine, the crazy candles, the fancy food he'd spent our money on, to feed Joy and her ex-husband, who would probably be stoned when he came, and Peggy and goodness knew who else.

There were about fifteen people in our apartment that night. They sat in circles, on the floor, but nobody sat on the couch. I guess it was too square to sit on the couch or on chairs. Rob talked more than most of the men, and when he came out to the kitchen, where I kept making more and more sandwiches (those people ate as much as they talked and drank) he told me, his voice low, that he was "pretty sure Joy was thinking straight now."

I was getting so upset that my hands shook as I put the squeeze-cheese on the crackers.

"How can you tell if she's thinking straight? She always acts goofy, if you ask me!"

"She's wearing a bra," Rob said solemnly. "That means her conflict is resolved."

Horse feathers, I thought, and I squeezed cheese all over the kitchen wall, by mistake.

They began drifting away around ten, which was the time the week-night parties usually began to break up. But tonight, Joy had gone to sleep in a chair, her head nodding on her plump neck, and Peggy was asleep on the couch, wearing what I had come to think of as her minnow pants. There were a few others in the living room, sitting cross-legged, arguing about something I didn't care to hear about, so finally, I poured a glass of milk for myself and went to bed.

I slept, dreaming of the way it had been when we still lived in our little home town, when we had that cute, rented house and my folks came over once a week for dinner and Rob's folks came over once a week and our life was full of order and good, old-fashioned decency. When I thought of how my parents would react if they knew about some of these characters—Joy and some of the others, it made my face burn with shame. I wished I had never found this place and even more, I wished I'd never wished my husband would stop being square and Get With It. Because now that he liked wine and black candles and long conversations about love and politics and honesty and things like that—he seemed to have somehow moved away from me. He didn't seem to see me at all—especially in bed.

I was asleep when Rob got in bed. I knew he'd had too much to drink; I could tell because it took him a long time to get his shoes off. Suddenly, I felt a tremendous need for him. I rolled over and put my hand on his face—that had always been my kind of shy signal that I was ready to make love. Even though I'd usually waited until after dinner and after dinner dishes, just like Rob said I did, still, I always gave my little signal.

"I love you," I whispered, and I realized that for some reason, tears flooded my eyes. "Rob—did you hear?"

"Love," he said "L-O-V-E." He sat partway up in the near-darkness. "Becky—did you hear us talking about different kinds of love tonight? About how a man can love one girl in one way and another in a different way and yet, he's really not unfaithful to his wife?"

I didn't feel like rehashing one of those involved, get-nowhere conversations about love. So I said nothing, and when my husband's arm slid around me, I began to feel desire rise in me.

"What I mean is," he said gently, "I could care about one woman in a sexual way—and about another in a way that was only friendship, or the desire to make her feel better. But my real heart would still be with you, Becky. I'd give to those others—and they'd be giving to me but my real, inner self would really only relate to you. You see. . . . "

I sat up and looked down at him. Suddenly, I didn't feel sexy anymore. I felt scared.

"You'd give to who? And they'd give you—what? What're you trying to say, Rob?"

"Joy and Peggy," he said. "Honey—I talked to them and they both decided it's a good idea. The four of us. I can make Peg feel like a woman again—and that's all she really needs. And Joy—with me, she doesn't have to come on sexy, because I happen to really understand her. But I wouldn't be taking any of my love from you, Becky. In fact, with the four of us, I'd be even more loving, because love multiplies and grows."

I was out of bed, standing over him, screaming like a banshee. "Are you asking me to let—to let two other women in our bed? Are you trying to mumbo-jumbo me into being part of some kind of—orgy?" I began screaming. "Well you can go right ahead and have your orgy—but I'm not going to be a part of it! You can let your love multiply and grow, but it isn't going to multiply in my direction, because I'm not going to be around!"

It didn't take me long to pack. I was crying, and Rob was sitting on the edge of the bed looking ashamed and horribly embarrassed, and finally, I was on my way out, the suitcase thumping against my leg. Joy was sitting in the chair, looking scared to move, but Peg was still asleep on my couch. At the door, I put down my suitcase, then I went over and grabbed Peg's leg, tugging at her minnow pants, until she tumbled onto the floor. She sat up, staring at me in shock.

"Get out of here," I said evenly. "You stink like a fish, did anybody ever tell you that?" I turned around and glared at Joy. "And as for you—you're fat! Fat, fat, fat, fat! And lazy. No wonder you turn men off!"

I went on out, down the stairs, because I knew Joy and Peg might use the elevator and I didn't want to say anything else to them. When I got outside the building, I walked along with that suitcase still banging against my left leg and finally, before I got to the bus stop, I stopped and breathed hard and then for some reason, I turned my face toward the building where Rob and I lived.

He had opened the window of our bedroom. As I watched, he knocked out the screen with his fist and then he stuck his head out, looking for me. He looked so frantic, so much like a little boy that suddenly, I felt my mouth twitch. And the more it did, the more I began to see things more clearly. Joy and Peg—two jokes, the kids we partied with, a lot of good-natured youngsters who meant no real harm, Rob's orgy idea, nothing to leave him for—not really.

Because it was true that both of us had been pretty rigid and unbending, with our small town ideas about how to think, ideas handed to us from our parents and never questioned by either of us. But Rob had changed—at least he'd learned how to accept people who were weird, and he'd been willing to be friends with them. I was the one who had only wanted a change of scenery so I could forget my sorrow—I was the one who hadn't been able to change. When Rob had told me I only made love after dinner, after dinner dishes and when there was a full moon, he hadn't been very far wrong.

I looked back at Rob. He had seen me and he just sort of leaned there in the window, looking down at me. He looked so alone and so unhappy that suddenly, I just let my suitcase go and I began to run.

He was halfway down the stairs when I was halfway up. He gathered me into his arms and together, we walked the rest of the way to our apartment—and our bedroom.

That night, I left the girl who could only make love four times a week, if the dishes were washed and if no really good TV was on—behind forever. In her place was a new girl—sensual, loving, passionate, not afraid to express herself with her man.

We had an orgy, all right, and I'm not one bit ashamed to say that—an orgy with just my man and me. And if you haven't tried that kind of all-the-way giving and loving with your husband—you really should!
THE END

Male, female, the third sex and

THE FOURTH SEX—
My Husband!

Sure, 40 years later we can all have a good laugh at Katie and how she isn't able to figure out the truth about Brian on their very first date, when he tells her, "That gold dress suits you to perfection! You ought to wear lots of gold, green, and topaz... and stick to simple lines to show off your beauty." And that he really, really likes interior decorating. To be fair, she's only 18 when they start seeing each other, and not much older when they impulsively get married.

True Love and True Romance both have their share of stories about naive women who discover their husbands just aren't that into them. (This is at least more sensitive than the luridly titled "Why Do They Whisper My Husband Is a Queer?") The "fourth sex" turns out to be bisexuals, "able to physically love either sex," except that "they always have a stronger leaning towards one sex ... and can only find true happiness in that kind of relationship."

Heck, for 1972, the idea that same-sex relationships could lead to "true happiness" was practically progressive. Katie's feelings of pity for Brian ("there is still no real place in this harsh world for those like him") seem hopelessly retrograde to us today, but at least she's moving on without resentment.

Nightmares do come true! That's what I was thinking as I sat in my lawyer's office that day telling him I wanted to divorce my husband, Brian. I wanted to divorce Brian—yet I still loved him! Yes, even after everything I could still feel that way. What's more, he loved me too! Then why the divorce? My lawyer, Ted Hobson, was asking that very same question, his dark eyes full of surprise. Ted was the same age as Brian—twenty-nine—and he also lived in Magnolia Court, the apartment complex we lived in. He'd met us around the pool, in the game room and tennis court, and I suppose to him we looked like a very loving couple.

Now he was shaking his head. "But—why, Katie? I mean, this really surprises me. You and Brian—you always seemed so— well, close."

Tears of shame and misery misted my eyes. "I-I can't discuss it, Ted. P-please don't ask me to."

"But you need grounds for a divorce, Katie. You know that." Ted dropped his professional front completely then and reached across the desk to take my hand. His expression was very gentle, very sympathetic. "Can't you talk about it, honey? Maybe it would help."

I put my hands over my face. How could I talk about it? Yet I was going crazy keeping it all locked up inside me. I could never discuss this with my widowed mother, that's for sure! Anyway, she lived a good distance away. And as to friends—all my old friends had drifted away since I married Brian.

Ted came around the desk and took my hands away from my face. "Listen, I think we could both use a drink." He glanced at his watch. "Four o'clock. Let's cut out and beat the crowd to Arnie's, okay? Come on—it'll make you feel better."

In the cool, dim atmosphere of Arnie's, I was able to talk about it, finally. I had to talk to somebody, and Ted was sweet and understanding.

My story really began four years ago, when I was eighteen and in my first job as a receptionist with Allied Land Development. Talk about a job where you meet big, husky masculine types! Wow! Builders, construction workers, guys selling machinery, you name it. And all with one thing in common—they were very much—male!

Brian, the day he strode into the reception room was no exception. Big, husky, bronzed—and so handsome he took my breath away. Those vivid blue eyes of his widened when he saw me. "Hi! So they finally took my advice and improved the place."

"Sir?" I blinked up at him.

"I see the sour puss receptionist they used to have decided to retire. It's an improvement." He flashed me a smile exposing flawless white teeth and handed me his card. Brian Stapleton, he was, and he was a sales representative for Landway Construction Machinery.

One more he-man, I thought, but my heart was beating strangely in my chest. I found I could hardly take my eyes off Mr. Stapleton as he sat waiting to see my boss, Charlie Decker. He was fashionably dressed; his slightly longish hair caressed his collar in back; lazy blue eyes. And under that pale blue jacket—muscles!

I felt faint. Can you understand how it was? I really did flip for the guy at first sight. Oh, I'd had a few boyfriends, kids my own age, and they always put me off with their loud, bragging talk, their clumsy kisses, and the way they came on so strong. Mom had brought me up strictly—there had only been the two of us since Dad died when I was eight—and I'd been raised to value the love I had to give. The last boy I'd dated steadily had almost made me forget my upbringing. One night in his parent's beach cottage, we almost went too far. I would have too—except that he was so overeager and furtive that it completely turned me off. Soon afterwards we broke up and for some reason I'd given up fellows my own age. I found myself attracted now to older men like Brian Stapleton! The next time Brian came in I made myself be extra nice to him, extra friendly, but it was a few more months before he asked me to have dinner with him. Over the meal in an Italian restaurant, he told me he had an apartment in Ridgefield, that he travelled around the state selling machinery, and he made a good living at it. I wasn't surprised to hear that. He had everything it took to be a salesman—intelligence, good looks, charm! Brian was a great conversationalist too, I discovered that night, and took a big interest in everything—including my outfit and hair! "Black hair and green eyes—enchanting," he said with a smile. "That gold dress suits you to perfection. You ought to wear lots of gold, green, and topaz, Katie. And stick to simple lines to show off your beauty."

See what I mean? He made me feel like a million dollars; that he had eyes for me alone. On our next date, some three weeks later, I found out he did oil-paintings in his spare time. He was also interested in interior decorating and had a good friend in the business. "If only your apartment was in Ridgefield," Brian sighed, "I could get Terry to redo it for you. He has fantastic taste! A real big talent!"

"I'd love to meet him and see his work."

Once more came that beautiful smile. "Well, who knows, maybe you will—" and a funny expression came into his eyes, as if he'd just thought of something startling. I wanted to press him to tell me what it was, but decided against it. I had the feeling that he'd duck out quick if pressured. That night I prayed Brian would kiss me, but he didn't. He was a gentleman in all respects. I thought of inviting him into my modest little apartment—Mom had moved to Florida to live with her sister—but thought better of that too. After a long, clinging handshake, it was good night. Easy, chickie, I told myself when I closed the door behind that gorgeous hunk of man, just play it, oh so cool! Something about Brian, a certain remoteness, warned me it would have to be that way. As it turned out, I was right. We dated on and off—maybe twice a month- all that first year and still he didn't kiss me! Crazy! I know you must be thinking that, yet somehow it wasn't. You see, Brian was such a great guy, took such a big interest in my career, appearance, apartment and so on, and was so wonderful in every way that it didn't seem so odd. And too, one night he half explained it by saying, "There was another girl, Katie, last year. We—well, I'm still recovering from it."

"Want to talk about it?" I whispered.

But he shook his head. "Not now, okay? I'd just as soon forget it."

I took his hand and squeezed it. "I understand, Brian. And it's fine with me."

Quite suddenly, as if overcome by a surge of emotion, Brian turned and our lips met. Then, with a groan, his arms were around me at last. But just as suddenly he let me go. There was the strangest look in his eyes, almost as if he were about to cry! He stumbled to his feet and stood looking down at me and the words came blurting out. "Don't see me again, Katie! You—you're a sweet girl—and I'm afraid I'll hurt you."

"I'll take my chances!" I jumped to my feet and went back into his arms. He stood for a moment as if frozen, then once more his arms went around me and our lips met. But when he released me he turned, with a strange cry, and rushed out the door.

I didn't see him for three whole months and it was hell! By this time I was totally gone on the guy. I called his apartment in Ridgefield. One night I finally got him. "Oh, Katie," he sighed, "why did you call? We can't see each other again. I—don't ask me." And he hung up.

My pride was hurt. I stewed for a week, then called him once more. This time a woman answered and at the sound of her voice I felt as if a dagger had slashed through me. "Who is this?" she asked a second time.

"Uh—Kathleen Sanders. W-who is this?"

"Bobby," came the lisping voice. "Just wait a minute, please. I'll see if Brian's here."

Bobby? A boy—or a girl? In a minute the voice was back to say, "Sorry, Brian isn't here, but I'll tell him you called."

Several more weeks went by and I suffered helplessly as I waited for the telephone call that never came. Finally I became disgusted with myself. Perk up, you nut! I scolded myself. Stop the big tragedy act! Brian Stapleton wasn't the last man on earth. I would get over him. I would! I should have been given an "A" for the effort I made to put him out of my mind. To help myself I had a flurry of dates with other guys. But none of them showed the same interest in me as Brian had. They didn't give a hoot for the decor of my apartment or the color of my dress--just as long as it had a low neckline!

But, very gradually, a little of the first sharp pain was fading. I was beginning to think I would live-- when Brian walked into the office once more and blew everything sky high! He seemed so pleased to see me and we had a big night on the town—dinner, dancing, the works! Later, in my apartment, he kissed me over and over. "Katie, darling, you don't know how much I've missed you---"

I grabbed a playful handful of his hair. "Then why did you stay away so long, you big lug?" I was half laughing, half crying in my happiness at having him back. Then I had a thought and looked at him mock-sternly. "Who is Bobby?" Brian blinked, then laughed. "Oh—Bobby! He's just a guy who lives in an apartment across the way. He's harmless."

The minute I heard the word "guy" I relaxed back in his arms and snuggled closer. There was no reason in the world why another man should cause me a moment's jealousy!

Brian had a suggestion to make. "Look, we could see each other more often if you lived in Ridgefield. Why don't you try to find a job there?"

I was ecstatic that he would want me close to him! A couple of months later I had a new job in an insurance company in Ridgefield and was installed in an apartment building just three miles from where Brian lived. I wished I could have moved into his complex, but they were much too expensive for me.

Our romance bloomed for several months. The only bad thing was his frequent trips out of town, often over weekends. Once, annoyed at not seeing him four Saturdays in a row, I said, "Honey, I fail to see why you have to be gone on weekends. What can you possibly sell then? Businesses are closed then."

He stared at me hard, flushed a little, stammered, "Look—I like to get to a-a town ahead of time and—and prepare."

"Prepare? What are you talking about, Brian? You have your spiel down cold by this time."

"You make me sound like a-a dull record, playing the same song everywhere I go!" His eyes were surprisingly angry. "As a matter of fact, I vary things depending on what company I'm trying to sell. And you have to have time to get yourself jazzed up."

"You need Saturday and Sunday to get yourself to a point where—"

"Okay, Katie, enough!" Brian interrupted. "I don't have to explain my methods to you. Can't you just take my word for it? Do I have to go on the witness stand?" He flared up at the end, his voice rising, and threw his hands dramatically into the air. Then he grabbed his car keys off the table and stomped out!

I sat staring after him for several minutes, numbed by his outburst. The following morning he called to apologize. I hadn't slept all night and went weak with relief until I heard what he was saying.

"—no good for you, Katie, believe me. You deserve much better. I'm not going to see you again. One day you'll thank me." And he hung up.

I called him right back. "Why don't you let me be the judge of whether you're good enough for me or not?" I was in tears. "Why are you doing this to us, Brian? Every couple has fights—"

"We're not like every couple, Katie," he sounded as if he was crying himself. "I-I—Excuse me, please."

Once more he hung up. For three whole weeks I suffered, this time determined to forget him. Obviously, Brian was not interested in marriage. He'd made that all too clear. So why get hung up on a guy like that?

It was no use! I loved him, was crazy about him. Somehow I must make him see it; see we were really so good for each other. On impulse, I went into a store and bought two thick, juicy steaks, a bottle of wine, a couple of red candles. I appeared on Brian's doorstep an hour later, arms laden with goodies. I'd cook him a delicious dinner, we'd drink the wine, then we'd talk and—if possible, make love! For once I'd make Brian forget he was a gentleman! I'd coax him into letting himself go.

I rang the doorbell. I knew he was home because there was romantic music coming from inside the apartment. And sure enough in a moment the door opened—only it wasn't Brian!

A small, slim young man stood there dressed in pink pants and a lacy white shirt. His hair looked almost too black, his skin too peachy. "Yes?" he asked in a voice that was more like a whisper.

Momentarily flustered, I stammered, "Is Brian—I mean, may I—" my eyes drifted beyond the cute young guy and into the room. Brian was squatting casually on the white fur rug, a record player at his feet. There were several other men in the room and it looked like some sort of bull session, only—

"Katie!" Brian leaped up, ran to me, and for some reason was as flustered as I was. "This is a-a surprise."

I stared at him. "Am I-I interrupting s-something?"

He glanced back into the room. "Listen, fellows, I—don't let me break up the card game. I'll be right back." And then Brian grabbed my arm and practically carried me to his car. We got in and he took the groceries and dumped them in the back. The next minute we were driving to a nearby cocktail lounge.

Once we were seated with a drink in front of us, Brian said, "You should have called before coming around, Katie. You know how men are when a card party is going on." His laughter did not seem real. What was more, I'd seen no sign of cards, only records, those men, and the smell of incense burning somewhere.

"That man—the one who answered the door," I began haltingly. "He—he seems odd. I don't know quite how to put it, but—"

"Oh—Bobby! He's a funny one," he agreed disarmingly. "Works in the theatre, you know, hence the makeup." So that explained it! "When we've nothing better to do we get together for a few drinks and a game of cards." Brian waved a hand casually.

When we've nothing better to do? Hurt, I looked down into my drink and there was a long, awkward silence.

Then, suddenly, his big hand was over mine and Brian was saying, with a catch in his voice, "God, Katie love, what am I going to do about you?"

I hadn't planned to say it, but it came bursting out anyway. I raised eyes, brimming with tears, to his and said, "I love you, Brian. I love you."

His face twisted as if with pain and he groaned, "Baby, don't say that! You don't know—"

"I know all I have to, Brian. I know you're a very wonderful guy and—and I don't know why we have to do this to each other."

Our eyes met. Brian's fell away first. He signaled the waiter for fresh drinks and when they were set before us, he sighed again, twiddled with the stem of his glass. I could tell there was a tremendous struggle going on inside him, but I was keyed up too. So overwrought I could hardly stand it. I'd just said I loved him. I'd opened my heart. Was this all he could do—sit and fiddle with his glass!

"Forget it, Brian!" I snapped. "Just forget what I said a minute ago. I-I won't bother you again—" I jerked to my feet, spilling my glass, and ran out of the lounge. It was raining and somehow, when I reached the sidewalk, I slipped. The next thing I was falling into the road.

There was a horrible squeal of tires, the honking of a horn, and then I was struck on the side. I flew through the air, tumbling over, and sagged in a heap on the wet curb.

"God! What happened?"

Through a dark haze I felt strong arms carefully lift me, draw me against a broad chest. It was Brian. Even half dazed I recognized the scent of his imported cologne. As he soothed me, stroking gently with his loving hands, he cursed the driver of the car heatedly. "Just took off, damn him! Didn't even get to see the make of the car or the license plate."

I was taken to the hospital and Brian rode with me. He was so upset, blaming himself for everything, that I realized, finally, what I meant to him. I didn't feel all that bad, to be truthful, but I was weak—I pretended to be worse than I was just to get his loving sympathy.

Finally, after I'd been examined and placed in a hospital room for observation (I only had cuts and some bad bruises). Brian came in to see me. My bed was screened off from the others and the minute he was behind that screen he took me into his arms. "My poor little Katie! I should be whipped for driving you out into the rain like that. If anything had happened, I'd have—have died too," he added.

I caught his face close, smiling contentedly, "You do love me, don't you, Brian?"

Then, at long last, he admitted it. "Yes, I do. I love you very much." And as if he wanted it out fast before he had time to think about it, he rushed on, "Will you marry me, Katie? Would you be willing to share your life with a guy who's so far from perfect?"

"Oh Brian, darling, who wants perfection?" I cried, holding him very close to me. "Perfection is dull!"

"I hope you go on thinking that," Brian said quietly, a funny almost sad look in his eyes. But the next minute he was smiling. He kissed me over and over. "Get well soon, okay? I'll make all the arrangements."

We were married the following month. Mom flew up for our quiet wedding. A couple of my old friends came. But the bulk of people were Brian's friends, men he associated with in business or got to know through his other hobbies. They all seemed happy for us and wished us well. Mom thought Brian was wonderful! As we got into the car for our honeymoon trip, Mom cuddled me against her for a moment, whispering, "You're a very lucky girl, Katie. I know you're going to be happy together."

We certainly were on our two week honeymoon! That first night when he came to me in our moonlit room, he was like a young god—whose love turned me into a goddess. Lots of girls don't enjoy their honeymoons, but I loved every second of mine and was sorry when it was over. Our last night in Atlantic City we splurged on this great club—African decor, exotic, beautiful black dancers, a fantastic combo to dance to. I was positively glowing by this time, blooming from the long days and nights of love. I wore a low-cut black dress that Brian had chosen, very plain, but very form fitting. The slim, attractive man at the next table couldn't take his eyes off me. What's more, he was obvious about it! He raised his glass to me, smiled himself sick, sent me hot, sensuous glances that almost made me laugh.

But Brian didn't laugh. He got furious—so furious he made me leave the place before we'd finished our meal! On the way out he passed the other man's table and glared at him with pure hate in his eyes. It was as if they'd been lifelong enemies!

I giggled and clutched Brian's arm possessively. I was sorry to leave the club so soon, yet flattered too that my husband was so jealous. And he did the very thing I wanted—was ready for—took me back to our motel and made beautiful love to me the rest of the night.

When we returned to Ridgefield, I moved into Brian's spacious apartment in Magnolia Court. When I think of how very happy I was those first few weeks, it brings bitter tears to my eyes. Brian was a good husband. He worked hard, was sweet and kind and considerate in every way, showered me with gifts and clothes and perfume and anything else I desired. One day he came home to announce, "I had lunch with Terry! Would you like him to come and redecorate our apartment to suit you?"

"Terry?"

"My decorator friend. Remember I told you about him?"

"Oh—yes."

"What kind of decor would you like? How about French Provincial?

Or maybe something more exotic—Spanish. I think red leather walls and heavy dark, carved furniture would be nice, don't you?"

I laughed aloud at his interest and enthusiasm. How many men, I wondered, would take such a close interest in something like this. I knew we could afford to have the place done over. Brian had a good bank account and made big money.

"Sounds great!" I said happily, not realizing it was the very last thing I needed—Terry!

Then, before I even met him I discovered I was pregnant. I've never seen a man so happy as Brian was that day I gave him the good news. He turned white, then red, swept me off my feet in a fit of wild ecstasy. "I'm to be a father!" he laughed. "A daddy! You've made me the happiest man in the world tonight, Katie—"

"Well," I giggled, "you had a little to do with it too, darling."

"When Terry comes to decorate, we can turn the spare room into a nursery for the baby! Go downtown and pick out everything the baby will need and remember, only the best for my son!"

Oh, those were such fabulous days! Love was beautiful! We got along beautifully too. Not a single ripple to mar our joy in each other—until Terry McNair came on the scene.

From the minute we were introduced, I knew—with a start of surprise—that the man didn't like me. As a man, Terry was a strange one—tall, slim, long wavy black hair and dark eyes and obviously plucked eyebrows. His clothing was immaculate. His nails polished a delicate pink. His hands were in better shape than mine; they were soft, snow-white, limp!

Terry forever waved his hands around as he spoke in that high, simpering voice of his. He took absolutely no notice of my wishes, but danced about the apartment giving instructions to his assistant, a slight boy with blonde ringlets. "I see this room in shades of purple, Rodney! Yes, pale lilac walls, deep plum carpet, and the bedcover a stark white"

"Uh—Terry," I said several times, trying to break into the rapid-fire flow of instructions. "I-I would like our bedroom in pale blue—"

"Blue! Blue!" He turned his head haughtily, wrinkled his nose and pinched his pink mouth tight. "You would make this lovely room blue!

Nonsense! It has to be purple! It's a purple room. Blue is so—so dull; so ordinary." It was like a slap in the face and I fell silent.

We moved into the living room. "Orange!" Terry screamed, startling me so that I jumped. "Oh, this is such an orange kind of room. Yes, write that down, Rodney. Orange—with dark green draperies, a brown shag rug—"

"Uh—Terry," I tried again.

"Yes?" He looked at me over his shoulder.

"I'd like this room in white and gold."

"But everybody has white and gold! It's so—"

"I know—ordinary," I finished for him, my patience beginning to wear mighty thin.

Suddenly Terry tossed his folder of fabric samples into the air, wheeled on me, and said dramatically, "Do I tell you how to cook? How to wash the dishes and polish the silver?"

"No, but—"

"Then please don't presume to tell me how to decorate!"

My face burned. "Listen, Mr.—whatever your last name is, this happens to be my apartment—"

"Brian's!" he corrected smoothly.

"And I am Brian's wife! You will use the colors I tell you to use—"

"Never! I refuse to turn my friend's nice apartment into a-a cheap imitation of every other apartment in this city. Not even for you, Mrs. Brian. Give your husband my regrets—and my sympathy." And he waltzed on out, nose in the air, malice gleaming in his small black eyes.

Brian was surprisingly upset when I told him about it later. "You should have gone along with him, Katie," he said with a frown. "Terry is a wonderful decorator, with excellent taste."

I made a face. "Orange walls! A purple bedroom! Ick!"

He looked at me and there was this odd expression in his eyes, almost a look of distaste. "That sounds fine to me. Who are you to argue with the taste of the man who had decorated the best houses in town?"

I stopped trying to make light of it then. I could see he was upset, and it puzzled me. But I thought it best to smooth the whole thing over. "You don't really care what I pick out, do you, darling?" I smiled. "Men aren't concerned with all that—"

"What are you trying to say—that all men are blind oafs who only care about football, beer, and bed?" His tone was bitingly scathing and it stung me.

"No, but—"

"I happen to be interested in how my home looks, do you mind? Now get on the phone and call Terry and apologize. He came down here as a favor—"

"Apologize!" I sputtered. "You must be crazy! I'll never apologize to that—that queer!"

His face went white. It was a minute before he could say, "What did you call him?" His voice was a hoarse whisper.

"A queer! A fairy! However you say it!" I screamed. "It's true and don't deny

He grabbed my arm, hard, twisted it a little. His skin was mottled pink and white, his eyes enraged. "Don't you use that word in my presence, Katie! Never again, d'you understand?"

I flinched from the look on his face, from the way he was twisting my arm.

"You—you're hurting me!" I gasped. "Let me go!"

He did and strode right out of the apartment. Over his shoulder, he yelled, "I'll come back after you call Terry!"

"Never!" I yelled back. "I don't want that—that bug in my home ever again. He makes my skin crawl!" The door slammed off its hinges.

I fumed the rest of the night. It wasn't so much that Terry was, well, the way he was. What bothered me was his high-and-mighty attitude. His lifestyle was his own business, but his rude snobbishness was something else.

I had absolutely no intention of calling the man. And the more I thought about it, the more I wondered why Brian was so upset. After all, what was Terry to him? True, he was a friend, but when he insulted your wife how friendly could you continue to be?

My mind took me down a dark path. Suddenly I was thinking of the beautiful Bobby and his make-up and curled hair, of Terry and his pink nails and plucked eyebrows, of his adorable assistant with the blonde ringlets—and of all the other beautiful young men who seemed to hover about our apartment. I had a hideous thought—Brian? Oh no! God, no! Not my darling Brian. Forgive such a thought, dear God, I whispered aloud. Please forgive me. Because I knew beyond the shadow of a doubt that my husband could not be one of them. Brian enjoyed making love to me, he enjoyed a woman's body! Those other men they could not.

Well, I soothed myself, we happened to live in an apartment complex near the arty section of town, a part of the city that attracted unusual types. That was all. No need to get alarmed about it. And as for Terry, well, Brian was the loyal kind, for which I was glad. And he hated to hurt anybody's feelings.

So if it meant that much to my husband, why couldn't I call and apologize and get it over with? Was it such a big thing? Worth having a fight over?

I ended up calling Terry. Brian and I made up in bed! After that fantastic session I laughed at myself silently for even halfway thinking that he could be like them. I vowed never to doubt him again.

As we settled deeper into married life Brian's absences from home increased. There was a stretch where he was gone five weekends out of six! He was often on the road during the week too, and it wasn't long before he was away oftener than he was home.

I stood it for just as long as I could, then one night I complained. "I just can't see why you have to be gone on the weekends!"

He groaned loudly. "Oh, not again! I explained about all that. I'm sorry, you'll just have to live with it. 1 warned you that things wouldn't be perfect!"

He was right about that, and perhaps I was expecting too much. As it was, Brian was a wonderful husband when he was home! Which was less and less often lately.

In July, three young men moved into the apartment next door to ours. The apartments were side-by-side, with the bedrooms on the top level. Anyway, Ken and Victor and Pat were nice enough, very polite, very well behaved for the most part except that, soon after they arrived,

I noticed that all their visitors were other men!

Because we were so close—right next door—we soon became friendly. Before I knew it, they were dropping by at all hours, staying to eat with us, to have drinks, and to talk. As I said before, they were perfect gentlemen, yet . . .

Victor was the odd man in that trio, I soon noticed. He was only about twenty years old, with long dark brown hair, pale gray, limpid eyes. He especially liked to discuss things with Brian and seemed to need his advice on just about everything. Sometimes, when Vic was in our apartment, I'd turn and catch him looking at me in a funny way. Then he started calling me "angel" and "princess" and so forth. In the kitchen one night when we had a few friends over, he slipped in beside me and offered to help me carry the dip.

Up close Vic was quite handsome. Then, as I handed him the dip, he suddenly leaned over and kissed me on the mouth. At that instant Brian came through the swinging doors and caught us. I closed my eyes, waiting for the explosion. But it never came!

Brian chuckled awkwardly. "Oh I came in for some ice."

My face was burning but Victor didn't look upset. He flashed Brian a big smile, then headed for the living room. Brian and I didn't get a chance to talk until later, when everybody left, then he said with a grin, "Our friend Victor seems to have quite a crush on you, Katie."

I don't know why, but his easy tone, his treating it all so casually bothered me. Before I knew it, I flared up, "Look, Brian, I'm tired of all these men who seem to hang around our place. I want you to-to discourage them."

He laughed. "Discourage our friends? What kind of"

"We hardly have an evening to ourselves anymore! Either you are away, or when you're home we never can be alone together, just the two of us. I'm sick of it and . . ."

"Simmer down, will you?" Brian stripped off his shirt and tossed it on the bed. "Can't you take a little flirtation? You should be flattered that a young, good-looking kid like Vic made a pass at you."

I was stunned! His casual, couldn't care less manner really floored me. He acted as if he didn't care!

"You want other men to flirt with me, don't you?" I accused. "It gives you a-a cheap thrill! Maybe," I was really worked up now, "maybe you'd like to stand by and see us making"

"Shut up!" Brian roared--and slapped my face. "You uptight little bore, you . . ."

But he didn't finish. With a strange, agonized cry, he grabbed his shirt and his car keys and bolted out the door. I stumbled after him, falling over things in the dark, but he reached the car and jumped in and shot off down the street. "Brian!" I screamed, racing headlong out the door—and plunging down the short flight of steps to the hard paving below! Something struck me a breathtaking blow in the stomach--the ornate stone planter— and for a second or two I lay there writhing, unable to draw a breath. And when I could breathe, I was overcome by a gripping, grinding pain tearing through my stomach and back.

"Oh—God!" I choked. "The baby!"

From nowhere a shadowy figure appeared—Victor. "Lie still!" he shouted. "I'll call for an ambulance!"

The horror of that trip to the hospital will stay in my mind forever. Yes, I lost the baby! They fought for it, but it was no use. After that they gave me a needle that plunged me into total darkness, and I was glad. I woke up in a white hospital room and lay motionless, afraid to move lest I bring the horror back. I tried to tell myself that it didn't happen, that my baby was okay. It was just a bad dream and in a minute I'd wake up and be fine. Over in a corner of the room I heard low, muted voices—Brian's and Victor's!

Brian sounded terrible. "I should never have—married her," he told Victor brokenly. "She deserves—so much more. I thought it would work. I wanted it to work, but—I should have known it was useless. I love her! Can you believe that, Vic? I love Katie very much, in a way, but still I—" his voice choked off to nothing.

"You tried to make a go of it," Victor said soothingly. "But you know now that you're not for her—or any woman."

What on earth were they talking about? I struggled to sit up, moaning, "Brian—"

Then—at last—I saw them, standing there holding hands. Holding hands! I stared at them stupidly for a moment and time hung heavy in the silent room. Our eyes met and, oh God, I knew.

I slumped back against the pillow and closed my eyes and a hopeless cry tore out of me, "No, Brian! Oh dear God, no! Not you, Brian!"

He ran to my bed and sat down and took my hand in his. There were tears in his eyes.

I twisted my head from side to side. "You were a-a real husband to me. You were a real man—you are a real man!"

Brian buried his face in my lap. "I told you, a long time ago, it wouldn't work, Katie. Lord, I tried! How I tried —"

"But you were a real husband!" I grabbed his head and lifted it, wild in my confusion. "You were a husband in every way. Not like—like those others."

"I'm bisexual, Katie," he said bluntly. "I can—can love men or women."

I understood at last. Either one could satisfy Brian. He was a member of the fourth sex!

"But—" I limped on, "you really prefer men?"

He nodded miserably. "I'm so sorry, Katie! I wanted so much to go straight; to be a good husband and to father a child. I thought—I prayed it would work."

"But it didn't?"

He sighed, shook his head.

I threw myself back, turning my face to the wall, and sobbed brokenly. The doctor came in and they left. I knew, in my heart, that it was the end for us. And I couldn't-didn't want to—believe it! It was a week before I could leave the hospital. Brian paid all expenses, sent huge bunches of fresh flowers every day, but he didn't come back to see me. He did send one very sweet, very sad note. He would always love me, he wrote, always remember the beautiful, brief time we had together.

The day I left the hospital I asked my doctor about men like Brian. He explained that, indeed, there was a fourth sex. Some men, he went on, are able to physically love either sex—men or women—and even father children. Yet even so, they always have a stronger leaning toward one sex, often men, and can only find true happiness in that kind of relationship.

Women too, bisexual women, are the same—able to love both sexes. Able to become wives and mothers, yet secretly hunger after women, and only with other women find true fulfillment.

This stunned me. Oh, I knew about true homosexuals, but not about the fourth sex, who could give such a good imitation of being something they were not!

My life was in a shambles when I left the hospital. Brian had promised to make it easy for me to get a divorce. I told that to Ted as we sat in the cocktail lounge and I bared my heart to him.

"I'll make the divorce as smooth as possible," Ted promised, covering my cold hand with his big warm one. "And I'll help you all I can."

He was as good as his word! It was fortunate he was single because no wife would have put up with the long hours he spent on my behalf. Not only was Ted my lawyer, but he helped me find another small apartment, helped me move in, and took me out so I wouldn't sit at home brooding.

Just the same I had many long, sad hours~usually late at night—when I couldn't help thinking back to the good times when Brian and I had first been married. He had been such a wonderful husband, interested in everything, but perhaps too interested in some things to be entirely normal.

Anyway, I feel sorry for Brian and wish him nothing but luck and happiness. I don't hate him or despise him, far from it! If there's anything I feel, it's pity. Because there is still no real place in this harsh world for those like him. We're divorced now and I'm still seeing Ted. Tonight, when we went out to dinner, Ted complimented me on my dress. "Hey, that's kind of cute. Green looks good on you."

I stared down at my dress, and laughed, "Ted, this is blue!"
"Green."
"Blue!" I giggled, shaking my head. Then I noticed where his eyes

were—not on the color so much as the fit. Sure, Ted was color blind! But when it came to the really important things, his eyes were okay!
THE END

MISS NOVEMBER AND MR. JOE NAMATH

One of the great things about this "mini-story" is that, with a couple allowances for style, it'd probably work just as well today if you swapped out Joe Namath and replaced him with David Beckham. This is a short one, so let's just dive right into it.

There she stands, hands on hips, shoulders back, feet wide apart. Stark. Except, of course, for a discreet twisted sheet hanging down between her legs. How I hate her! She's so damned coy. All the rest of them, too. Blonde, black-haired, red-haired, but all with those great big grotesque bosoms and sly, self-satisfied eyes, as if to say, "Look what I've got! You can't possibly compete with me."

And I have to go by them ten times a day, every time I go by Tony's workshop downstairs. It's Miss November I really can't stand. She's parted her long, angelic, straight blonde hair in the middle, and she has big blank blue eyes. It's really queer, the way men's minds work. If a naked girl has dyed blonde hair, they think she's PURE. That evil photographer just caught her by surprise; but she's really the innocent girl next door. Hah! Tony looks up from the coffee table he's working on. "Hey, Nora honey, what are you mumbling about?"

"Oh, nothing."

He laughs. "The competition's pretty rough, isn't it? I guess you didn't eat your vitamins when you were a little girl. You're still little!"

I pick up one of his oily rags and sling it at him. My face is burning hot as I stamp upstairs. I'm so foolish to let him see how mad those—cows—make me. He tries to get my goat and he succeeds every time. But wait till those gals get to be forty or so—they'll be sagging clear down to their toes. Try to tell Tony that, though.

Tony comes upstairs. "How about a beer, honey?"

I yank one out of the refrigerator and slam it down on the table.

"Hey, Nora, it isn't that bad, is it?"

"If you think cows are so great, why didn't you marry one?"

"Well, I married you when you were eighteen, my little heifer, and I thought you were still growing!"

I whack the bag of pretzels over his head and retreat into the bathroom, locking the door. An hour or two in a nice bubbly hot bath ought to calm me down. Really, I don't know why I get so mad. I succeeded in beating out all the big-chested competition when I married Tony, and those girls were real, not colored paper on the wall. I guess it's just that the girls on the wall look so bloody complacent. They'll never wrinkle or sunburn, and any little defects they have were whisked away with the photographer's airbrush.

The next day I was having coffee with Molly, my neighbor.

"I know Tony wouldn't tease me so much if he didn't get such a big reaction from me. I lose my temper every time," I complained.

"I know what you mean," says Molly. "My husband has every damned month hanging on the walls. I look at them and get so depressed. I think he really doesn't understand how all that perfection gets me down. After all, those gals have all day to work on themselves, and probably lots of money, too."

"And the whole bit is so phony. Those females—just happened to be unzipping their tight jeans when a photographer came along. They're really such wonderful daughters and have cute little nephews that they take to the zoo. Yuck!" I gag.

"Strange, isn't it, how the zoo bit is little and black and white, but there just happened to be 3' by 4' color film in the camera when the girls are showering," comments Molly.

"Oh, well," I sigh. "It looks like I'll be making the same complaints for the next fifty years. Unless girlie magazines all go bankrupt. Somehow I don't think that'll happen. But I do wish I could just once get Tony's goat the way he gets mine."

"You won't be able to do that, not unless magazines start publishing cheesecake pictures for women!" Molly laughs like mad.

I sit looking at her thoughtfully. "Say, Molly, would you like to drive down to that ancient bookstore downtown—the one that sells old books and magazines?"

Molly stops laughing. "What's in your head now?"

I tell her.

"You can't! Hey, Tony might really get mad."

"Why don't you do it, too?" I ask her.

Molly looks horrified. "I wouldn't do that. It wouldn't be dignified. Besides, my husband shocks easily."

"Shocks easily! With Miss November around? He ought to be able to bear up under any strain."

"No, no," says Molly. "It wouldn't be ladylike."

"Okay," I say. " 'I'll go by myself,' said the little red hen." And I did.

So now, nine o'clock in the evening, I'm sitting on the edge of the bathtub, with fifty magazines spread out on the vanity. Very, very quietly I snip, snip, snip, cutting out certain large pictures from weekly and monthly magazines. I hold them up to the light, chuckle and admire. Maybe there is something to this pin-up business after all. Tony bangs on the door. "Hey, what are you doing in there?"

I start guiltily. "Don't be silly. I'll be out pretty soon," I shout, flushing the toilet loudly. Hastily I pick up the brown paper bag full of mutilated magazines and thrust it in the vanity along with the Kleenex and toilet paper supplies. The scissors I slip into the drawer with my comb and rollers. The cutout pictures go in my wig box.

The next morning I get up thirty minutes early. Tony mumbles. 1 say, "Don't get up yet. I just have to go to the bathroom."

"Again?" he yawns.

"It's still yesterday," I say mischievously.

"Oh." he says, accepting the non-explanation and going back to sleep.

I hustle out to the kitchen with my equipment and go to work fast. Then I do the usual breakfast chores. Tony comes shuffling into the kitchen, eyes still shut but his nose following the coffee to the breakfast table. He sits down and his eyes start blinking open. First his eyes light on his hot cereal. No brown sugar. He slowly rises and opens the cupboard door. Magnificently bare, Joe Namath grins joyously down at Tony from the inside of the cupboard door. Tony's eyes open wide and stay open. He stands there. I wait. Tony has decided not to comment. He takes the brown sugar down and carries it to his cereal. No cream. Tony rises and, wary now, opens the refrigerator door. Tony and Tom Jones exchange hot somber glances. Tony grasps the cream pitcher and retreats to the breakfast table again. No coffee. He gets up, avoiding my eye, and goes to the percolator on the counter. Charlton Heston reclines, nudely sardonic, in his Roman bath along the wall behind the percolator. Tony unplugs the percolator and carries it to the table. Tony opens his mouth.

"Bring me my grapefruit," he says.

Silently I place it on the table to the right of his coffee cup. Tony glances up at the dining area wall, and finds himself staring at the statuesque naked rear of Burt Lancaster in "The Swimmer."

I say complacently, "You know, you're quite right about pin-ups. The different angles are interesting."

Tony gives me a long intense look, and goes back to his grapefruit.

So I go back to my grapefruit, and we finish our breakfast. Tony vanishes into the bedroom, and soon reappears, dressed for work. He walks into the hallway and I follow him to kiss him good-bye. He picks up his lunch from the hall table. On the wall over the hall table sits Omar Sharif, a foolish grin on his face, his legs strategically crossed. Tony turns and looks at me reproachfully. I reach up and peck him on the check, and breathe softly into his ear, "The competition's pretty rough, isn't it?"

CRASH! And I am looking at a closed front door.

I begin to worry. Have I gone too far? I go back into the kitchen and pace anxiously about. I pick up the brown sugar and put it away into the cupboard. Spectacular Joe grins reassuringly at me. Maybe things will be all right after all.

When Tony finally returns home from work, he retires to his workshop. He emerges for dinner, full of idle chit-chat, completely ignoring the impudent rear of Burt Lancaster. I answer gloomily. After dinner, down he goes into his workshop. Damned rabbit-hole. Ten o'clock. Tony passes me on the stairs, going upward and calling cheerfully, "Goodnight, Nora, honey!"

Suspiciously, I glare after him. I continue on down to his workshop. Maybe—if I rip them all up . . . but there'll be more next month. It's no use.

Good heavens! Why, there are only five or six up on the workshop wall! I look closely. Mia Farrow! I look at the others. Slim, tiny, delicate and alluring. No wonder he spent all evening in the workshop. No wonder there are so few pictures up. He was hunting through all these magazines looking for Mia Farrows and Audrey Hepburns. I begin to chuckle. Bless his heart. Maybe I can find a picture of Dustin Hoffman or Woody Allen for the kitchen. Tomorrow. Right now I rush up the stairs to see Tony.

As I turn the bedroom door handle a thought flashes through my mind. That picture of Joe Namath—maybe I'll keep Joe Namath tucked away someplace. THE END

**My friends, my relatives, everyone thinks
I'm a monster**

I DON'T WANT CUSTODY
OF MY CHILDREN

How did the romance magazines address the feminist movement and women's liberation? Many of the women in True Love and True Romance stories have office jobs—at least until they get married. But "I Don't Want Custody of Our Children!" reverses the pattern: When Judy's husband tells her he's in love with another woman and wants a divorce, she's so fed up with being a housewife that she immediately agrees—as long as he takes the kids. Now, a year later, she's got a job and an apartment in Manhattan, and a little black book "filled with the names and telephone numbers of attractive, eligible men." But is she happy?

Of course, Judy needs to be back on the path to marriage and family by the end of the story, but by 1971, it was too late to simply ignore the lessons of feminism. So, as you'll see, she eventually sets out on a middle course that might allow her to have it all—so the next time she gets married, she and her husband will have an equal partnership.

"**B**ut," the young lawyer said earnestly, "this is most unusual. I mean, in an uncontested divorce action, the mother always gets custody of young children. Unless, of course, she can be proved to be an unfit mother."

"Judy's anything but that," my husband Mark said eagerly, leaning forward in his seat. "She's a wonderful mother. A marvelous mother."

"I really think," the judge advised gently, "that you ought to give yourself some time to think this over. To hand your two little daughters over like this—"

"But I'm not 'handing them over.' I'm just letting their father have them. Their father and, of course, their stepmother."

We had gone into the judge's chambers for this final meeting. A great, vaulted room with sunlight streaming through the white Venetian blinds, glinting off the aluminum water carafe on its little matching tray. The judge, too, was rather young and impressive in his flowing black robes. He tapped well-manicured fingers against the mahogany desk for a minute before sighing deeply, before saying, "Well, if that's what you're sure you want I have no choice but to grant the divorce and give your husband full custody of the children. You are to retain visitation rights. It's all most unusual, however. Why, I've had mothers sit in that same chair and sob their hearts out as they begged me to give them custody. I just wish I could understand you, Mrs. Littler...."

My young suburban friends, all housewives just as I had been, have become my ex-friends since the divorce. At first, they'd meet me in New York for lunch when they were on a shopping trip and always, toward the end of the lunch, they came back to the thing foremost in their thoughts.

"The only thing I can't understand, Judy, is why you let Mark and that woman keep your children. Why," indignantly, "I'd fight Harry"—or Joe or Ed or Bill —"tooth and nail before I'd let him have my children."

And then, just the other day, Mark called. He called me at my office. He was at home, as it turned out, babysitting with the children while his wife was visiting her mother, who had been taken ill in her Washington, D.C. home. His voice had sounded frantic over the phone, even a little desperate. It made me realize how my voice must have sounded when I had called him at his office in the middle of a busy, exciting working day to plead for help with some trying domestic problem.

"Judy," he said, "you just don't realize what you're doing to these kids. Sure, they love seeing you weekends and going shopping, or to Radio City Music Hall, but they need a mother, and they need her here."

"But they have a mother," I replied sweetly, "and she is there. There's no reason why Eleanor can't take care of the children just as well as I can."

"Now, look, Judy, I know you're doing this just to punish me; to hurt Eleanor; to make trouble for me in my new marriage. But if you'd—"

"Look, Mark," I told him, my voice hardening, "you were the one who wanted the divorce and I gave it to you. I told you I didn't even want any alimony. All I wanted was the same thing you wanted—namely, my freedom. Freedom to be myself, which is what I've got."

The buzzer on my desk lit up and I said hurriedly—as he had cut me off hurriedly many times. "Sorry, Mark, but my boss is buzzing for me. I have to run. Kiss the children for me—" and I hung up to go hurrying off in response to Mr. Meader's signal.

It wasn't until I got home that night, bone-weary from an exceptionally hard day, that I began to think about it again. Kicking off my shoes, I sat in the big armchair near the window, a tall, cold drink on the table at my side. My apartment is small, but charming. It overlooks Gramercy Park and now, in early May, the bright new buds are on the trees. Children skated along the street, calling to one another. Nursemaids pushed baby carriages, heading homeward after their day, in the park. Other young men and women like myself hurried along the wide, sunswept streets beneath my window. They, too, were returning from work they found satisfying, to open a door on a pleasant, if small apartment. This is a building of mostly singles. The few children who live here were born after their parents moved in and the management, as a rule, discouraged them from staying.

My married friends who have come here have chided me with, "But aren't you lonely?" To which I say, quite honestly, "Heavens, no!

What time have I got for being lonely?" There's my brand new color TV staring back at me from across the room. There's my hi-fi playing a lovely Chopin Etude. There are my textbooks from the school where I'm studying accounting and real estate law so I can be more valuable to my employer. In my oversize alligator handbag tossed onto the bleached mahogany table, there's my little black address book filled with the names and telephone numbers of attractive, eligible men and bright, busy, amusing business women. Women who, like me, earn good salaries; take pleasant, carefully planned vacations each year; keep fit in exercise classes; go to museums, art exhibits, the theatre. Women who see nothing particularly unnatural in my decision to yield up my children to the care of another woman. Women who say, "If I had to sit home all day listening to nothing but daytime TV and the prattle of little children, I'd be under the care of a psychiatrist."

And that, I think, is exactly the point I had reached that Monday morning just one year ago today. I think it sitting here watching the sun set over the spires of Manhattan. I think it sipping my drink and going back over it in my mind. I think it trying again to assure and reassure myself that I did the right thing for everyone concerned. Except, of course, Eleanor, who is only twenty-four and bitterly resents having been made an "instant mother" of two young children. I think it as I decide to pull out my stenographer's notebook and jot it all down. Maybe, once I have committed my little story to paper, I'll be able to understand better what I did and why I did it.

It was, I suppose, what might be called a typical Monday morning. A morning familiar to thousands, even millions, of harried young housewives. I had no way of knowing it was the morning of a day destined to be different from all other days in my life. At seven-thirty, just as I was thrusting my arms into a robe and getting ready to go downstairs and make breakfast, the phone rang. Mark was showering and shaving, and so I picked it up. It was a collection agency telling me we were three months in arrears on the car payments. That was Mark's department, but I promised they'd have a check by the end of the week.

"If we don't," the voice at the other end snapped, "we'll have your car."

Downstairs, bright spring sunlight was flooding into the pretty blue-and-white kitchen and the milkman was at the hack door—with another overdue bill. "Sorry to bother you so early in the morning," he apologized, "but the company's getting real tough on collections these days. Too many bum checks and dead beats."

"Just let me get the coffee started and I'll write you out a check."

A bellow of pain descended from upstairs and four-year-old Debbie yelled out, "Mommy, make Susie stop hitting me. She punched me in the stomach."

I went to the foot of the stairs. "Susie, get back to bed at once. Remember, you're just getting over the mumps." And to Debbie, "Now go back to your room and get ready for the nursery school bus."

"I'm not going to nursery school today" she announced. "I have a stomach ache. Maybe I've got 'pendicitis like Daddy had."

"No such luck," I muttered under my breath. Maybe it was mean and callous, but at least a mild appendectomy would put her in the hospital for a week and give me a rest. There was no point in continuing the argument, which Debbie would win in any event by sticking her fingers down her throat and vomiting as her eight-year-old sister had taught her to do.

The coffee was perking, milkman waiting. I went to my little desk in a corner of the living room and wrote out a check. It left me with a balance of exactly twenty-two dollars to last until Mark's next payday.

I said, "Here you are," and the man tipped his hat, thanked me, went out to climb back into his truck and roll off down the driveway.

I envied him. I wished I could climb into a car or a truck and roll off. Instead I turned back to the job of fixing a breakfast which the children wouldn't eat. They always ended up with a handful of dry cereal. The table in the pretty breakfast nook was set from last night. I poured orange juice, lay slices of the extra thick bacon Mark liked on the griddle, broke six eggs into a bowl for scrambling, put bread into the toaster, called upstairs, "Breakfast! Come and get it."

Mark was flying down the beige-carpeted stairs, monogrammed

attaché case in hand.

He worked as a salesman for a big New York City printing firm and always had to carry samples.

"No breakfast for me," he called over his shoulder, shrugging into his topcoat. "I have an early appointment at the office."

"Then why," I demanded furiously, "didn't you tell me so last night?"

"Forgot. Besides, who in hell could enjoy breakfast with those kids screaming their heads off? I wish you'd learn to control them."

I wanted to hit him with the frying pan in which golden eggs meant for scrambling were slowly burning.

"I'm down here making breakfast, paying bills, answering telephones. Why don't you control them?"

"I'm taking the car," he said, ignoring that. "Have to see a few suburban clients today. I should make it home to dinner by six, if the boss doesn't call any last-minute sales conferences."

I turned off the grill and the frying pan and followed him to the front door remembering how, once upon a time, he had never left in the morning without giving my rear end a fond pat and me a deep kiss. All at once I found myself wondering when that had stopped. When, in fact, he had stopped seeing me. He certainly wasn't seeing me now as he climbed into our two-year-old station wagon and he, too, rolled down the driveway and off for an exciting, challenging day of work in New York. His secretary would bring him coffee and a danish and the morning paper. At noon, he'd be somewhere having a two-hour lunch with a client at the company's expense. Then, I would be carrying a tray up to Susie, who wouldn't eat it, and fixing a lamb chop for Debbie, who would secretly feed it to the dog beneath the table. Then I'd gnaw on a cold chicken leg in between running up and down stairs from the cellar where I would be feeding laundry into the washer-dryer. I'd be making beds, running the vacuum, answering the always-ringing telephone, and racing the clock to have everything spick-and-span. I'd have dinner cooking when Mark turned his key in the lock at six o'clock.

All right, what next? A breakfast tray for each of the girls.

Debbie poured her cereal down the toilet. Susie vomited hers back up. I poured myself some black coffee, lit a cigarette, told myself, "Steady," and prepared to face the day.

The washer-dryer was broken again. When I flipped the switch, all that happened was a low, growling, grating sound and no sprays of water gushed forth. I turned it off and went upstairs to call the repairman, who said he couldn't possibly come before Friday. That meant I'd have to wash out some essentials—socks, shirts, underwear, dresses for the girls—by hand in the laundry tub. I remembered that I'd forgotten to turn on the dishwasher. When I did nothing happened except a cloud of thick, acrid-smelling smoke that poured out at the top and sides. I pulled it out, peered inside, and saw that Debbie had put her plastic doll's tea set in the tray. The heat had melted them and now they were clogging the mechanism. I'd need a knife, boiling hot water and time to dig the gooey mess out. I thought of rushing upstairs, pulling Debbie out of bed and spanking her bottom. What good would it do? I'd still have the mess to clean up plus a crying, howling child on my hands. After close to an hour I had it cleaned out, but when the washer was turned on again, the rancid odor persisted. I'd have to wash the dishes twice.

The front doorbell chimed and when I opened it I found a man in white painter's garb standing there, informing me that Mr. Littler had commissioned him to paint the kitchen today. I assured him, smiling grimly, that that was impossible. I had a very sick little girl and no time to clear the cabinets or move the kitchen furniture around.

He shrugged. "Okay, lady, but this is the only time I'll have for a month and your husband told me to be sure to get it painted. He seemed real worried about getting it done."

I said, "That's funny. He didn't say a word about it to me." I opened the door wider and said, resignedly, "All right, come in. But you'll have to start with the breakfast nook and you'll have to move the furniture around yourself. I'm trying to get some laundry done."

He said again, "Okay. It's your nickel. I get seven-fifty an hour."

I said, "I wish I did," and stood there at the open door as he

149

carried his ladder, his paint buckets to the kitchen. It was a pretty day. Soft, cloudless. It was a pretty, tree-lined suburban street. Well-cared for lawns, well-cared for homes although, like ours, none was very expensive. A typical middle-income suburban community. I wondered how many of the wives in those white or pink or yellow-painted houses were feeling as desperate as I felt this morning. I was really letting it all get to me: the sense of loneliness after Mark had stormed out without his breakfast; the endless demands on my time; the utter thanklessness of being a wife and mother.

"Oh, now, come on," I told myself firmly. "Let's not start to wallow in it. Just be glad you have two pretty little girls and a handsome, loving husband with a decent-paying job."

But my self-lecture wasn't working. Why, I wondered, heading back up the stairs where the doors to the children's rooms were mercifully closed so I could be spared the mess I would see when I finally got around to opening them. Why was this morning different from other mornings? Why, today, was I feeling a kind of desolation, almost as though Mark had left for good? It was the way he had acted, of course, storming out without breakfast, blaming me for the children's noisy behavior. As though they were my children, and I could damn well take care of them myself. Well, I thought, suddenly furious, *damn you* as I tugged at a sheet. *Damn you for acting so superior, as though you were the only white man living on the block.* That thought made me giggle while I shook pillows out of cases and put them on the window sill to air out. I lingered there, as I had downstairs, seeing the golden forsythia in bloom, smelling the lilacs, remembering a time when Mark and I had first met at the little community college we both attended. On a day like this we would stroll across the campus, hand in hand, and he would recite some poetry of Rupert Brooke's. Or else we'd just sit beneath a tree eating our sandwich lunch and thinking how wonderful it was to be young and in love.

The last time I had asked him to read some poetry out loud to me, he looked up from the printing textbook he was frowning over and said, "Are you nuts? That's kid stuff." Then, as though seeing me for the first time, he'd tickled, "By the way, you ought to do something with your hair. You're too old for a pony tail."

I was twenty-eight.

The phone rang and a photographer asked whether I wouldn't like him to come and take some "studies" of my two beautiful children. His company was running a contest, and— I cut him off with, "Sorry, they're both in bed with mumps."

The painter called up to ask whether I'd mind clearing out the cabinets now as he was going out to sit in his car and eat his lunch. Debbie appeared at her door in her pajamas to say she was hungry.

Over her head I saw the indescribable litter of her room. She'd also been using her Magic Marker on the wallpaper.

"I'll bring it up to you on a tray. The kitchen's all torn up by the painter."

Susie didn't want any lunch. Just a coke. A coke is bad for you, I started to say and thought, So what? Forget it.

At four the phone rang again, waking Debbie from her nap. It was Mark, asking whether the painter had come. When I said he had, Mark's "Good!" seemed all out of proportion to having the kitchen painted. What had made it so important to him all of a sudden?

Then he said, "This is a good night for us to eat out, then. Get a sitter for the kids and call a taxi and meet me at the Red Mill."

The Red Mill was the most expensive eating place in town and we had only twenty-two dollars in the checking account. Besides, how could I get a sitter at the last minute like this? And didn't he realize most sitters wouldn't want to sit with a child just getting over mumps and still infectious? I hated the sound of my own voice pouring out my housewifely woes and yet I seemed helpless to control it.

"For Christ's sake," Mark snapped, "you're always complaining that I never take you anywhere, and then, when I offer to, all I get is one great big long bellyache. We'll charge the damned dinner, then, and call a visiting nurse, I don't care what it costs," he roared across my protests. "Just get one. The Mill, at seven," and he rang off.

I stood there, hand on phone, wondering vaguely what I would wear. It had been two years since I'd bought myself anything new except things to wear around the house. I lifted my eyes and peered into the gold-framed mirror above the telephone table, and decided, objectively, that I looked like hell. I was having my period and my hair always looked exceptionally dull and listless at that time, all the golden highlights gone out of it. If he'd called me earlier I might have been able to manage a date with the hairdresser. But who would stay with the children? Oh, to hell with it. He never really saw me any more anyway.

I ran my hands down along my body and felt that telltale roll of fat bulging above the girdle. I'd meant to join Weight Watchers, but who has the time? My face that once had a model's high cheekbones, looked plump and matronly with the definite beginnings of a double chin. As soon as the kids were well and back at school, I promised myself, I was really going to do a job on myself. I'd run an ad in the paper and offer to type letters and manuscripts for local businessmen in order to pay for it. I still had my old portable from college days. Mark would he pleased when he heard what I was planning to do. He was always saying, "If you're so bored all day, why don't you get out and do something?"

My spirits rose a notch. The painter came in to say he'd done all he could for one day but not to let the kids get into the wet paint, "Because I'm not doin' nothin' over unless I get paid for it."

I called the visiting nurse service and was told a nurse would be there at seven. But she was to do no cooking and the charge, because of illness in the family, would be ten dollars for the first three hours and five dollars an hour after that. I agreed. I'd fix TV dinners for the children then close and lock the kitchen door. By the time everything was finished and I was ready for my shower, it was half-past six. As the taxi drew up before the door. I called goodnight to Miss Tolley and the kids and fled before another problem might present itself.

The town clock was just chiming seven when the taxi deposited me at the door of the Red Mill. I found Mark sitting on a red leather stool at the little circular bar, having a martini and watching the news. He looked smooth and handsome and pleasantly relaxed as he greeted me with, "The hem of your dress is down."

"Oh, damn! There wasn't time to look in a full-length mirror before I left."

"And what in hell have you done to your hair? It's all frizzed up. Looks like a bird's nest."

"That's because I had to use the curling iron on it. There wasn't time to wash and set it properly."

"Will you have a drink here or wait and have one at the table?"

"At the table. I'm starved. Spent my lunch hour cleaning out cabinets for the painter." He had paid his, bar bill and was steering me by my elbow toward the darkened room in back when I said, "And by the way, what's the big rush about having the kitchen painted? We've waited two years. Why couldn't it have waited another month?"

"Because I might be putting the place on the market. I'll tell you about it at the table." I've read the phrase, "I was stunned into silence," but I never knew before what it meant. Put the house, put our home, on the market? Why? Had he lost his job or something?

A waiter pulled out my chair for me. Red shaded lamps glowed softly on the red-and-white checked table cloths. Muzak was being piped in. I listened to someone singing, "Raindrops Are Falling on My Head." More than rain drops were falling on my head. The roof was falling in.

He didn't even let me finish my martini before he leaned across the table, his blue eyes boring steadily into my dark ones to say gravely, gently, "Now, Judy, I don't want you to take what I'm about to say too hard. What I'm about to say is really going to make life more rewarding for both of us. Let's face it," he was taking little sips of his martini in between the phrases. "Neither of us has been getting much fun out of life lately. You look like hell and I feel like hell and—well—the spark's just gone out of it, that's all."

My hand was shaking as I returned my glass to the table. "The spark's gone out of what?" I repeated stupidly, although I knew. I knew before he spoke the words. Maybe I'd known for a long time.

"Out of our marriage," he was answering my automatic question. "Lately, when I make love to you I find I have to close my eyes and think of someone else to make it really exciting."

Without thinking, just responding to the awful hurt be had

dealt me, I emptied the rest of my martini in his ruggedly handsome, smiling face. Carefully, saying nothing, he took the handkerchief out of his breast pocket, mopped up his face, signaled the waiter and ordered two more drinks.

"Yes, sir. And would you like to order now?"

"I guess we might as well. What'll it be?" to me.

I found the most expensive thing on the menu and ordered it. Filet mignon, medium rare, baked potato with sour cream and chives, and to hell with the bulge above the girdle for tonight.

Across from me, Mark closed the over-size red menu, and said, "Make that two, and let's have a bottle of Cabernet Sparkling Burgundy." He smiled across at me as the waiter moved away. "The last supper," he said. "Might as well make it a good one. And now, let's get down to business. I guess by now you've gathered what this is all about—that I want a divorce. A nice, quiet, friendly divorce that will give us a chance to make a new life for ourselves while we're still young enough."

"Who is she?" I asked dully. "Anyone I know?"

"No. A girl I met at a publishing party last New Year's Eve."

"And you've been having an affair with her." He nodded. "And she's the one you think about when you close your eyes."

He nodded again, saying, "But you must have guessed something was wrong. Our love-life's been pretty lousy lately, even for you."

"What do you mean, even for me?"

"Well," he said, working on his fourth—or was it his fifth?— Martini, "you never did like it very much, even in the beginning. Maybe because you were a virgin when I married you. Maybe I haven't been a very good teacher."

"Maybe you haven't," I agreed, wondering with new stabs of pain and jealousy in what way she was "better at it" than I. How did women differ when they were making love? What made one woman a good lover and another a poor lover or, at least, an indifferent one? After the divorce I must do some experimenting on my own and find out.

"I gather your new love isn't a virgin then."

"No, she's divorced, in fact, although she's very young. Twenty-four. He was almost twice her age. She met him when she was modeling. He's a rich cloak-and-suitor. One of those." Whatever that meant.

The steaks arrived on their sizzling platters. The wine nestled in its silver bucket of ice waiting to be poured. The Muzak played, "I'll Be Seeing You." All too appropriate. We lifted our glasses and toasted one another.

"To you," he said. "May you find real happiness with someone, and soon."

I said politely, "Thank you," but I didn't wish him happiness. I wished him on the far side of hell. And her, too. Her name was Eleanor. She was tall, blonde and blue-eyed and always eager to go places, do things. Ski, swim, dance, drive her little foreign sports car at crazy speeds, laughing when it made him nervous.

"She's wonderful, she really is. Even the kids are going to like her."

"That's good," I said, "since she's the one who's going to be raising them."

He lowered his wine glass and stared at me across the table. "Are you nuts or something? What would she do with them?"

"What will I do with them? You said you'd probably be putting the house up for sale."

"That's right. Because I'm going to need the dough. In today's market we should be able to get twice what we paid for it. Eleanor will lose her alimony when she remarries."

"Poor girl. My heart bleeds. Anyway," I said, almost cheerfully, "that's the deal. I just made up my mind. You want a divorce, you get custody of the children. I'll go back to business school, take some brush-up courses for my steno and typing, find myself a job, a cute little apartment in New York and whee! As you say, a whole new life."

Of course, he didn't believe me. He thought it was a joke, or a threat, or a trick. He'd had the whole thing worked out so neatly in his mind. My parents own a comfortable old farmhouse in New

Hampshire and they were always saying how lonely they were, how much they missed me and the children since they were too old to travel much anymore. So I and the children could go there to live, "for a while, until I get ahead financially—and you decide where you want to live and what you want to do."

That was to have been my life, struggling to raise two children without a father while he and Eleanor moved into a charming New York apartment. We would sell the furniture and split what we got for it because Eleanor had made it clear she didn't want to live with another woman's furniture. Eleanor certainly sounded like a girl who knew what she wanted and was accustomed to getting it. What she didn't want was another woman's children. But she was going to get them if she wanted to have their father.

Mark said wildly, "You don't know what you're doing. To me, to the kids. You're their mother. You can't just walk out on them like that."

The lawyer said, "This is all most unusual." The judge had the session with me in his chambers. I stuck by my guns and Mark and I took turns explaining it to the children. Daddy was going to have a new wife and Mommy was going to live in New York and work. Grandma and Grandpa would come and stay with them for a while until Daddy and his new wife came back from their honeymoon. Then maybe Daddy would hire someone to help care for them and they'd come in to spend every weekend with me.

"We'll go to lots of movies and I'll take you shopping for pretty clothes and we'll see museums and all kinds of things."

Mark had listened, frozen faced. Not until I called the taxi and had my luggage stowed in the back seat with my mother crying quietly in the background just as she had at my wedding, did Mark really believe I meant it.

It's been a year now, and what friends I have left report that Eleanor and Mark fight like hell, even in public. She hates the suburbs, the house, the children, the dog, the cats. He didn't sell the house because where could he go with two young children and a lot of animals? The children are flourishing, though, and love their weekends with me because I can be a companion, a fun person, instead of the exhausted, over-worked woman I had been.

The bills are Mark's problems now, not mine. I make a hundred and twenty-five dollars a week, and all I have to do is pay my rent and utility bills. There are several attractive men in my life who take me out to dinners and lunches and love the fact that I don't want to get serious. I don't want to get serious because every day away from Mark and the nightmare of bills, laundry, sick children, and chauffeuring that my life had become makes me see one thing clearly. Mark and I loved one another and, I think, still do. But we'd lost one another in the welter of unpleasant things our life had become. My endless complaints; his seeming indifference to my loneliness; my terrible boredom. We weren't Mark and Judy any more. We'd become Mommy and Daddy.

Last night, Mark called me and asked me if I'd have dinner with him tonight. "There are some things I'd like to talk over with you. Eleanor," he added hastily, "knows all about it and she approves."

"Then, fine," I said cheerfully. The full length mirror on the back of the bathroom door told me I'd lost all those bulges, thanks to diet, exercise and massage. I'd shed ten pounds since coming to New York and taking an executive secretary's job in a big real estate firm. I go to school three nights a week to learn about real estate law so I can be more efficient in my job. I'm never bored, never lonely. And if, as I suspect, Mark and Eleanor have reached the end of the line, and Mark wants me to give our marriage another chance, I'll say "yes," and say it eagerly.

This time our marriage will be fun. This time we'll both climb into the car in the morning and head for New York leaving someone thoroughly competent to care for the children. Someone who likes caring for young children, who's trained to do it. And Mark and I won't talk about taking the dog to the vet or how much it's going to cost to have the washer repaired. I'll talk about my busy day and he'll talk about his, and when we come home together our home won't seem like a trap to either of us but like a haven. With two salaries the bills will be kept in order. With two separate, exciting lives our marriage will be kept in order.

Maybe a lot of marriages could be saved if the wife just refused, as I did, to accept custody of the children. If she insisted on her right to be a free human being, just as her husband wanted to be. I don't know. I only know it seems to have worked for me. For us.

The phone is ringing now, and it will be Mark telling me when and where to meet him. I look radiant, well-groomed, happy, as I go to answer the ringing phone. Don't you really think my little experiment was worth whatever money and even suffering it cost?   THE END

WHY NOT? WE USED TO BE MARRIED

Many stories in True Love *and* True Romance *from the early 1970s are about young women going through wild times, getting into trouble, and resolving to straighten out their lives at the end of the story. Here's a story about what might happen after that. Angie's got a safe, stable marriage now, but then her first husband—the one she married straight out of high school, and divorced less than a year later, when she got tired of living on the wrong side of the tracks—is back in town, and he promises he's ready to clean up his act, too.*

The morning I found out that Keith Ryan was back began just like any other morning—or rather, like most of the mornings I'd known since I'd married Jim Kessler. I woke up, opened my eyes, and knew it must be nearly seven, because I could smell coffee perking. Jim was an early riser; he didn't get up until eight on weekends, and he seemed to think getting up at that hour was kind of naughty.

My husband—my "new husband," my mother called him—was thirty-three, ten years older than myself. Jim wasn't really too old for me because at this point in my life, I needed an older, mature man . . . at least that's what I told myself. Jim was organized, cautious, kind—a good, solid man who worked hard, paid his taxes and was faithful to his wife.

I put my hands over my head and stretched. I'd turned out to be what I used to laugh at, what Keith and I used to laugh at—a housewife, living in the suburbs, a churchgoer. Yes, I was now a member of a group of married people, all older than myself, who played cards at each other's houses on Saturday night.

Keith, my first husband, and I hadn't referred to that kind of life, that kind of person as being square, because we thought the word "square" was too square. Earth People, we called them.

We used to lie in bed, there in our shabby apartment over on Rohan Street, and we'd watch the Earth People going to the Church Of Holiness, there across the street. Sometimes, we would have a hangover from too much beer-drinking at Sam's Attic, the place where we liked to go with our equally kookie friends, and sometimes, I would have a headache from joint-smoking.

Marijuana was a big part of our life together. Both Keith and I had begun smoking it as seniors in high school, and when we eloped, the summer after graduation, our life really didn't change much. We had been lovers before; we had been users of grass and once in a while, acid. We had loved to speed around on Keith's motorcycle, me on the sissy seat in back, and we had loved camping out, sleeping under the stars, cooking over an open fire. We did those things before we got married—my mother knew I was involved in a sexual affair but she really didn't care. And we continued to do them after we were married.

Only something went wrong. We began drinking a little too much and we got kicked out of our kookie pad because the local sheriff raided us and we were both put on probation because they had found a whole group of us kids sitting around high on grass. All of a sudden, the whole scene—the motorcycle, the dirty, crummy apartment with the cushions on the floor, the dusty stack of records, the way-out magazines Keith subscribed to because he liked to feel he was a rebel felt wrong.

More and more, I began to feel less and less satisfied. I began going over to my mom's to wash my hair, because the sink in our bathroom always had roaches crawling up and down the drainpipe. My mother, remarried after years of being divorced and alone, began to worry a little. She and her new husband didn't really want me around all the time.

When I was going with Keith, when I was married to him, I was no problem to my mother. Now, all of a sudden I tried to burden her with my new thoughts and feelings about Keith, about my marriage to him, and about being a hippie. Maybe Keith and I didn't have shoulder-length hair or anything, but all the same, we were a couple of hippies at heart.

People in town resented the area where we lived, and after having been married to Keith for less than a year. I began to resent it too. We began to fight—I stayed off pot and acid and stopped drinking beer because I hated the way I felt physically when I used those things.

Keith didn't understand what was happening, and when he finally realized I wanted to divorce him, he stayed drunk for nearly a month, shut up in that filthy apartment, the rent due, no job, until finally, they took away his motorcycle. He left town right after the divorce, and I went to live my my mother and stepfather. When I met Jim. I'd married him as quickly as he was willing.

Jim was an Earth Person: he had a good job and he drove a new car, not a cycle. He also shaved and bathed each morning, and he didn't drink or smoke. He'd been married once before, very briefly. The girl had been killed on their honeymoon.

Now, smelling the coffee, I got out of bed and smoothed down my short hair. I was supposed to go over to Richmond today, to shop for drapery material. I'd been married to Jim for two years by now, and during that time I'd learned to sew. In fact, I'd made curtains for most of our little house and for my mother's house too. Now, my mom seemed like a kind of middle-aged kook to me, with her efforts to keep looking young, the hard-drinking crowd she and her husband ran around with, and their interest in things like skydiving and boating. But then, maybe I was just getting to be Ultra Earth People, like Jim was.

He was eating his breakfast, reading the paper, sitting there in "his" chair at our dinette table, and the sun slanted in the window in precisely the same pattern it did every morning.

"Hi," he said, and he went back to his paper. "Don't forget to water the grass while I'm gone, Angie."

Gone. I'd forgotten. This was the morning Jim was leaving for

Camp Malcomb, down near Anderson, for his annual two weeks tour of duty in the Army Reserves. I hadn't actually forgotten, because I'd spent all week getting his shirts and things ready, it was just that I'd forgotten this morning, because I was sleepy, probably.

"I feel guilty." I said, kissing him lightly on the top of his head, where his hair thinned a little. "I should have gotten up to cook for you."

"I like to cook." he said. He'd finished his coffee. "I'll miss fixing your breakfast for you on Sundays."

That was a little ritual of ours, Jim's bringing me a tray on Sunday's. It had been his idea, and it had been such a switch from the hung-over Sunday mornings I'd spent with Keith, that I'd gladly gone along with it.

Jim left for camp at nine and I quickly straightened up the house and got dressed to go to town and get the curtain material. I had plenty to keep me busy during the next two weeks. My new draperies, lunches with some of my neighbors, my work at church in the Young Adults' Sunday School class. We were planning a big picnic in two months, up at the town's park, and I was on the food committee. My mother made fun of that—the fact that I was so active in church work while she was trying so hard to be a kind of aging swinger. But I didn't really care. I was happy with Jim.

Still, for some reason, I was kind of glad to see him leave for camp. That surprised me, the sudden, crazy feeling of freedom I felt when he walked out that door. I knew he would fasten his seat belt, pull out of the driveway and wave at me as he drove off, then, at the corner, he would honk his horn, probably twice.

And he did all those things, right on schedule. When I shut the front door, I realized that I felt somehow glad he was gone. Not gone forever—I couldn't stand that: he was my husband and he'd been very good to me. But gone for two weeks. I glanced at myself in the mirror, there in our little hallway. My eyes had a peculiar glow to them, a kind of expectant look, like a naughty child. Stop that, I told myself firmly. Start thinking about curtain material and stop that!

I was nearly out the door, on my way to town, when the phone rang. I knew it would probably be my mother; she always waited until she thought Jim was out of the house before she called me. Then, she seemed to feel she could say nasty things about him. since he wasn't in the house. It was Mom, all right, and her voice sounded oddly excited. I figured maybe she and Joe, her husband, had been spending more time out at the airport, or on the boat they'd bought.

"Angie," Mom said, "can you talk?" Pause. "I mean, is he there?"

I nearly smiled. Since I'd met Jim, I'd come to realize that in many way, my mother was like a spoiled child. She'd allowed me to do a lot of things in high school that a really good parent wouldn't. She'd never ready condoned my pot-smoking, but she'd sort of looked the other way, too involved in her own life to bother much with me.

"Jim's gone to camp, Mom," I told her, "for two weeks."

"Two weeks!" I heard her draw her breath in. "Do you suppose Keith knew that, Angie?"

I frowned. "Keith?"

Actually, I didn't like it when Mom mentioned him. She was always doing that, bringing him up, talking about something he had done that she thought was kookie or cute. I didn't want to hear about those days with Keith and I'd told her that. But since she didn't like Jim—she thought he was a stay-at-home, conservative bore—she still brought Keith's name up every chance she got.

"He's back," she said, that thread of secrecy and excitement still in her voice. "I saw him! Or rather, Joe and I saw him. He's working out at the airport."

I closed my eyes, unsure of my reaction. I had thought that Keith would never come back to Batesville. He always hated it, at least, he said he did. In high school, he couldn't wait to take off for New York or Florida or the hip scene in San Francisco. But then we'd married and for some vague reason, we'd stayed here. Maybe because down deep, I liked little towns, especially this one.

"What on earth would he be doing at the airport?"

But I think I knew, even before she told me. Anywhere there was something off-beat or dangerous going on, trust Keith to try it. He was, Mom said, working around the hangars, doing odd jobs, sleeping out there on a cot. And he was learning sky-diving for free.

I tried to put that out of my mind, the fact that Keith was back, but all day, I felt kind of jumpy. It was as if any second, I expected him to turn up. But then, I reminded myself that it was Jim, not Keith, who wanted togetherness to the nth degree. Jim was the one who sat next to me in church, in Sunday School, at the movies, called me three times a day every day and loved sitting close to me on the couch to watch T.V. Loved having me in our little house, having the house cozy and buttoned up, and there we'd sit, watching T.V. Keith had never been like that. Keith had always believed in freedom and doing your own thing.

Still, I had that strange feeling that Keith was going to show up, and when he did, I wasn't really surprised. The only thing that surprised me was my reaction to seeing him again. I was just crossing Main, waiting for the light to change, and as I walked across the street, I sensed something—a kind of closeness, a feeling that Keith was watching me. It was spooky. Then, when I got to the drugstore, I suddenly heard his voice. It stopped me dead in my tracks.

"Angie? How are you?"

He was sitting in a car. It was a yellow sports car, with the rear end raised for speed—a hot-shot's car, a kid's car, the kind Keith used to spend hours working on. I hadn't seen him for over four years, but I saw at once that nothing had changed for him. The car was four years newer than the one he'd bought before he bought the expensive motorcycle, and he was four years older; but he looked the same and the car looked pretty much the same.

"I'm—fine," I said slowly.

He looked handsome—Keith had always had that going for him. When I was about fourteen years old, I used to watch him go off the diving board up at the park pool, and just looking at him used to make my breath catch in my throat. Keith's eyes met mine. His eyes were a kind of blue-green, and now, they seemed darker than I remembered them. It could have been his deep tan that made them look that way. Or it could have been emotion. They always did deepen in color when he got mad or excited . . . or when he wanted to make love to me.

"You look great, Angie," he said softly. "Just great."

I managed to smile. "You look the same."

I took a small breath. About a million memories seemed to come flooding down on me, so that for a crazy instant, the scene that was real—the town and the stores and the people and the curtains I'd come down to buy—all that didn't seem real. For a brief moment, I was thinking of the good times, the Sunday mornings in that crummy little apartment, the time he'd brought me a wilted violet and I felt like bawling because that seemed so sweet to me.

Then, I noticed that he wasn't wearing any shoes. And he had on jeans, with both knees torn out. I stared, and all of a sudden, the stores and cars and streets and sounds came back to me. I was married to Jim, and this kook was somebody I had once been married to. Our worlds were very different now.

"I guess you could say I'm not exactly dressed up," he said, smiling a little. "Could I buy you a beer or something, Angie? For old times' sake?"

"I don't drink beer," I said cooly. "Not anymore."

His eyes narrowed. "You telling me you're straight now?"

"I'm not telling you anything!" He always could upset me quickly, make me mad, make me cry. Now, as I went into the store to buy my curtain material, I felt tears burning my eyes. Why in God's name did he have to come back to town?

That night, after Jim had called to say Hi, I thought about it. About the reasons why Keith might have come back. I hadn't told Jim he was back, maybe because I felt the less said about my days as a hippie, the better. My husband knew I'd been married right after high school and that the marriage didn't work, but he didn't know much more than that.

Keith may have come back because he had relatives here. His father still lived here, a peculiar man who drank too much and who used to run the card game downtown, the one that was illegal. And there was a cousin of his still living here.

Surely he hadn't come back because of me. Had he? When there's been no contact during the years since our divorce, no letters, just one crazy Christmas card with a drawing, in violet ink, of a flower like the one he'd picked for me that day? That card had come from New York City—somebody had told me Keith was living there in Greenwich Village.

I slept badly that night. When I woke up, the phone was ringing. I knew it probably wasn't Jim; he'd be too busy at camp to call me at this hour. But it could be one of my friends from church. I'd be better off talking to somebody—

"Hey, Sack-Out." Keith said, his voice deep and teasing. "You gonna sleep all day?"

That was his old, pet name for me, his old way of getting me out of bed after one of our parties. Sometimes, he'd whisper those words to me and before I could take my head from the pillow, we'd be making love. It's over, I told myself now. Over long ago—

"You shouldn't call me," I told him, my voice thin and sharp. "Keith—you've no right to—"

"Since when do we bother about rights, Angie? Remember..."

I closed my eyes. "I don't want to remember that apartment we lived in. I don't want to remember any of that."

There was a small silence. "I thought it was great," he said finally. "And you did, too. Sometimes."

"Yes. Sometimes." I stared at the front door. The tiny window in it was streaked; I really should get busy and wash windows. But somehow, I didn't care.

"I want to see you," he said, his voice urgent. "Just for a little while. I want to talk to you. It's about—well, I need your advice. Nothing wrong with that, is there? Hell, Angie, we've known each other since we were kids, right?"

Maybe it was that I'd ended up not buying that material to sew on, and maybe it was that I didn't want to spend the day washing windows instead of sewing, like I'd planned to. I didn't know. All I knew was, I told Keith okay; he could meet me at Sadler's and we'd have a coke and he could ask me about what had happened to so-and-so. Like he said, we'd been friends before we were lovers or husband and wife. So what could it hurt?

He was waiting for me when I got there. I wore a cotton dress and heels, and the picture I'd presented to myself when I left the house was that of a young, well-dressed housewife. Keith slouched in the booth; he needed a shave and the t-shirt he wore was absolutely shapeless. He grinned as I slid into the booth, then he threw a pack of cigarettes between us. The same brand we used to smoke.

"I don't smoke anymore," I said, sitting stiffly in the booth. I hadn't been in this place since before my divorce from Keith. Once, when I was about fifteen years old, I used to think this place was terribly exciting. All the big wheels from the high school used to gather here to gossip. But now, I saw that it was dirty, a crowded smoky little room, with a tile floor that looked as if it had never been washed. And the kids seemed awfully young and loud-mouthed to me, shooting back and forth across the room.

"You look great," Keith said, his eyes watching me. "Angie, if I told you that I used to get high on speed and dream about seeing you again, would you believe me?"

"Sure," I said evenly. "The part about your getting high on speed, anyway." I looked around me. "This place is awful. And once, I used to think it was fun, coming here."

He was watching me, looking at me. I could almost feel the questions in him, the wheels turning, the decision being made.

"You've changed," he said finally, "You're like—somebody else."

I raised my chin a little. "I am somebody else, Keith. I'm married now, and I live in a clean, pretty little house and I grow roses and I've learned to sew and—"

"My God," he said, and he grinned at me. He looked, in that instant, like a charming, smiling kid, a little boy who thinks the whole world is out of step but him. And I found myself smiling back. It always had been hard to hate Keith. Keith just wasn't very hateable.

We ended up taking a ride, because all that smoke bothered me. I sat beside Keith, there in the front seat, wondering why I was doing this, but when we took off and headed for Alberton, a pretty little resort not far away, I told myself the ride would do me good. If it didn't scare me to death first. Keith drove as he'd always done, like a madman, but when I suddenly put my hand on his arm as we skidded on a curve, he looked at me with that new look of question and then, miraculously, he slowed down.

We parked at drive-in and he talked about New York, about a buddy of his there who had died while on drugs, about the reasons for coming home.

"I guess," he said slowly. "I got—lost, Angie. And I want to find my way back." His voice was low and anxious and without wanting to feel that way, some chord was touched in my heart.

It just—began to get to me," he said. "Living like that." He shrugged. "Maybe I want to be straight too. Like you."

"Sure," I said, finishing my sandwich, "That's why you wear that shirt with the spot on it and those jeans with the holes and no shoes. And you drive this souped-up car—"

"The change has to begin inside a guy," he said quietly. "Then, before long, it begins to show on the outside. I've got a job now. They take out taxes and everything." He grinned.

"Big deal. Keith, you've always been kind of—different. I'm not so sure you belong back here, in this little town."

"Wherever you are," he said softly, "is where I belong."

I should have known he would kiss me, or try to. Now, as he did, while he was doing it, I think I knew he probably had planned this. But in his arms, for a wild moment, I forgot. I was the same girl I'd been a long time ago, very young, easy to excite, a kookie little girl who'd met her perfect match. Keith's girl.

"Take me home," I said finally my voice shaking. I stared out the windshield. "I'm married, Keith. I've changed."

"I've changed, too," he said. "Maybe I don't look different right now, but like I tried to tell you, Angie, a big change has started in me. I took that job at the airport because I figured maybe I could learn to fly a plane, but yesterday, I decided what I really like is to work on motors. A guy could get a job as an airplane mechanic, right? He could go to school and learn how to service those big jets, right? That's got to be a union job—I'd make good money, enough to support—"

"A wife," I said, my heart pounding in my ears. I didn't dare look at him. "I'm already a wife, Keith."

But when I got out of his car, downtown (I didn't want my neighbors talking), I couldn't stop thinking. What if, four years ago, this change had come over Keith? When I'd gotten so sick of pot parties and getting kicked out of dirty apartments and never enough money for food—what if then, Keith had gotten fed up too? I promised myself that tomorrow, yes, tomorrow, I would go downtown and buy the curtain material and start sewing.

But I didn't. I talked to Jim on the phone that night, but still, I said nothing about Keith. Jim sounded tired. They'd been at the rifle range all day and it was hot as blazes there at camp. They were going out on maneuvers in the morning, so it would probably be five days or so before he could get to a phone. Did I have plenty of money, was I okay?

Never once, when I was married to Keith, did he ask me if I had enough money for anything. Unless it was when he asked me if I happened to have any money so he could buy some joints for us to smoke. His way of solving a problem had always been to get into the hazy, unreal world of drugs or alcohol.

I kept thinking that way, about how different my present husband was, how lucky I was. I thought that way all day, and I made myself wash windows. When I started sewing the curtains, they'd be clean. I called my neighbor, checked on a committee I was to be on later, at church, and fixed myself a sandwich.

I knew, I think, that when that knock came at my door it was Keith. I almost didn't answer it, but in the old days, he used to do wild things like kick doors down and smash dishes, if he got angry or especially if he thought another man had looked at me.

I opened the door. Then I just stared.

It was Keith, all right. All dressed up, wearing clean, obviously new slacks, a sky-blue sports shirt, loafers and, wonder of wonders, a tie. Not a fancy one—it was one of those nice, loosely tied knitted kind, but it was still a tie.

"It's me," he said, smiling into my eyes. "Didn't I tell you I was going straight?" He leaned against the doorway. "I gave up drugs before I left New York, Angie, no kidding. I never was really hooked. I drink a little booze now, that's all. Listen, I've got something great to tell you. Can you go for a ride?"

We drove to the pretty little resort town where we'd driven the last time. Only this time, instead of pulling into a drive-in, we went to Orley's Inn, a beautiful big restaurant that sat high on a hill, overlooking the lake. There were candles and there was even a fireplace.

"It doesn't seem like—us," I said. The glass of wine had made me feel warmed, even a little giddy. I had forgotten to eat much that day. I seldom bothered much with food when Jim was out of town.

"It isn't us," Keith said, his eyes serious. "It isn't the old us. Or maybe I should say the young us." He reached for my hand. "I've grown up, honey. I've been all over, made that hippie scene, tried all the damned drugs and the kicks and now, I'm back here because I know what I want." His eyes deepened. "I know what I want, Angie. I didn't do anything right before. I messed our whole scene up. I messed our whole lives up."

I started to protest, but I didn't. This boy had once stolen my hat when we were kids; he'd teased me in the winters with snowballs and in the summers by shoving me into the park swimming pool. I'd fallen in love with him when I was still a little girl, and we'd married when we were still children, really.

"We belong together," he said, and his hand closed over mine. "You're still my girl, Angie."

My voice didn't sound like my own. "I'm—Jim's wife!"

"No," he said gently, and with great conviction and certainty. "You're not. You've never been anybody's wife but mine."

When we were in his car, he pulled off the highway, as I knew he would. When he began taking off my clothes, I think we had both already decided that this was what would happen. I felt the old stir begin in me; I'd forgotten his little love tricks. Little, sexy things he did—different things from what Jim did.

"My God," I said, when I opened my eyes. I felt a rush of shame and sorrow flow into me. "Oh my God—I've been unfaithful to Jim!"

I didn't get to say anymore. Keith talked all the way home. He said that from now on, he'd prove to me more and more that I was right for him, that he was right for me. He was beginning mechanic's school at night so that he could continue to service planes. He had an apartment, on the other side of town from where we'd once lived. He was different now, mature, ready to face life. He'd put drugs and booze and that all behind him. All he needed to "keep straight" was me.

And after all, we had grown up together, fallen in love, married, been happy for a time. When we made love now, Keith reminded me that once we'd been married, once we'd shared a life and a marriage bed. He was, he told me, no stranger who wanted to make me feel guilty about Jim. He was the boy—no, the man—I should still be married to.

Jim was to come home on Saturday, his Reserve Duty finished for this year. He wired me the time he'd be home, and Keith and I decided that Keith would come over an hour before Jim was to get home. That way, together, we would tell Jim. We would tell him we should have waited to grow up—tell him I went into my second marriage out of fear and loneliness—tell him, in short, that the little girl with the shabby clothes and the little boy who used to grab her woolen hat on cold winter mornings still belonged together. Angie and Keith. I didn't pack my things. I would wait until Keith and I had explained it all to Jim, logically, firmly, kindly. Jim would understand; he would not be emotional or violent. Jim, after all, was mature. So I didn't pack. There would be plenty of time for that.

This time, Keith and I were going to do things right. After the divorce, we would remarry, and we'd invest in a small house, probably a house like this one . . . I heard the car outside, heard it pull into the driveway, and for a moment, I felt panic seize me. I wanted to run, but I reminded myself that Keith and I had stopped running. I opened the door and stepped quickly outside into the darkness. I wrenched open the car door and tried to begin. I couldn't see Jim's face, but it was just as well, because I hated to see hurt well up in his brown eyes.

"Jim, I have to tell you—my first husband is back and I—we—"

"Angie!" His hand reached out and grabbed mine. "Hey, it's me. It's Keith, not Jim!"

I stared. Yes; yes, of course. How could I have made such a dumb mistake? My husband wasn't due in for another hour; Keith was to come first, so we could face Jim together. But the white shirt, the cufflinks that had gleamed in the light from the dashboard, the neatly folded jacket—it had seemed so much like Jim.

I felt my eyes widen. Where was the charming, dirty, care-free, wonderful boy I had loved years ago? Where was the mixed up, pleading, cute, naughty maverick I had lived with and loved for a little while?

Gone. Just as the kid with the high voice, the Keith of twelve, was gone. And the Keith of fourteen, who used to ride me doubles on his bike. The rebel was gone; he had been replaced by this earnest, hardworking young man who had his hair cut short and who didn't look very good with short hair, combed straight back. It gave a certain sharpness to his features that made him look hard and calculating. His hair was beginning to show signs of thinness.

I felt tears flood my eyes. "Keith," I said, and my voice shook, because I really was sorry to know that the charmer, the kook, was gone forever, and that one day a bald, middle-aged man here in town named Keith Ryan would be talking about the horrors of smoking pot. "Keith. I can't go with you."

He reached for my hand and I let him take it. "Maybe you're right. Angie. Maybe when people grow up they just don't go around breaking up marriages."

We kissed for the last time, Keith and I. I knew, by the time I was back in my house, by the time I was fixing a snack for Jim, that I hadn't fallen in love with Keith all over again. I'd simply remembered what it had been like once, a long time ago, to love a young boy.

That was a while ago, my crazy, comeback romance with Keith, but I still see him from time to time. He belongs to our church, and his wife and I are on the same bake committees sometimes. When my son was born, their little girl was born, just down the hall.

It's over; the past is over. I've grown up and so has Keith. And if my Jim sometimes seems to want to stay home too much, to fuss over me too much, to worry over our son too much—I just have to remind myself that Jim's first wife died before she got to be a wife, that she was killed in their car on their honeymoon, and that Jim has suffered in his life.

Mostly, I remind myself how lucky I am. And how happy.
THE END

WE'RE JUST TWO GIRLS IN LOVE–WITH EACH OTHER

We've already seen how True Romance dealt with gay men in the early 1970s–now here's a story about two Lesbians. (The word was still capitalized back then.) Except that these women aren't really lesbians. Well, Edie is, but she and Cara, the narrator, are strictly platonic roommates. "We shared something much more than physical passion," Cara explains. "We shared emotional peace and fulfillment." More impressively, given the era, Cara is accepting of Edie's sexuality... although she's still convinced Edie could be quite pretty if she just allowed herself to be more feminine.

Of course, Cara will find her way back to men and marriage eventually. And though readers today might bristle at her suggestion that Edie will be able to find the same happiness someday, at least it's a sympathetic portrayal.

They say there's always one consolation when you've hit bottom—you can't go any lower. But whoever said that was wrong, as Edie and I were finding out. Painfully, wretchedly, when we thought at last we'd found a way of life. We knew it because of the rain pelting down on us, now that we'd been locked out of our furnished apartment. We knew it because of the street hoodlums, aimless adolescents who had nothing better to do with themselves than jeer at two helpless women, and throw whatever bits of refuse they could find on our littered street, and yell vile names at us.

"Hey, Butch," yelled fourteen-year-old Mike, whose mother had a succession of "husbands" drifting in and out of her flat, "hey, Butch, which one of you is the father of the baby?"

I ignored them. All of them, the young adolescent hoodlums, already schooled in their cheap superiority, their scorn of anyone who was in any way different from what they accepted as the norm. Why? Did Edie and I, living our quiet lives, locked away by ourselves, with only each other—and the baby—for company, threaten them?

In a way we did. We were different, all right. Edie and I had made lives for ourselves without men. Men in the ordinary sense, that is. As lovers, companions, supporters, givers of emotional fulfillment. And was this a threat to them, to the Mikes of this world? What better had they to offer us than what we gave each other? They and their older brothers—

I remembered the first Mike in my life. Oddly enough, he too was fourteen years old, though his name wasn't Mike. It was Allen. He carried my books home from school, walked me up the stairs of the small building in which my family had an apartment, and on the landing he tried to kiss me. Well, that in itself wasn't bad. I must say I liked the idea of Allen kissing me. He was sort of good looking, and nice, and seemed gentle and mannerly.

It was what he tried afterwards that disturbed me. I was frightened at his touch, all over me, it seemed, his grinning face, the hotness of his eyes. I slapped him away.

After that I didn't let any of the boys walk me home for quite awhile. Then other things held my attention, so that I didn't even think of boys for awhile. Mom got terribly sick, and I spent a lot of time looking after her, as well as doing all the household chores.

My father looked at me once, in a funny way, and said, "You fill your mother's place. Almost."

I didn't understand then what he meant, but I had an uneasy feeling. I didn't like the way his eyes followed me about the room, whenever I was near him. And when, finally, Mom had what they call a "merciful release" from her suffering, some instinct made me get out.

I had no idea where I was going, or why, but right after the funeral I packed whatever I had in a single suitcase and left. I found myself a room, and got myself a job. I lied about my age, and made such a good waitress that when the manager of the diner found out I was under sixteen, he said he had great regret in firing me, but to come back when I was older. He couldn't, he explained, take the responsibility of keeping a girl so young working in a place like his.

So I took the bit of money I had managed to put away and went to New York. I was quite sure that in a crowded city no one would pay much attention to how old I was. Even so, I did all I could to make myself look older, wearing a lot of makeup and dark clothes.

That did it. My disguise worked so well that I got a job in a swank cafe in one of the city's best hotels. I thought charging fifty cents for a cup of coffee was ridiculous, but it didn't seem to keep the customers out. In fact, the place was always crowded, and some of the customers were very important people indeed.

I was waiting table one afternoon, after the lunch crowd had thinned out, when a very distinguished man came in and ordered a sandwich and coffee. When he paid his bill, he did it with a credit card, and my eyes nearly popped when I saw the name. A very high-up politician. Very, very impressive. And even more so when he looked up at me, smiled, and asked if he could have the privilege of calling me sometime.

Could he! This was the first time anyone really respectable had asked me out. I mean, I'd had the usual run of men, the type who were mostly just trying to prove something to themselves, how irresistible they were, and how any girl was fair game. But this one! Someone older, distinguished, well known ...

I should have known. I heard the line about how his wife didn't understand him, how a man in the public eye had many cares, knew many people, and was essentially lonely. As I look back now. I realize how naive I was to have fallen for that. But I did. And where I fell was flat on my face.

We had an affair that lasted for about six months. And then, suddenly. I didn't hear from him. Not a single phone call, not a line, nothing. And he was still in the city. It hurt me, it really did, because I had genuinely cared for him. What really cut me to the quick, though, was the way he came in one day, with a young girl, quite obviously not his wife, and sat down at my table! I asked one of the other girls if she'd mind taking that table, without explaining to her. But she must have seen enough in my face to simply take over without question.

Once again I went through the same feeling I'd had before, when that kid had tried to go as far as he thought he could get away with. I shut myself up within myself, hurt, bewildered, wondering what on earth I had done wrong. It didn't last. I was young, and by the time I got to be eighteen I was beginning to understand what the world was about. That you had to take chances. You could stumble, fall, skin your knees, get up and try again. And it wasn't too hard to try again when Gary came into my life. He was a medical student, bright, full of fun, intelligent, and with a deadly seriousness about his future professional career that I found refreshing, after seeing so many wisecracking smarties in the coffee shop all day, every week.

"We can't get married," he said to me, quite as if the fact that we eventually would was to be taken for granted. "Not now. When we do marry, I want to be able to support my wife. A doctor can. A med student can't."

Honestly, that didn't matter to me. Gary and I were in love, and wasn't that the important thing? We were the only two people in the world for each other. When Gary took me in his arms, I was home; I was safe; I was sheltered, with the world shut out. His lovemaking was unlike anything I had ever known; it made me feel as if never before had I been alive, whole, completely and uniquely myself. All he had to do was touch me, and I felt a fire running through me. And it wasn't as if we ever sated our passion; he could make love to me, and I would drown in a sea of delight, and be satisfied and even exhausted, and yet would welcome his lovemaking again, if he cared for it, the very next minute.

One didn't need a marriage license for our kind of love to be sanctified. At least that was how I felt. And, since we hated to be apart from each other for any time that wasn't occupied by my work or his study, it just seemed a natural thing for Gary to move into my apartment. The arrangement was ideal. He had quiet during the day, when he wasn't attending classes, and since I worked the afternoon to dinner shift, he could study right through the evening. The nights were our delight, and he was always there. It was heaven on earth.

Our heaven lasted two whole years while Gary completed his studies. Then he told me he had an offer he couldn't refuse to go into a big hospital, for further training and study.

"How marvelous!" I said.

"That's one of the best training grounds in the city!"

"I knew you'd understand," he said, beaming. "I knew you wouldn't stand in my way. You'd never nag or fuss."

"Well, of course, darling," I said. "When on earth did I ever? All I want is the best for you."

He kissed me. "That's what makes you so adorable," he said. "That's why I'll never forget you."

My heart sank. "Forget me? You sound as if~ as if you're going away."

He smiled easily. "Well, in a way, yes. The hospital has accommodations nearby for its personnel. And with the grind I'll be having— well, they think it's better if I live right nearby, I'll always be on call."

I knew that wasn't so. I knew that some of Gary's fellow students, who had already started interning in hospitals, were living some distance away from where they worked. With the apartment situation in New York, you took what you could get. I knew, then, that I had come to the end of the line with Gary. He was easing himself out of my life, just as he had eased himself in.

I didn't cry when he left. What was there to cry about? It was as though there were no emotion left in me. I felt old, dried out, wrung out, used up. This time, definitely, I was through with men. There

179

wasn't one you could trust. They were all alike. Henceforth I would live alone, be alone. That was going to be my life.

But life had a few surprises in store for me. I began to feel nauseated in the mornings, but I put that down to my general nausea with life. And then there were the unmistakable signs. When I finally could ignore the whole thing no longer, and went to a doctor, I thought the earth would slide out from under my feet. It was one thing to be afraid I was pregnant; it was quite another to have it confirmed.

What in the name of all that was holy was I going to do? At first I thought of an abortion. That seemed the easiest, most practical way out. I could go to a clinic, sign up—but the thought of it made me shudder. This was life I was carrying inside me. And yet what other way was there for me?

I woke up one morning knowing that it had to be done soon, or not at all. I made up my mind. It was a lovely spring morning, still cool, but with that promise of warmth that made the heart ache with its promise of joy and sunshine. I put the moment off as long as I could by walking through the park, on my way to the hospital. Suddenly the nausea hit me, and I sat down on a bench holding my head in my hands, trying to give myself time to overcome it.

As if through an amplifying system. I could hear the cries of children, very small children, romping, shouting, and generally being full of noisy vigor. And I was on my way to~ I couldn't bear it! I just couldn't stand any more of life's cruelty. I wanted out, out from the whole thing!

I must have gotten my wish, even if only momentarily, because the next thing I knew my wrists were being rubbed, by strange, strong hands, and I was coming out of a deep, endless blackness. I looked up into the face of a friendly angel— or so she seemed, with her golden hair like a halo around her face. And when she stood up, saying, "Now sit there. I'm coming right back," she rose to what seemed to me a towering height. She came back with a soft drink from a nearby vendor, and held the paper cup to my lips while, I took slow sips.

I remember blurting out, "I wish I were big and capable like you," and immediately regretted it.

A funny look came over her face, as if she had withdrawn all
expression from it. She was like something carved out of stone. But she
smiled, then, and said. "And I've always wanted to be small and dark
and delicate, like you."

I laughed, and said, "I do very tough work. I'm a waitress. That
takes plenty of endurance."

"Good," she said. "Now let's go have a cup of coffee someplace and
you can pull yourself together."

I had already called in to say that I wouldn't be in that day, so it
didn't matter that we spent two hours over that cup of coffee. I found
myself telling Edith—"My name is Edith, but of course my friends call
me Edie"—the whole story of why I had fainted. Gary, the baby,
everything.

"Men!" was her first comment. It wasn't what she said, it was the
way she said it. As if, to her, it was a dirty word. Since that was pretty
much the way I felt, too, I didn't see anything objectionable or unusual
about her attitude.

"Well, Cara," she said, when I'd finished, "there's one thing pretty
clear to me. You don't really want that abortion, do you?"

"No," I said soberly. "Not really. But I don't know what else I can
do. I can't raise the baby myself. You see, I don't have much money—"

"I should think you would have made good money in tips.
Waitresses usually do," she said.

I nodded. "Oh yes," I said. "I did indeed. But Gary was always
needing something, and I paid the rent and expenses—"

"My God," Edie said. "The whole bit!" Then she repeated the dirty
word. "Men."

We were both silent for a moment. Finally she said, "Look, I have a
suggestion. You can say no if you want to reject it. But one thing is
sure! You can't go on living alone. You need someone to help you, to
look after you. Why not come and live with me?"

"How kind of you," was all I could think of to say.

Her mouth twisted. "It's up to you. I think, Cara, that you and I
can get along." She put her hand over mine. "And there need be no

strings attached, if you don't want them. We can just live together like two friends."

As if a light had been turned on, 1 had a sudden flash of understanding. "You're a Lesbian," I said calmly, unemotionally, as if I had mentioned her lovely golden hair.

In the same way, she answered, "Yes. Does that bother you?"

"I don't know." I said. "I honestly don't know. And furthermore," I added. "I don't think I care." So, as simply as that, it was decided and done. I moved into her apartment.

Two women sharing an apartment was a situation so common in that crowded, expensive city, that it couldn't possibly cause any comment. And Edie was as good as her word. About everything. She pampered me as if I were a baby myself. She made me give up my job instantly, saying that it wasn't good for the baby, me constantly on my feet and lugging heavy trays. Edie made enough money to support us both in a modest fashion, and she shared it generously with me. She was a marvelous cook, and she saw to it that I ate. And ate and ate. "If not for yourself, then the baby." And, because she planned our menus carefully, I didn't put on too much weight.

When the baby was due, she acted better than any father I had ever heard of. I remember one of the girls at the coffee shop laughing as she told us how she had had her baby. Her husband, who adored her, had been busy doing a crossword puzzle when the pains started. "Bill," she kept saying, "I've got to get to the hospital. Now. Instantly!" And Bill hadn't even looked up, just said, in an irritated voice, "Wait a minute. What's an eight-letter word for a sailboat?" Of course, he did get her to the hospital, but barely in time.

Edie had everything organized in advance. My suitcase was packed; she got a taxi and had it wait at the curb while she came back upstairs and got me, she saw me installed in my room, and waited outside, quietly, patiently, until young Sam was born. The baby, I had decided, was going to be Sam, either way. My mother's name had been Samantha.

Edie's hatred for males certainly didn't extend to this tiny one. "He's just a little fella," she cooed. "He never hurt anyone."

And sometimes, when we got home, I wondered who was really Sam's mother, me or Edie. Her affection for him was genuine, and she looked so gloriously feminine, playing with him, cleaning him, when I had had just one diaper too many to cope with, and just generally loving him, that it was hard to believe that she was what she said she was.

I wondered, sometimes, if she wasn't right about being a homosexual after all. She started to caress me once, and I gently refused only because I was through with anyone, anyone at all, making love to me. But her caress was so soft, her kiss on my lips so tender and warm, that I began to understand why it could be that some women could love other women, and never a man. And I didn't condemn such a love. But, even if I were to eventually, it was not the time, not yet. We shared something much more than physical passion. We shared emotional peace and fulfillment. And she told me that she was getting as much from our relationship as she was giving. More, she said.

"I guess I just like looking at you," she said once. "You're everything I never was. You're pretty, and sweet. Not like me. I was always a big lummox. When I was a kid I was a fat, pimple-faced horror."

I thought for a moment she was going to strike me, she was so enraged by what I did. I laughed. That was all I did. I stopped abruptly, when I saw the expression on her face. I wiped the tears of laughter from my eyes and tried to explain.

"I couldn't help thinking how silly it was, for you to want to look like me," I said. "When you're so gorgeous now. Whatever was wrong when you were a kid, you grew out of it."

Her mouth tightened, and I went on, hurriedly. "Oh, I know by now what you think of yourself. You think you're still a fat, homely kid. I don't know where you got such a notion, because you're beautiful." And, because we had learned to speak plainly with each other, I added, "And not because I love you, either."

She still stared at me, her mouth tight. I just kept on talking. "I'm not the only one who thinks you're special. You didn't see that young doctor at the hospital who came to check up on me after Sam was born. He could hardly pay any attention to me for looking at you."

"Probably wondering just what I was doing there," she said, bitterly.

I shook my head. I was bitter myself, a little, as I said, "No. Believe me, I know admiration in a man's eyes when I see it. I saw it then. For you."

"Pooh," Edie said, and I didn't try to argue with her anymore, just then. But in my mind's eye I could see her, if only she'd let herself go. She had a magnificent figure; not small and cute, like mine, but large-boned, with a kind of majesty about her. When she relaxed at home, she moved gracefully, easily. It was only when we were out, among strangers, that she walked like a disgruntled goose.

And her face she had regular, classic features. What I wanted to do was to make her let her golden hair grow long, then wear it up in the back in a French twist. She would have been incomparable. Like nobody else, like only Edie, gorgeous and unique!

It happened again, and again I couldn't convince her. When Sam was three months old I took him to the pediatrician for a checkup, and since Edie worked in the afternoons at the library, she came along that morning. Dr. Nash came out to see me in, and he gave Edie a long, thoughtful look. I mentioned it to her later, but she made nothing of it again.

"Probably looking for the baby I should have had in my lap," she said.

I couldn't understand it, and I said so. "Edie, I don't think you really have your heart in this business of being a Lesbian. You have never pushed me into your way of life, though you keep telling me it's the only way. And you have so much warmth and love in you, you're almost more of a mother to Sam than I am."

She shrugged. "And how'd you get the baby in the first place? Some bum took you for his convenience, then ditched you. No, Cara, that's not for me. If ever I thought a man could have a lasting disinterested relationship, I might change my mind. But I know the creatures aren't capable of it." Her mouth twisted in a mirthless grin. "Look at my father. Married my mother young, used her to help build up a business, and then left her for a slut who wanted only his money. My mother," she added, "never wanted anyone but him, even after he left. The idiot."

"Who?" I said. "Your mother, or your father for having left her."

This time it was Edie who laughed. "Both, I suppose. My mother was a very pretty woman. I guess that wasn't enough for him." Then she stopped, realizing the tactlessness of what she had said.

"No," I said. "Being pretty isn't enough."

I don't know how long we'd have gone on, in our comfortable way, if Sam hadn't gotten sick. He frightened me so, poor infant with his fever and his constant weak wailing. I rushed him to the pediatrician, who gave him a long, thoughtful examination, and then said, "Now I don't want to frighten you, but I think we'd better check little Sam into the hospital. Just for observation, mind you."

But I was frightened, terribly frightened. Nothing could happen to him nothing—not to my baby! It tore my heart out to leave him in that room full of pathetic little ones, all so tiny and bewildered. The nurses were kind but firm. I could come early the next day, to be with him and comfort him, but now I must go.

I was sitting huddled in a chair, as if trying to get back into the womb myself, when Edie came home. I sobbed in her arms and told her all about my fears for Sam, and she was more comforting to me than a mother could have been.

It was when she kissed my hair and laid her hand comfortingly on my shoulder that I suddenly noticed not only that our window shades were still up, but that our neighbor across the window shaft was watching us. I had never particularly liked this neighbor, a rather flashy young man, and more out of sheer annoyance than anything else I got up and pulled down the shade. I had no way of knowing what that simple normal gesture was to cost Edie and me later on.

The concern that filled us both at the time was the diagnosis on Sam. Apparently there was some digestive blockage that hadn't been evident before. Sam had been a fussy eater, with a tendency to colic, but while it was distressing, it hadn't seemed too overwhelming. The doctors had hoped that, as sometimes happens, the condition would correct itself in time.

Now Sam would need treatment. And we couldn't take him home, because he was so tiny. He needed long hospital care. It was best for him, of course, though it was rough on Edie and me. I would spend as much time in the hospital as I was allowed, and Edie would come in after work and join me. When we came home, together, we were both punchy with exhaustion and worry.

"Drunk!" I heard a woman mutter in disgust one evening, as we came into the entrance of our apartment building. I turned around, in a half-dazed way, to see who was drunk. There was no one else around, and the woman was glaring at Edie and me.

"Got rid of the baby, I shouldn't wonder!" I heard one day, through the air shaft. "Got in the way of their carryings-on," another voice added. "Them two—it's scandalous! They shouldn't live here, with decent people!"

I was glad Edie wasn't there at the moment, to hear that. She had gone out to get us some cold cuts for our supper, while I made coffee and a salad. When I heard the doorbell ring, I thought she might have forgotten her keys, or been too laden down to fish for them. So I opened the door without asking who was there. As soon as I did, I felt an intuitive shock of fear go through me. It was the young man who had been watching us through the air shaft window. He pushed his way in, grinning nastily at me.

"Girlfriend's out, huh?" he said. I didn't say anything. "Thought I saw her put her coat on. Maybe she'll be gone a good long time, huh?"

"What do you want?" I said, trying to keep my voice steady. I didn't know why my heart was pounding so. I just knew I didn't want him anywhere near me.

"Now," he said, "that's no way for a nice girl like you to talk. Because you are a nice girl, aren't you?" There was a sickening emphasis on the word girl. "You have to be," he went on. "You had a baby. So you've been with a man. With lots of men, maybe. Liked it, too, I'll bet!"

Now the fear that was inside me began to take shape. As if he had spoken the words, I sensed what was in his evil little mind.

"Get out," I said again. "Get out, or I'll call the police!"

He started laughing in a way that made my blood run cold. "Call the cops!" he roared. "That's good! The likes of you!"

Suddenly he clapped one hand over my mouth, and with the other he threw me to the floor. It was so brutal, so sudden, that for a moment—only for a moment—I was stunned.

Then I started to fight. I must have bitten his hand, because suddenly I had a salt taste in my mouth, and through a haze I saw something red. Then he started slapping me, punching me. He had already ripped my skirt when I heard the door open. Oh thank God, Edie was home! There was a thud of packages being dropped, and suddenly the weight that was over me went limp. Edie had given him a savage chop that should have knocked him out, but didn't. He was reeling, muttering such obscenities as I hope never to hear again. Between Edie and me we shoved him out the door, praying that would be the end of it. He was lucky to have gotten out alive. I had to hold Edie back; I pretty much felt like killing him myself, but that would have been completely senseless, and once I was rescued from him, I wanted only to be rid of the threat.

But that was far from the end of it. He stood out in the corridor, yelling that he was going to tell the whole building what we were.

"They know anyhow!" he screamed, like a demented creature. "Everybody knows what you are!" From there he went into language that would shock a longshoreman.

We heard doors popping open, excited comments, a general hubbub in the hall. Then there was a hammering at our door. Our landlord shouted in furious tones that this was a respectable house, and he wasn't going to have any such carryings-on.

Edie opened the door, and said, "Take a look for yourself. He tried to rape my roommate."

"Yeah, sure," the landlord sneered. "I know how you girls fight. I'm not having any of that in my house. He already told me about it. How he heard you fighting and tried to break it up, and you nearly killed him."

"Too bad we didn't!" Edie said, and slammed the door shut. We debated calling the police, but how can you prove attempted rape?

We decided to forget the whole thing, and hope it would blow over. Far from it. In no time, it seemed, we were served with an eviction order. We were "undesirable tenants." I'd have left, and gladly, but Edie said, "We'll fight this."

With her characteristic energy, she found a lawyer. He said it would be a difficult case to fight, because she would have to disprove the charges against us.

What Edie said was, "They'll have to prove them."

Apparently there was some blunt talk between Edie and the lawyer, because he asked her if she were indeed a Lesbian. And she answered, instantly and honestly, "Yes. I am."

She was laughing when she came home. "I finally found a man who isn't afraid of me," she said. "He's going to take our case."

But we lost. Two of the neighbors swore that we were always fighting, and that we mistreated the baby so badly he was in the hospital. Lies, of course, but it was their word against ours. And their word won.

I was sick—sick over the depths of depravity to which human beings could sink. Even Edie couldn't say, "Well, what do you expect of men?" because these two who lied about us were women. Without giving us time to find another place, we were thrown, with all our possessions, into the street. How glad I was then that Sam was in a hospital!

I don't know what would have happened to us at that point, if our lawyer, Mark Haddon, hadn't helped us. Even Edie seemed defeated—Edie, who'd always stared life right in the eye. I had never seen Edie so low, so completely depressed, and my heart ached for her.

And then Mark truly became our friend. Just his presence was soothing. He said, "I've found you temporary shelter. A friend of mine has a big house, and he's willing to put you up till you get a place of your own."

Edie was looking at him suspiciously, but he paid no attention. Fortunately, since we had been in a furnished apartment, our belongings didn't take up much room, so Mark was able to move us in his station-wagon. Then he took us both out to dinner. I kept staring at him, then at Edie. I felt all mixed-up inside. Funny. I liked Mark a lot—but I was supposed to hate men.

We moved into his friend's house, and we began the round of apartment hunting. Mark said to me one night, "Are you and Edie still planning to live together?"

It hadn't occurred to me not to. I explained to him about the baby, how Sam would need all my attention when he came home, so that I wouldn't be able to work, and so forth.

And then Mark surprised me. Very quietly, he said, "Have you thought of marriage?"

I smiled a twisted smile at him. I didn't want to tell him I was through with men who were nothing but heartache, when he had been so good to me. When, actually, he stirred some long-buried feelings in me. He went on blandly, "Think about it, Cara. And when you decide men aren't all stinkers, let me know. I'll be waiting."

I was sure he was making fun of me. I burst into tears. Then his arms were around me, and he was saying, "Cara, honey, I know a real manhater when I see one. You're not. And—believe it or not—neither is Edie."

I gasped out the only thing I could think of, "But—the baby!"

He laughed. "In some civilizations, a man won't marry a woman until he's sure she can bear him children. Let's have a dozen more."

I couldn't believe it. So much kindness, so much tenderness, from a man! For six months longer I still couldn't bring myself to believe it. We were married Christmas.

By that time, Edie was seeing a psychiatrist. A man psychiatrist, no less! At first, she wouldn't go, saying things like, "You men—you're all alike—think you have all the answers!" But I begged her to go.

"It can't hurt," I said. "If the psychiatrist doesn't know what he's talking about, you can forget all about him."

More to accept the challenge, than anything else, she went. Edie had always met life as a challenge, ready to fight it, and she would meet this one, too.

Nothing really happens overnight, though sometimes it seems that way, and it didn't with Edie. She came to me one day, after a session with the doctor, laughing in wry amusement.

"Do you know what that idiot said? You won't believe it. He said it wasn't men I was afraid of. He said I'm terrified of other women! Can you imagine?"

For a long time she was hysterical about that one, but after awhile I saw for myself how the truth was coming home to her. She no longer regarded all women as if they were her mother, women who would degrade her, scorn her. Edie had been able to show affection to me, because when she met me I was so helpless, so obviously unable to fight. I was no threat to her.

She began to blossom. When she played with little Sam, who was finally home, a healthy happy little boy, it wasn't with the desperate affection of a woman who knew she would never have babies of her own. Oh yes, Edie truly loves Sam, and is like a second mother to him. Because Edie has a lot of affection to give, I hope that someday she may find the right someone to give it to. I'd like nothing better, as I once told her teasingly, than to see her through her first pregnancy!

When I said that, Edie's smile wasn't bold and mocking. It was shy, reserved. She turned her head away. And I knew that real feeling, which she had so long denied herself, was coming into its own with her. She was still unused to it, unable to cope with her deep and very womanly emotions. But I think, just as the miracle happened with me, it will happen to Edie. Nothing will ever make me happier, than to see Edie, whom I truly adore as a friend, find a perfect life of her own, with a man who will love her as Mark loves me. THE END

To save my marriage I'd do even this...

THREE IN A BED!

In the photo that accompanies this story, a young girl sits on the floor, wrapping herself tightly in a bedsheet, as two bearded biker types loom menacingly above her from either side. This scene, as they say, does not appear in this story.

Oh, Joe's a biker all right. "This is my first love, baby," he tells Mandy when he takes her for a ride on his motorcycle shortly after they've met. "You'll be second. Dig?" But his love for Mandy grows stronger; they may decide to get married as a joke, but the relationship goes well—at least until they fight over buying a new bed. Joe gives in, but as Mandy finds out later that night, there are some strings attached to the deal.

"Three in a Bed!" wants to have it both ways. Once Mandy reconciles herself to the threesome, it's a powerful sensual experience: "I wanted them both over and over," she says. "There seemed to be no way of satiating my womanly hunger." The morning after, though, she's filled with remorse. It's a common strategy for *True Love* and *True Romance*: People were already talking about wild sex and "free love" so openly that you could no longer pretend there wasn't something compelling about it, but you could at least try to brand it as dangerous and steer readers back to righteous monogamy by the story's end.

V room! Vroom! Joe gunned down on the accelerator, and we were off! I tightened my grip around his waist and hung on tight, thrilled by the sensation of speed as we caromed through the streets and by the feel and the essence of Joe. I remember a brief, giddy notion that we were one—Joe, I and his big powerful bike.

I felt free and content. Even the occasional pinch of my kidney belt wasn't enough to detract from the exhilaration of soaring over the road with my guy. And with my helmet and goggles on I enjoyed a smug satisfaction that no one—only Joe—knew who I was. Not even my own father would recognize me, I thought.

By now we were out of the city limits and going at a fast clip. I was glad because I wanted the great feeling I had to last. But, obstinately, thoughts of my dad kept pushing their way into my mind. We had had a terrific blow-up earlier, and I had rushed out of the house defiantly.

"I'm almost eighteen, and I'll do what I please!" I shouted at my father.

"Then you won't be living in my house!" Anger shot through his voice and his eyes. He slammed the door hard.

The argument, as usual, had been over Joe. Dad hadn't liked him from their first meeting. At first, I was defensive about Joe. But gradually I became defiant. Joe had dropped out of school in his junior year, two years earlier. But he had a good job as a trucker. I was proud of the fact that he had bought his own bike and had his own apartment. Dad didn't agree.

"He's a no-good hippie, Mandy. He won't do right by you, mark my words!" For a moment a look of sadness came over his face. I couldn't admit it but I knew that his concern for me was real. He just doesn't understand, I told myself. He's not young and he doesn't understand. Dad thought anyone with long hair and blue jeans was a no-good hippie. If he had had his way, I'd be wearing Shirley Temple curls and a Girl Scout uniform, at least one inch below my knees!

"Before your mother left us..." he'd start. "I promised her. . . ."

"Oh, Dad, not that again," I moaned. That phrase was Dad's euphemism for 'died' and sometimes I wished he'd say it just once. She didn't 'leave' us. She died.

I had no real memory of my mother. I had been only five or six when she became ill and after many months she died. The word 'mother' meant to me a hushed, sad feeling and a house filled with friends and relatives being overly attentive and kind. And the memory of my dad becoming quietly drunk as he sat at the kitchen table, his sad eyes glazed with tears that somehow didn't fall.

Soon after that, Dad went back to his job in a life insurance office, and a housekeeper, Mrs. Martin, came to live with us. I resented her from the start and over the years it deepened. We battled constantly about what I should wear, where I could go and who I could see. I became convinced that she was poisoning Dad's mind against me. I wanted her out of our house and off my back. I determined that either she'd leave or I'd simply take off.

"I've had enough of your cheeky ways, young lady." Mrs. Martin's voice was strident and I wished there was some way to silence her. We were in the midst of a particularly heated exchange about the mini-skirt I was wearing.

"Good!" I countered. "Then you can leave! Go find someone else to make miserable!"

Her look was a cool, detached appraisal. "All right, Mandy, I'll leave. Your father can mail me my pay that's due. But just remember my warning. You better change your wild ways, or you'll never be a lady!"

She didn't wait for the answer about to explode from my lips but went directly to her room and began to pack. Minutes later, she was gone.

It was great getting at least one person off my back. Dad was upset about Mrs. Martin's leaving, but I convinced him I was old enough now so that we could get along without a housekeeper.

But I soon realized that Dad felt he had to be twice as strict with me as before. I determined to leave home just as soon as I graduated high school. I was taking a commercial course and I knew I could get an office job.

Then I met Joe. Pow! It was like an explosion. From that moment on nothing else mattered.

I had gone with some friends one evening to a coffee house just outside town. It was a groovy place with a live rock group who were blasting away as we walked in. My eyes narrowed, trying to adjust to the swirling strobe lights playing through the smoke-filled, darkened room. For a second or two I couldn't see how crowded the place was but could feel the crush of bodies. We slowly moved through the crowd toward a table. There were young people in bells, jeans, minis, maxis and tassled vests filling what seemed like every inch of space. Everyone was doing their own thing, singing, dancing, talking—some just smiling and watching.

I felt a hand gently, but firmly grip my arm. I turned to see who had hold of me.

"Hi." His voice was deep and authoritative. "Hi." I smiled tentatively, a little confused. He was sitting at one of the tables and smiled up at me. "Have a seat."

I could feel myself start to blush as he looked at me steadily. "But I..." I glanced in the direction my friends had gone.

"Forget them. They won't miss you. But I would." With that he gave a tug on my arm and sat me down in the chair next to his.

He looked directly into my face then. "You're my kind of chick."

It was as simple as that. I stopped blushing. Somehow I knew exactly what he meant as I looked steadily back at him. I would be his chick and he would be my fellow. A slow excitement began to build in me, the delicious feeling of anticipation.

"I'm Joe," he offered.

"Mandy."

"Let's cut this scene."

Without waiting for my answer, he abruptly got up and headed for the entrance. Obediently, I followed. Echoes of the blaring music followed us outside. Joe nodded in the direction of the parking lot. "This way."

He headed toward a large, shiny object whose metal reflected both the moonlight and the neon light of the coffee house. As we neared I could make out that it was a motorcycle.

"This is my first love, baby. You'll be second. Dig?" It was a matter-of-fact announcement.

"We'll see," I thought to myself. The female instinct in me reacted as though I had just been challenged, rather than warned.

Joe straddled the big bike and reached for two helmets that were hung on the handle. "Here," he said, handing me the smaller one. "Put it on."

I did as I was told but couldn't resist asking: "Do you always carry a girl's helmet along?"

"I don't like my broads with scrambled brains, baby. Sit down, shut up and hang on." He revved the motor.

Again, I obeyed. I was embarrassed to admit that I had never been on a motorcycle. But then the bike started to move so there was no time for me to do anything but close my eyes and wrap my arms around his chest. It soon became obvious that Joe didn't believe in gradual initiations. He gunned the accelerator until we reached a speed I didn't know was possible, the roar of the machine seeming like a protective curtain between us and any possible danger.

"We're here." The bike had slowed briefly and come to a stop as suddenly as we had started. He waited for me to dismount.

Confused, I hesitated momentarily. I felt a ripple of impatience flow through his muscles. Instinctively, I released the bear hug I'd held him in throughout the thrilling ride from the coffee house. I sensed that Joe had a very definite way of letting his displeasure be known, and I decided I'd have to learn quickly not to cross him.

"I said we're here, baby. Don't be a drag."

I was trying to get off the bike as quickly as possible but my legs felt a bit unsteady. Now, my irritability showed. "Where? Where is 'here'?"

He gave me a look which I was to learn meant "cool it" and said, "My pad."

"Your own?" my voice must have sounded incredulous. It was just that I hadn't met anyone till now who had his own place.

"Why not? I've got the bread."

He took my arm and guided me up the first flight of some rather rickety stairs. He pushed open the first door near the landing.

"Don't you lock it, Joe?"

"What for, baby?" He switched on an overhead light. I glanced up to see it was a naked bulb. "Anybody need what I got they can have it." He paused meaningfully. "Except my bike, of course."

I looked around the room. It was pretty bare except for a broken overstuffed chair and a beat-up table with two unmatched wooden chairs.

"Yeah," I agreed. "I see what you mean."

I heard the door close behind me and the click of a lock. I turned to see Joe smiling at me. "When I need privacy, click—privacy." He took off his leather jacket and hung it carefully on a nearby hook, saying: "Let's get comfortable."

"Cool." My earlier confidence was returning and I began to feel relaxed. I took off my pea coat and hung it next to his.

Joe headed toward the tiny kitchen and opened the refrigerator.

"A little wine and a little music. Great combo."

I followed him into the kitchen and looked around for a couple of glasses while he uncorked the wine.

"Follow me," Joe said, walking through the living room.

"How do you like it?" he asked, flicking on two switches. One illuminated the bedroom in a dim light from two lamps on either side of a mattress on the floor. The only things on the mattress were lots of pillows and a big, soft-looking quilt. The other switch obviously controlled the music which swelled forth from four speakers, one in each corner of the room.

"That's what you call stereo, baby," Joe announced, smiling at the sound.

"Wow," was all I could say.

We sat on the edge of the mattress and leaned against the wall. Joe took the glasses from me and filled them with the deep red contents of the bottle. The soft music of a jazz quintet filled the air around us and we sat quietly for a while, sipping the wine and listening.

Finally, I began to grow a little puzzled. Joe made no effort to touch me or to move near me. He just sat listening to the music and drinking from his glass. Then he reached over and touched my hand, almost brushing it with his fingertips.

"Nice and easy does it, baby."

Any earlier anxiety I had felt was dispelled by the confident and intimate sound of his voice. I knew then that Joe understood that I had never been in this kind of situation before and that his patience and gentleness would make it natural and easy for me. I pushed all thoughts of guilt from my mind. Even what I'd say to Dad when I got home seemed a far-away problem at the moment. The wine began to make me feel warm and lightheaded. My shameless desire for Joe began to blossom like a paper flower made to unfold in a glass of water.

Joe pushed off one high boot with the help of the other and then bent over to remove the remaining boot. I followed his action, kicking off my sandals.

Together, without a word, we both slowly removed our clothing. Joe took my glass and refilled it.

"Stand up and turn around."

I stood on the mattress and slowly revolved, knowing his eyes followed my every movement. A feeling of unabashed female pride came over me. I had waited for this moment for what had seemed like years—for someone I desired to look upon me, literally photograph me with his eyes, and find me totally desirable.

"Outa sight!" His expression was one of pure admiration.

I gave a silly half curtsy and lowered myself to a seated position again. Joe put down his glass, reached over and took my face between his hands. Pulling me toward him, he gave me a sweet kiss on the mouth.

I kissed him back—openly, honestly, but not sweetly. "Joe..." I pleaded.

"Easy does it, baby. Remember?" He ran a finger softly down my back as he spoke. "A little more music, a little more wine. . . ."

I began to squirm as my body, alerted to his touch, sent an S.O.S. to all my nerve endings. The only thought I had was my need for him - now—that very moment.

But still he waited—nibbling at my ear lobes, gently kissing my shoulders, my neck and breasts. Soft moans, an almost purring sound, came from deep within me. I wondered crazily how much ecstasy it would take to blow my mind completely.

Slowly, he aligned his body with mine, and with his free hand, arranged pillows around me. He carefully lifted me onto the pillows and we were, finally, one. At that moment, I knew that my life depended on him—nothing would ever be the same. Pleasure, happiness—there must be some word, I thought, a word that conveyed what I felt. But I could think of no word that was adequate.

Later, we lay resting, side by side.

"You're my chick, Mandy."

"Yes, Joe. I know."

We fell into a contented sleep, the music softly accompanying our deep breathing.

The morning light inching through the Venetian blinds startled me and pained my eyes. It took a few moments before I could remember where I was and how I got there. As I recalled the events of the night before, the memory of Joe swelled in my mind. I reached toward him. My touch caused him to stir. Automatically, he pulled me toward him, opened his sleep-heavy eyelids and smiled.

"Morning, chick."

"Good morning, Joe."

Within moments we were totally awake as our passion for each other, having subsided through the night, rose again to wondrous heights.

"Joe," I spoke quietly as we rested.

"Yeah, baby."

"When I get home my father's going to kill me." The picture of facing my dad was beginning to form in my mind and it was a sobering one. Quickly, I got up from the mattress, began gathering my clothes and headed toward the bathroom.

"I've got to go." Through the closed door I could hear Joe saying, "Don't be so uptight, Mandy. Or you'll get to be a drag."

When I had dressed and came out to say good-bye Joe was again sleeping soundly. I quietly set the alarm of the small clock atop an orange crate in the room so that he wouldn't be late to his job. Then I rummaged through my bag for a paper and pencil and wrote down my address. I signed it with x's and propped the paper near the clock.

Dad seemed more hurt than angry.

"Well, Mandy, I'm glad you decided to come home." He looked directly at me as he spoke. "I figured you were all right or I would have heard."

I determined not to lie to him.

"I met a wonderful guy, Dad. And I was with him." I said it, but I couldn't return his gaze. I looked away as I spoke that last.

"'Wonderful'?" Dad looked puzzled. "A 'wonderful' guy keeps my daughter out all night?"

I started to answer, to tell him how I didn't care what he said. That I knew I loved Joe and that he was what I wanted. But as I began, the sound of a motorcycle engine roared through the window and then stopped. I looked out the window and saw that it was Joe.

"It's Joe, Dad. Now you can meet him." I rushed to the door and opened it, smiling. "Hi, Joe. Come in."

He was halfway up the porch, removing his helmet as he walked.

"Dad," I said proudly. "This is Joe. Joe, my dad."

Dad put out a tentative hand toward Joe, but a look of disapproval belied his friendly gesture. If Joe sensed this he didn't show it.

"Happy to know you, sir," he smiled directly into Dad's face.

I tried to act casual, and I insisted Joe stay for dinner. I kept thinking that if Dad had a chance to know him they'd get along fine.

Joe ate hungrily and, in response to Dad's questions, proudly told how he had quit school because he wanted to be independent. "I've got a good job," he finished, "and I pay my own way. Even paid cash for my bike."

The evening ended quietly with the two men saying a polite 'good night' to each other.

As I walked out on the porch with Joe he squeezed my hand softly. "I'll be here tomorrow after work. We'll drag a little on the bike."

The next few weeks Joe and I were together as much as possible. And each time he called for me Dad became angrier. Many of the nights I stayed at Joe's and Dad didn't even bother to ask where I'd been. Then came the final, terrible blow-up with Dad that ended with my storming out of the house. I had promised to meet Joe in town and we were going riding on his motorcycle. We had stopped at a diner where a lot of the guys with bikes hung out. Although the ride there with Joe on his bike had made me feel free and happy, I just couldn't get the quarrel with Dad out of my mind.

"Come on, baby. You're draggin' us all with that look on your face." Joe hugged me, trying to cheer me out of my mood.

"I'm sorry, Joe." I tried to smile, but I guess it didn't look very convincing.

Joe insisted then that I tell him what had happened. I did. I told him everything, including what my dad had said about Joe and how he had as much as told me not to come back.

When I finished Joe looked serious for a minute and then he began to laugh. He threw his head back and laughed gleefully, as though he knew some delicious private joke that only he could appreciate. "Well, I don't see what's funny!" Now I was indignant and hurt. Here I was so upset I couldn't enjoy myself and he just laughed at the story of my misery.

"We'll freak him out, baby. Don't you get it?" This seemed to make him laugh harder.

"No!" Now I was angry. "I don't get it!"

"I'm sorry, baby." His laughter quieted. "We'll get married!" Another explosion of laughter. "Out of sight, man! That's so far out, it's in!" Again, laughter.

I was beginning to get the joke. It did seem pretty kicky. After all, except for a piece of paper and repeating a few words we were already as good as married.

Two hours later we stood before a justice of the peace. We'd traveled on Joe's bike to a neighboring state where there was no waiting period and Joe had awakened the man. At first, the justice must have thought it was a joke, too. He looked at us both standing at his door in our helmets and jeans and shook his head wonderingly.

"You're serious now?" He rubbed his eyes as though to clear them.

"Yeh, man," Joe assured him. "We want to join the straights."

Ten minutes later we were married. Joe paid and thanked the man, who still looked a little disbelieving, and we were off on the bike. I called Dad from Joe's apartment (now our home) and told him the news. I could tell he wasn't happy to hear it, but he did wish us luck.

The next few months were great. I loved being married. After Joe left for work each morning I'd clean the apartment and go out to market. I began to fix the place up with new curtains and a rug. I urged Joe to let me buy a couch from Good Will and then I bought some fabric to make a slip cover for it. I thought it was fun being a wife, especially Joe's. Our nights were filled with love making, and it was delicious waking up with him next to me each day.

"Joe," I cooed one morning as he struggled to leave me and the warmth of the bed. "Couldn't we get a real one?"

"A real what?"

"Bed."

"What the hell you call this?" he answered defensively.

"It's a mattress, Joe. Just a mattress. I want a real bed—a frame, a head, a foot, a box springs and a mattress. That's a real bed."

"Don't I remember you telling me how groovy this was?" he demanded. "Damned women—you're all alike! You been changing this place inch by inch ever since I let you move in!" He looked really angry and his voice got louder. "I dig the way I live, and I don't need no broad changing things!"

He stomped toward the bathroom and turned to face my angry voice.

"Let me move in?" I screamed. "You married me, remember? It's as much my place as yours. And I want to live like a human being!"

What followed next was so awful that only bits and pieces of it remain in my mind. Joe and I said things to each other that were so cruel and hurtful I was left dazed and stunned when finally he left for work. All I could do was throw myself down on that damned mattress and sob.

Neither of us alluded to that scene or to the mattress for the next few weeks. At first, we maintained a reserved truce. But gradually we relaxed and before too long our desire and love for each other smothered the residue of ill-feeling that remained from our earlier combat.

I was trying to resign myself to simply doing things Joe's way, to living the kind of life he liked. I had just returned one day from buying some of Joe's favorite foods at the market when our building superintendent stopped me in the hall.

"Had a big delivery for you, m'am. You'll find it all in your bedroom."

Totally baffled, I thanked him and rushed upstairs and into our bedroom. There I saw a huge, gorgeous, king-size bed—complete. I rushed over to touch it and sit on it to make certain I wasn't seeing things. Once I knew it was truly real, I rushed out again to buy all the trimmings—sheets, pillows, blankets and a beautiful bedspread.

When it was time for Joe to come home that night I had his favorite casserole cooking in the oven, wine chilling in the refrigerator, a pretty at-home gown on and incense burning in our newly furnished bedroom. I felt good—as only a woman can when she knows she's fulfilling, her role as wife and lover.

The door opened just as I was adjusting the stereo. I turned in happy anticipation to greet Joe but stopped abruptly when I saw he was not alone. Puzzled, I waited for an introduction, if not an explanation—I had thought this evening would be ours alone.

"Mandy, this is Freddy. Freddy, Mandy."

Freddy looked me up and down appraisingly and half nodded to Joe. "Hi," was all he said to me.

I looked at Joe for some kind of reaction. Normally, he wouldn't have allowed any guy to look me over the way Freddy had just done. But he had not only allowed it, I thought I could detect his smiling agreement to Freddy!

"Freddy's gonna stay for dinner, Mandy. O.K.?"

I sensed that this was a fact, not a question, and gave the answer I knew was expected of me.

"Sure, Joe. Anything you say." I remembered that I hadn't thanked Joe for the bed. "Joe," I smiled. "It came. And it's just beautiful. Want to see it?"

Joe's face seemed to harden imperceptibly. "Naw. We'll see it later." He turned to Freddy. "Right?"

"Anything you say, Joe, baby." Again, I could feel Freddy's eyes on me.

By now I was not only confused but I began to experience a kind of free-floating anxiety. Something was happening that I couldn't quite understand. I felt that something was expected of me, but I didn't know quite what. Nervously, I used the excuse of checking on dinner to escape the eyes of Freddy and to give myself a moment to think.

After dinner, Joe announced that we'd have the wine in the bedroom. He took the bottle and Freddy and I obediently followed him. With an expansive gesture, Joe turned to Freddy and asked, "What do you think of our bed, man?"

"Crazy." Freddy walked over to it, sat on the edge and nonchalantly pulled off his motorcycle boots. "Crazy."

Joe looked pleased as he sat on the other side of the bed. With a finger he beckoned me to join them. "And lucky Mandy can sit right in the middle." He patted the spot where I was expected to sit.

Something told me not to cross Joe. That if I did I'd regret it. I joined them on the bed. Joe poured wine for us all around and reached over to press two switches. One dimmed the overhead light, the other released the music from the stereo.

We sipped our wine slowly, none of us talking.

"This bed is really boss, baby. I can see why you were so insistent." Joe broke the silence. "Can't you, Freddy?"

"All right, man." As Freddy answered, his hand slowly caressed my ankle and moved slowly up my leg.

Again, I looked at Joe for some sign, some reaction. There was none. In desperation, I drank down all my wine and asked Joe for more. He filled my glass and as I raised it to my lips I could feel Joe's hand exploring my thigh while Freddy put his mouth close to my shoulder and began kissing my arm and neck.

I drank the wine quickly. Through the warm glow filling me I hazily realized that we—the three of us—were about to do something that I had to go along with, or I'd lose Joe. Even as the thought became clear to me, Joe and Freddy were alternately undressing me. It happened to be Joe who removed my final garment.

"Stand up and turn around, baby."

Shyly, at first, but then with a brazen pride, I stood up before the two of them. As I turned, they undressed quickly, without taking their hungry eyes off me. Each of them reached up for me then, and we were suddenly a sea of arms, legs and mouths. I turned wildly from side to side, finding a waiting male whichever way I turned. Caresses and kisses encompassed me from my face to my feet, the front of me, the back of me. I no longer cared what we were doing but just that we were doing it! I reached the heights first with Freddy, then with Joe and then they became indistinguishable. I wanted them both over and over. There seemed to be no way of satiating my womanly hunger.

Finally, from sheer exhaustion, the three of us fell asleep, Joe on his stomach, with one hand resting on my thigh, and Freddy on his back, with his arm over my waist.

Morning came and I was alone. I looked about, slowly. The wine had left my head splitting and I felt dry-mouthed. Were it not for my conscience reminding me, I would never have believed Freddy had been with us. There was no trace of him. Joe had gone off to work.

I showered and made some coffee. As I sipped it I tried to believe that what had happened was really true. Worse, I had to believe that Joe had planned it. That he had wanted it that way. Finally, when I could no longer deny any of it to myself, I began to cry—softly at first, but then in great rushing sobs.

By the time Joe came home I had barely managed to tidy the house and get his dinner started. I had decided that we'd have a quiet dinner with no scenes and that we'd talk after dinner.

But Joe didn't agree.

"What's to talk about, baby? I got you a bed, didn't I? Let's go riding."

Once more, I sensed that Joe didn't want to be 'bugged,' as he put it. So I put on my jeans and boots and minutes later we were roaring off on his bike.

A week later, we still hadn't discussed the evening with Freddy. I was beginning to convince myself that I must have dreamt it all when one evening Joe again arrived home with Freddy. Then I knew I hadn't dreamt it. It had been real enough. And I also knew that this evening would he a repeat of Freddy's last visit. It was.

The following morning I packed my clothes and moved to a motel. I couldn't stay with Joe another day—no matter how much I loved him. I knew that if this was the way he insisted our marriage be it would only be a matter of time before we began to hate each other.

I sat down wearily in the motel room. I tried to figure out what to do next. I knew I'd have to get a job. I certainly couldn't go home to Dad. He had seen me a few times since Joe and I had been married, but he'd been only coolly polite. I lay down on the bed, closed my eyes, and wondered how I could exist without Joe. I felt as though I'd been cut in half.

The next thing I remember was a pounding on the door. I sat up, startled. I must have fallen asleep. I tried hard but I couldn't remember the day or the time.

The pounding became more insistent. "Yes?" I called out. "Who is it?"

"Open the door, Mandy. It's me, Joe."

I went toward the door, ignoring the stiffness in my muscles. I stopped myself when I got to the door. "What do you want?" I asked warily.

"Mandy, open the door, please. I want to talk to you." I had never heard Joe's voice sound so plaintive. I turned the lock and opened the door.

We stood looking at each other, neither of us speaking.

"May I come in?" Joe asked politely.

"Mandy, we've got to talk. This is crazy." Saying that, he stepped inside and closed the door.

Joe looked directly into my eyes. "Mandy, I've been a heel. I'm sorry. And I'm asking your forgiveness. Can you forgive me? I've searched this town to find you and ask your forgiveness."

I couldn't bear to look at him. "Joe, I can't forgive myself. How can I forgive you?" A rush of shame brought hot tears to my eyes. "Mandy,

I'm no good at words. But I know that what happened was all my fault. I acted stupidly, trying to get even with you. It's true, I want to live my own life—but with you." Now he was pleading. "I know I can change, Mandy, because this past twenty-four hours has been hell without you."

My tears fell without let-up. "But, Joe," I cried, "what we did—what we've done—we've sullied our own marriage!" Saying those words recalled such a sharp pain of guilt I wondered how I could ever feel free again.

Sensing my total despair, Joe took me in his arms. "Oh, baby," he begged, "we love each other. That's enough, isn't it? That and your forgiveness."

And then the two of us were alternately crying and laughing as we babbled loving terms to each other and each assured the other of forgiveness.

"Joe?" I pulled away and looked at him.

"Yeah, baby?"

"What if—what if I 'bug' you again?"

Joe smiled. "Listen, baby, when a guy has a chick like you, it's a treat to be bugged. In fact, it's a very groovy scene."

He looked around the room for my suitcase. Glancing at the bed he said, "Come on, Wife. Who needs this rented sack when we got a king-size one of our own at home? Let's split."

"Outa sight, man! Outa sight!" I laughed happily as we closed the door behind us.

THE END

THE PILL THAT FAILED

It produced triplets and a husband

Unplanned pregnancies were a staple of pulp romance stories, often showing the dire consequences of a young woman's choice to become intimate before getting married. So what happens when reliable contraception makes it easier to have sex without worrying about getting pregnant? Well, even "The Pill" wasn't perfect.

"The Pill That Failed" indulges in a bit of misdirection: The real focus of this story isn't Evie, the young girl who gets pregnant, but her older sister Marion. It's Marion who confronts the father of Evie's unborn children, Marion who agonizes over what's going to happen to them after they're born... and Marion who doesn't even realize that she's fallen in love.

When Evie, my young sister, paid me an unexpected visit I knew something was wrong. Ever since she'd moved out of my apartment the year before to go it alone, Evie had been very firm about my dropping in to see her unannounced, and she always called me before she came over. Now she stood in my doorway, a woebegone kitten with mussed blonde hair and a stricken look in her big blue eyes.

"What's wrong?" I asked apprehensively.

"Oh Marion, I'm in a jam. The worst jam of my whole life!" She burst into tears. I stared at her for a moment, thoroughly alarmed, then put my arms around her and led her, still sobbing, into my little kitchenette.

"Now just sit," I said firmly, helping her into a chair. "We'll have tea and you can tell me all about it."

Evie looked up at me through her tears. "You're a nut, Marion. Your remedy for everything is a cup of tea." She was sobbing again. The water was hot and I made the tea, wondering what on earth could have upset Evie so.

"Come on, honey," I coaxed. "Drink the tea. It will make you feel better."

To my surprise, she obeyed. After a moment she stopped crying. I waited, watching her. "All right now, what's the problem?" I asked. "Did you lose your job?"

"I'm pregnant," she said flatly.

All the breath seemed to leave my body. Pregnant? Oh no, she couldn't be! Evie was a bit wild, yes, but she wasn't stupid; I'd seen the birth control pills in her medicine cabinet.

I asked, still stunned. "Is it that Air Force captain?"

She chewed on her bottom lip, a habit from childhood. "No. We broke up ages ago. It's another man, Phil O'Brian. He sells insurance. His office is right across from where I work. We've been dating for months."

"Is he married?" I asked quietly. On at least one occasion, Evie had dated a married man.

She took a deep breath. "No. Phil is single. He intends to stay that way, too." Her voice quavered. "I—I was really serious about him, Marion. He seemed like such a nice guy. We hit it off just great."

"Evidently," I said dryly.

She pushed her hair back. "Oh Marion, don't go prudish on me now! I know you feel differently about sex, and all that. But it wasn't just sex, not this time."

Some of the first numbness began to wear away as I stared at my impossible little sister. Selana, you should have lived, I thought desperately. You were the only one who could handle Evie! But you're dead, and we need you so. . . Selana was my stepmother, Evie's real mother. She had died in a boating accident when I was twelve and Evie only six. Papa and I both turned to Evie for comfort because she was so much like Selana, beautiful and high-spirited. Only that was wrong, I guess. Evie was spoiled rotten.

"Have you told this—this man you're pregnant?" I asked.

Something flickered behind Evie's eyes, pain or anger—I couldn't tell. Her voice was firm. "Yes. He won't marry me."

Anger rose up in me. "Well!

We'll see about that. There are laws to protect girls against men like that!"

Evie smiled, a funny, warm little smile. "Calm down, sis. I need help, not righteous indignation. No law can make Phil marry me. All the law can do is make him support the baby and he already promised to do that. I'd sure like to sue the company that makes those pills, though."

I looked away. I didn't want to hear about Evie's pills. They were a symbol of the life she led. "How far along are you?" I asked.

"Almost four months."

I gave a little start. "That far?"

"Yes, and I just found out about it myself. You see, Phil and I had this fight about getting married. I decided the best thing to do was get away, change jobs. Working right across the hall from him there wasn't much chance of—well, getting over him.

"I applied for airline stewardess training and went for a physical. The doctor told me I was at least three months pregnant, maybe four! I told him it was impossible—that I took The Pill. He said The Pill wasn't one hundred percent successful." She started weeping again, silently this time, and somehow, her silent weeping was more terrible than hysteria.

I got up and put my arms around her the way I used to when she was little. "Don't cry, Evie," I said soothingly. "I'll help you, don't worry. You'll be just fine."

She clung to me helplessly. After awhile, she calmed down again and we started making plans. Evie would move back in with me immediately. She could work for another month; after that, we'd see. We talked of leaving town for awhile but in the end we both agreed that leaving was foolish. While my job at Meldone's Department Store as senior clerk wasn't the world's greatest, the salary was better than I would make starting over at a new job. Neither Evie nor I had any real savings, and what Papa had left when he passed away three years before had been eaten up by the medical bills from his long illness.

It was late when Evie left. Emotionally exhausted, I went straight to bed. I couldn't sleep, though. I tossed and turned, thinking about Evie. She and I were so different. Evie was twenty-one; I was twenty-seven. Maybe the six years between us was more important than I thought. It was almost as if we were different generations. Or maybe it was because Evie had gone to college and I hadn't—but how could two years of college make so much difference?

Or maybe it was because Evie was lovely to look at and fun to know. Men and boys had swarmed around her all her life; they rarely gave me a second glance. Oh, I had boyfriends. A few. And I had Ray. I brushed the thought of Ray from my mind. He would be shocked when I told him about Evie—but then, he doesn't have to know, at least right away. Anyway, it doesn't matter whether Ray's shocked or not. Evie's my sister. I love her and I promised Papa I'd watch out for her. Finally, I drifted off to sleep.

The next morning, I woke up determined to see Mr. Phil O'Brian. I had to find out for myself what kind of a man he was and just how much Evie could depend on him for her expenses. I'd heard that a delivery cost anywhere from three to five hundred dollars, not to mention the hospital expenses after the baby came. When we got right down to the nitty-gritty of the problem, Evie would need money more than anything. I took off work an hour early and headed for the office building where Evie and Phil O'Brian worked. I knew some people who worked with Evie so I went in the side entrance.

The insurance office wasn't a big place, but it was smartly decorated and the girl sitting at the desk in front looked like a model.

"May I help you?" she asked pleasantly. I clutched firmly at my handbag. "Yes. Mr. Phil O'Brian. please."

"Your name, please?"

"Miss Bagley. Miss Marion Bagley."

If the name Bagley meant anything to her she didn't show it. She picked up the phone, pressed a button and said, "Miss Marion Bagley to see you, Mr. O'Brian." She hung up after a brief pause, "Go right in, Miss Bagley. First door to the left."

I walked through the reception room down the hall to the first door on the left and knocked.

"Come in," a voice called. Suddenly, the nervousness that had been sitting on me all day lifted. I took a deep breath, opened the door, then shut it firmly behind me. A young man rose from his chair behind the desk.

"I'm Evie's sister," I said. "I want to talk to you."

We stared at each other for a long moment. He wasn't at all what I'd expected. He wasn't sharp or smooth-looking; in fact, he seemed downright rumpled in an attractive sort of way.

His hair was sandy, neither short nor long; his face was sunburned across the nose and cheeks, giving him a nice outdoor look. His dark business suit fit his broad frame neatly, and his grey eyes were direct and steady. He didn't smile.

"If you want to discuss Evie I suggest we go somewhere else," he said at last. His voice was deep; his words were easy, almost casual. He glanced at his watch. "Is right now convenient for you?"

"Yes," I said firmly, my eyes holding his.

"Very well," he answered. Then he picked up the phone and said something to someone about being back in a half hour. He held the office door open for me. "My car is in the parking lot," he said.

We walked silently to his blue sedan and again he politely held the door for me. He got in and started the motor. "Is there anywhere particular you'd like to go?" he asked.

I shook my head. "No."

"Let's make it Bircher's then. It's usually quiet there this time of day."

I nodded again. He didn't say anything else as he expertly steered through traffic. I didn't say anything either, but I stole glances at him. Phil O'Brian was no kid—he couldn't be bullied. Well, I certainly hadn't come to bully anyone, I thought quickly. I'd come to reason.

Bircher's turned out to be a restaurant and lounge. We walked through the dining room to a cozy little back room and sat down in a deep-cushioned booth. Phil ordered a whiskey sour for himself and a ginger ale for me. The drinks were served promptly. The waiter moved away. Phil offered me a cigarette.

"Thank you, I don't smoke," I said, trying to collect my thoughts, trying to remember all I'd planned to say.

Phil lit his cigarette. The back of his big hands were sunburned too. "You're not much like Evie," he said after a moment. I found myself flushing. What he meant was, I wasn't beautiful or sexy like Evie...

"We're only half-sisters," I blurted out.

"I know. Evie spoke about you."

"Well, you have the advantage," I said curtly. "I knew nothing of you until yesterday when Evie told me—told me—"

"—she's pregnant," he finished. His tone was suddenly as hard a mine. "Did Evie send you to see me?"

"No. She doesn't know I'm here. I came because I must know what you intend to do about my sister."

His expression didn't change. When he spoke, it might have been about the weather. "I told Evie," he said slowly, "that I'll pay all hospital and doctor bills. I'll support the child. But I won't marry her. I've never told her I loved her; I've never promised marriage. Evie was intimate with me willingly—no strings attached. I'm not denying that the baby is probably mine. Neither of us was seeing anyone else at the time. I am denying that I ever offered Evie anything more than an evening's pleasure."

Sudden, searing rage almost sickened me. "Pleasure! Is that what you think Evie is having now?" I sputtered. "Will it be pleasure for her to bear an illegitimate baby? Will it be fun when the child discovers he's a-a bastard?" My voice cracked and I paused, trembling with fury.

"Miss Bagley, if you'll just let me finish," he went on calmly. "Of course I realize this won't be a pleasure for Evie. But I certainly didn't plan it to happen. Evie assured me she was taking precautions and assumed she knew what she was talking about—"

"You assumed! Are you trying to say Evie deliberately got

pregnant?"

For the first time he lost his cool. I saw anger flash in his grey eyes. "No, I don't think that. I do think the whole thing is an unfortunate accident. It won't be pleasant for me, either. For one thing, there's my mother— I just bought a little place in the country for her and my three kid sisters. I'll have to give up my own apartment and move in with them to have money for Evie. My mother will want to know why, of course. It certainly won't be easy telling her—not to mention telling the girl I hope to marry someday."

"And who, pray, is the lucky girl?" I asked icily, hating him.

He blinked at me. "I don't know. I haven't met her yet."

I laughed. I couldn't help it. He sounded ridiculous. He reddened and his grey eyes flashed again. I quickly sobered. "Listen, Mr. O'Brian, I'm not interested in your mother or sisters, or your future wife. All I care about is Evie and the baby. Your baby, I might add."

"I'm willing to help, money-wise," he retorted quickly. "I just won't marry her. I don't love her. It's wrong to marry for any reason other than love..."

Fury possessed me again. "Don't speak to me of right or wrong, Mr. O'Brian. It sounds quite hypocritical coming from you. Frankly, I don't know what Evie ever saw in you in the first place! But I'm glad you've some conscience, at least. If you had refused money, I'd have gone to a lawyer."

His eyes narrowed. "Don't threaten me, Miss Bagley. I'm sorry for everything and I'll do what I can. But don't threaten me."

I rose, clutching the edge of the table, trying to control my anger. "Thank you for the ginger ale, Mr. O'Brian. Goodbye." And I walked out, leaving him staring after me.

When I got home, Evie was already there, moving in her things. We were busy for the rest of the evening. I didn't mention that I'd talked to Phil, but the next day I did see a lawyer after work. I was astonished to learn how difficult it would be to prove a paternity case in court. I went home very subdued. That night, I mentioned to Evie that I'd talked to both Phil and a lawyer. The news didn't cheer her any.

"Oh Marion, I could have told you what they'd both say! I'm not stupid, you know, in spite of what's happened. Phil's as stubborn as a mule. I'll get a lot more help from him if I don't try to push him. Let's just play it cool. Anyway, I plan to let the baby go for adoption as soon as it's born."

I stared at Evie, shocked. Somehow I'd assumed she would want to keep her baby. "You plan to do that?"

Her eyebrows raised. "Yes, of course. I certainly can't raise a baby alone. There are plenty of good, childless married couples begging for babies."

I tried to push away the funny pain in my heart. "But—but adoption, Evie. You'd never see your baby again."

"Why should I, if it's been adopted? Come on, Marion, you know very well a baby would be better off with a good father and mother than with me. Admit it!"

"I guess you're right," I said slowly. "Only it seems wrong, somehow. I wish you'd give it more thought. You have plenty of time to decide."

Evie sighed. "All right, Marion. I'll think about it some more but I don't expect to change my mind." She looked at me sharply. "And I don't want you getting all upset," she said firmly. "If I decide this whole mess bothers you too much I'll just move out again."

"Don't be silly!" I snapped. "It's your baby. You have to make the decisions."

And she did. In fact, after one more crying spell the night after she moved in, Evie's calmness amazed me. She worked a month longer at her job, then gave notice.

It seemed she started to show all at once; one day she was almost as slender as ever, the next day she had a round pot nothing could hide. After that she put an ad in the paper for typing at home. Immediately, there were calls, enough to keep Evie busy. I was glad, not so much because of the money, but because she didn't have time to brood.

One evening, as I left work, I found Phil O'Brian waiting for me outside the store. "I have to talk to you," he said seriously. I glanced away and started walking down the busy sidewalk. Phil fell into step beside me, making his steps match mine. "I've called Evie several times.

She won't speak to me. She just hangs up."

"Do you blame her?" I asked softly.

His eyes flashed. "Look, all I'm trying to do is discuss money matters with her—or somebody. I guess it'll have to be you."

I paused and we stood there on the sidewalk. He reached into his pocket brought out a check and handed it to me. "It's for two hundred," he said. "I made it out to you because I thought Evie might tear it up or something. I'll give you more later on."

I stared at the check. He seemed worried and ill at ease—a mother and three young sisters to support. Was his story true? Did he really support his family? I hadn't questioned Evie about that. Now I wondered as I put the check safely in my purse.

"Thank you," I said stiffly. "I can start paying Evie's doctor."

"Do that," he said quickly, shifting his weight uneasily. "Uh—how's she feeling?" People walked around us on the sidewalk, engrossed in their own affairs, their own problems.

"She seems to be doing all right," I answered, feeling something akin to sympathy for him. "Incidentally, you needn't worry about child-support later on. Evie plans to adopt the baby out."

His eyes widened in surprise. "She can't do that!"

I stared at him. "She certainly can!" I snapped. "As an unmarried mother, she's solely responsible for the baby."

His eyes flashed. "Now you listen—it's my baby, too. I've got some say about it!"

I felt the anger again, and a new frustration at his reaction. It was entirely unexpected. Why on earth should he care whether the baby was adopted out or not? "You're mistaken, Mr. O'Brian," I said coldly. "You have absolutely no rights. By refusing to marry Evie, you lost all legal claim to the baby. Now, if you'll excuse me—"

I walked quickly away, leaving him standing there on the sidewalk. When I got on the bus and put the fare in the box my hand was shaking.

I told Evie about Phil giving me the check. "He seemed upset when I told him you planned to give up the baby," I added.

Evie made a little face. "He would. In some ways, Phil is a

sentimental slob."

There was something in the way she said it. "Evie, are you still in love with Phil?" I asked softly.

"I don't think so. It would have been different if he'd loved me back. But he didn't. And doesn't now. I just want to forget him—to have the baby, and put the whole mess behind me. I still want to be a stewardess. I plan to apply again soon as I can."

I watched her take out two chops to broil for dinner. "Does Phil really support his mother and three sisters?" I asked, trying to sound casual.

"Yes. They just bought an old rundown farm outside of town. Phil took me there a couple of times. I think they're all crazy, wanting to live in the sticks, but they seem to like it. Phil's mother was raised on a farm. His sisters are nice, but awfully shy and stand-offish. I don't think they liked me much."

"How old are the girls?" I asked, frankly curious in spite of myself.

"I don't know. One's in her teens, the other two are still in the grubby stage. Phil's father died six or seven years ago. Phil had to quit school and go to work full-time to support the family."

I started to make a salad, still thinking about the O'Brians. "What's with the farm?" I asked after a moment. "A woman and three girls can't operate a farm, can they? I mean, Phil wasn't living out there at first—"

"They're raising chickens. Phil's mother knows all about that. But like I said, I think they're all nuts. If you don't mind, I'd rather not discuss the O'Brians. They all bore me silly. Do you want to go to a movie tonight?"

"Ray's coming over," I said, feeling oddly depressed. "We can all go to a movie, if you like."

She shook her head. "Thanks, no. I'll call Kitty." Kitty was one of Evie's girlfriends who hadn't deserted her and who called regularly. Evie had never said so, but I knew she didn't like Ray. Ray didn't think much of Evie, either, especially after he found out about the baby.

Not that we argued about Evie, Ray and I. We'd never really argued about anything and we'd been dating off and on almost two years. Ray was clean-cut, ambitious, and nice-looking in an average sort of way.

And he loved me. Not many men had ever noticed me and I wasn't getting any younger. I wanted to marry and have a family like any woman yet I kept putting Ray off. Why? I wondered. I was always avoiding a romantic showdown with Ray, but I couldn't do that forever, I knew. I was right.

Evie went to a movie with Kitty and Ray and I watched TV in my apartment. Right in the middle of a program Ray turned off the TV and said flatly, "Marion, make up your mind now—tonight—or I'm calling it quits."

Well, Ray was a habit with me; he helped kill some of my lonely hours. Words rushed to my lips, words of excuse—there was Evie; I couldn't think of marrying now because of her trouble. Later, later we would talk about us. But the words wouldn't come out. It isn't fair to Ray, I thought. Let him go.

"I'm sorry, Ray," I said softly, knowing I'd miss our quiet dates, our dinners together, the movies, the pleasant long walks. "I guess I just don't love you. At least not the way you want me to. The way you deserve."

He was hurt and angry. "I guess I knew it all along," he said harshly. "But I don't think it's because you don't love me. I don't think it's in you to love any man. You won't be bothered with me anymore. Good-by, Marion. Thanks for the laughs."

He was gone, the door slamming behind him. Evie came home and Kitty stayed awhile discussing the movie they'd seen. I set out cookies and made hot chocolate. After Kitty left, Evie helped me tidy up.

"You and Ray have a fight?" she asked casually, hanging up the towels.

I averted my face. "Sort of. He won't be coming around anymore."

Evie put her hand on my arm. "You might hate me for saying this, but I hope the break is for good. Ray is horribly dull. Oh, not that he isn't nice—he just isn't good enough for you. You can do better, Marion."

I leaned tiredly against the counter top. "Being dull isn't the worst sin in the world," I protested weakly. "I'm dull, too!"

"No, you're not!" Evie said firmly. "You just think you are.

Sometimes I think I should have been the older one—we'd both have done better."

I stared at her. Her expression was serious but I couldn't understand what she was talking about.

We went to bed early enough, but I couldn't sleep. Ray's words kept beating against my eardrums: You can't love any man. Any man. That isn't true, I thought, pushing my face into the pillow. I didn't realize how restless I was until Evie stirred in the twin bed beside me.

"Marion, you okay?" she asked sleepily.

"Yes," I mumbled. "I'm sorry I woke you. Go back to sleep."

I didn't want to talk then. I was afraid I'd ask Evie about love—how it felt to sleep with a man you were crazy about—but that's crazy, I scolded myself. You can see what love got Evie: an unwanted baby. She doesn't know anything about love, either, in spite of her affairs. Oh God, what's wrong with us? I'll probably wind up an old maid and Evie—what will happen to her? I tossed and turned for a long time and then finally drifted into an uneasy sleep.

I had a wild, unreasonable dream. I dreamed Ray was holding me and I felt excited and happy. But when I started to kiss him, there were freckles across his sunburned face.

"Let's have dinner out tonight," I suggested to Evie the next morning. "And are you taking walks like the doctor ordered?"

Evie looked down at her swelling girth. She was so big. "Yes, I'm taking walks," she said curtly. "I'm doing everything the doctor said. I'm not overeating or anything. I don't know why I'm so huge."

"It's probably just because you were so slender before that you seem so big now," I said, pushing away a finger of worry. "Anyway, take a nice long walk and meet me at six. We'll go someplace fancy for dinner, okay?"

Evie smiled, a pale, wan smile. "Sure."

At three Phil called to ask if I could meet him for coffee. It was my regular coffee break anyway, so I agreed to meet him in the coffee shop around the corner. We went to a back booth.

"What is it now?" I asked after the waitress had served us.

He pulled nervously at a paper napkin. "Well, it's—uh—I finally told my mother last night about the baby."

"Oh?"

"Yes. She had to know sometime and I got to thinking—I've decided to keep the baby. I don't want it adopted out."

I stirred my coffee. "You mean you've changed your mind about marrying Evie?" A look of torment passed through his eyes. "Marion, please try to understand. I can marry only once—for good. Evie and I couldn't possibly be happy together, but that doesn't mean I can't take good care of our baby. After Mother got over the shock she agreed with me. She thinks we should raise the baby. I'll be earning more money in the future, and God knows there are enough women in my family to take care of a baby." He paused, a pleading look in his grey eyes. "Will you talk to Evie? Explain how it is. We—my family—we want the baby. We'd love it—give it everything—"

I looked at him and the icy band of pain that had been squeezing my heart ever since Evie told me about giving up the baby began to melt away. Phil wanted his child! The baby would have a family of his own blood—a real father and grandmother and loving aunts. I found myself smiling.

"All right," I promised softly. "I'll talk to Evie."

"Thank you, Marion. I guess you think I'm the world's worst heel."

My eyes fell away from his. Yes, of course I thought he was a heel. He had used Evie for his own pleasure, then used religion as an excuse for not marrying her. If he was so religious, why'd he play around with her in the first place?

"Marion, I know I did wrong. I-I can't excuse myself," he went on, his voice low and earnest, almost pleading. "Going with Evie that way was against everything I've been taught. I never did anything like that before. Please believe me."

Suddenly the room was too close; I felt trapped, cornered. Phil's pleading eyes and voice pushed against me, compelling, threatening. I stood up abruptly. "I'll let you know what Evie says," I said crisply. "I'll be waiting," he said simply.

That night when I told Evie about Phil's plan for the baby, she exploded. "It's insane! I refuse to even discuss it. I want nice parents for my baby—a nice, normal mother—not a crazy old woman on a seedy chicken farm!"

My heart sank. "But Phil's mother isn't old, Evie. She's only middle-aged. Besides, Phil will marry eventually."

Evie whirled on me, her mouth set in a grim line. "Yes, that's another thing! Maybe his wife would hate the baby."

I wrung my hands helplessly. "Evie, be reasonable. Phil wouldn't marry a woman who'd hate his child."

"Sis, you don't know a thing about men—not a thing! You think all men are basically like Papa. Well, they're not. They're vile and nasty and they all want one thing—" She stopped suddenly. "I'm sorry, Marion. I don't really mean that. I was just blowing off steam. But I do mean what I say about Phil and the baby. The idea is ridiculous. My answer is no."

I felt weary, more tired than I'd ever felt in my whole life. "Have you signed anything yet?" I asked, dreading her answer.

"No. Dr. Brandon suggested that instead of a regular agency, I might want to arrange the adoption through him. He knows four couples who want babies." Her voice was flat, final. The kitchen table was set. "Let's get on with dinner, shall we?" she asked crisply. "I roasted a chicken."

I forced myself to smile, to eat, to dry the dishes. The following day I phoned Phil, and he met me at the same coffee shop. I gave him Evie's answer. The corners of his mouth tightened. "I'm not surprised," he said slowly. "But surely I have some rights. I'll see a lawyer and sue Evie for—well, I don't know what. A maternity suit, that's what!"

I stared at him. "I don't think that's legally possible," I said softly, thinking how fantastic the whole situation was. "We'll see," he muttered stubbornly.

I never did find out what his lawyer told Phil, or if he ever saw one, because the situation abruptly changed. The next day was Friday and Evie had her regular appointment with Dr. Brandon. She came home pale and shaken.

"For heaven's sake, what is it?" I asked.

"You'd better sit down," she said in a funny, quiet voice. I stared at her. She plopped down heavily beside me. "Dr. Brandon just told me I'm going to have twins."

"Twins!" My voice rose hysterically. "Is he sure?"

She nodded. Her face was white, making her eyes seem huge. "Yes, he's sure. That's why I'm so big." I saw fear glistening in those big, blue eyes. "Sometimes there's trouble with twins in a first pregnancy."

The fear clutched at me, too. "Dr. Brandon said that?"

"Yes. He's going to have another specialist in, when the babies are born."

"Oh." There was a small silence and I could feel the fear spread out between us. Evie reached over to pat my hand.

"But he said not to worry, sis," she said trying to smile. "I'm in excellent health and there hasn't been any problem so far. The only thing—" She paused, frowning. "It complicates the adoption. Not everybody wants twins. Sometimes twins are smaller and they have to stay in the hospital a long time."

"Oh," I said, my brain whirling. "Twins —but there aren't any twins in our family, Evie!"

"No. I don't think they are in Phil's, either, unless it's way back. Dr. Brandon thinks it might have been the pills. He says there's a slight increase in multiple births among women who use them."

I stared at her, trying to make sense out of the new situation. "What will you do now—about the adoption?"

She chewed on her bottom lip. "I think I'll wait until after they're born before I sign anything. If anything goes wrong and my babies aren't adoptable, I wouldn't want them raised in an institution. Once I sign them away, I'd have no say-so about their lives."

"Not adoptable? What do you mean, not adoptable?" I asked fearfully.

She made a helpless gesture with her hand. "Oh, you know—retarded, or something."

"Retarded?" I echoed. Suddenly, I stood up. I held my hand out to Evie, helping her up, too. "Now, that's a silly and morbid idea," I said firmly. "Your babies won't be retarded. They'll be nice and healthy in every way—why shouldn't they be? Dr. Brandon is only taking precautions to make sure everything goes well. Just stop worrying. Come lie down and rest."

She followed me obediently into the bedroom and I helped her undress and get into her nightgown. She settled down without any fuss. I left the room, closing the door softly behind me. I didn't want to use our phone in case Evie overheard, so I hurried down to the corner drugstore phone booth.

I called Dr. Brandon first. He told me essentially the same thing he'd told Evie. Still, I felt better after talking to Dr. Brandon personally. Then I dialed Phil's office. He had already left but the girl there gave me his home number. I could have waited until Monday but somehow it seemed terribly important that Phil know about the twins as soon as possible. A woman with a soft, lilting accent answered the phone and then Phil was there.

"Phil, I don't like to call you at home but I had to. The doctor told Evie this afternoon that she's carrying twins!"

There was a long silence on the other end of the phone. "Marion, did I hear you right?" he asked finally.

"Yes. Twins—"

"My God, I can't believe it!" he gasped. "It's fantastic."

I took a deep breath. "Fantastic or not, it's twins. I'm terribly worried about Evie. She's depressed and morbid. I think you should try to talk to her."

"But she won't even speak to me."

"I think if you came to the apartment—not now—tomorrow afternoon when she's rested. I don't want you to upset her. If you could just talk to her calmly without getting angry—"

"I'll try. I'll really try, Marion."

"About four, then."

"I'll be there," he promised and I hung up. When I got back to the apartment Evie was sleeping soundly. She slept for two hours but when she got up she still seemed depressed. At dinner she picked at her food, staring off into space. We sat up very late watching TV, but when we went to bed I still couldn't sleep. I tossed and turned, worrying and

THE PILL THAT FAILED

brooding. Twins—how could Evie give up twins? Twins were so special. Maybe Evie would change her mind; maybe she'd decide to keep them herself or let Phil have them. Twins —two helpless infants coming into such a crazy mixed-up world—the whole thing was so wrong . . . Finally I slept.

Evie and I had a late breakfast the next morning and then we took a walk to the park. It was a lovely Saturday morning. Children were out playing, the sun was bright and the air sweet and fresh. A little color came into Evie's cheeks. After lunch she napped again while I straightened up the apartment. After she got up and dressed, I brushed her hair.

"You used to fix your hair so nice," I said, scolding just a bit at the way she'd let herself go.

Her eyes met mine in the mirror. "And I will again, as soon as I feel like a human being. Right now I'm just serving a sentence. When it's over I'll live again."

The sharp ring of the doorbell cut her short. I hurried to answer it. Phil stood there, looking uneasy. Quickly I told him to come inside, then shut the door behind him. Evie came to the doorway. Her face paled when she saw Phil.

"Now, Evie, it's all right," I said hurriedly. "I asked Phil to come."

Her eyes narrowed. "Why?"

"Because you two have to talk, that's why," I said nervously. "Evie, it is Phil's baby, too—uh, babies," I corrected myself quickly. "He's helping to pay for everything. The least you can do is hear him out."

Evie glared at me. "I want you both to sit down," I went on, ignoring Evie's expression. "I'll get tea, and then we'll all have a nice talk."

Evie seemed to hesitate. Phil sat down gingerly; Evie sat down, too. I hurried to the kitchen for the tea. I was so fumble-fingered I knocked the sugar bowl over and had to clean up the mess. When 1 got back to the living room with the tea tray there was nothing but silence. Evie and Phil just weren't saying anything to each other. I served the tea and then sat down on the divan beside Evie.

"Evie, Phil was very surprised to hear about the twins," I began, breaking the thick silence. "I mentioned that twins, might complicate adoption."

Evie turned an icy gaze on me. "You tell Phil just about everything, don't you?' she asked, her voice as frozen as her eyes.

"Marion's only trying to help," Phil broke in. "She's thinking about you and the babies."

Evie's lips flattened. "She's not helping me by dragging you here! I told Marion to tell you that you taking the baby is impossible—even more so, now there's two babies. In the first place, I want them to have a real father and mother. In the second place, I don't want them to have your religion. In the third place, I won't let them be buried alive on a crummy chicken farm!" She paused, looking at Phil. "Need I go on?"

"No," he said, meeting her gaze squarely. "Will you marry me, Evie?" he asked. His voice was steady, matter-of-fact.

Evie's eyes widened briefly, but she quickly regained her composure. "No," she said curtly. "I wouldn't marry you for any reason. I'd much rather be dead."

Suddenly I realized I'd been holding my breath and an icy lump inside my chest melted away at Evie's answer. Evie set her tea cup down, then stood up, head held high.

"Now, if you two will excuse me, I'm going to my room." In spite of the huge burden she was carrying she walked out with dignity. In that moment, I was very proud of Evie, but I wasn't sure why.

"I'm sorry, Phil," I said softly. He nodded and his eyes looked weary and defeated and suddenly he didn't look young anymore; somehow, he was prematurely old.

"It's all right," he said, getting up. "Thanks for trying."

Evie would hardly speak to me for a whole week, but then she got over her mad and we were friends again. The weeks passed swiftly. I still talked to Phil over the phone and had coffee with him occasionally and he gave me some more money for Evie's expenses. Our conversations were always short. We really didn't have much to say to each other. All I could tell him was how Evie was feeling; that she planned to wait until after the babies' birth before she made adoption arrangements.

It was a sad, dreary time for all of us. Evie's labor pains started late one evening, almost a month early. Dr. Brandon rushed over, examined Evie and took her right to the hospital. I was left in the waiting room to chew my nails and worry. When Evie had been in the labor room for two hours I broke down and called Phil. I couldn't stand the strain of waiting alone. Somebody had to be with me, somebody who cared. Just as Phil arrived, Dr. Brandon came to the waiting room looking for me.

"Is—has—?" I asked incoherently.

"Labor is progressing nicely," Dr. Brandon said easily. "There's nothing to worry about at this stage. Most first labors take a long time. Just try to relax. We'll let you know as soon as anything happens."

"Yes—yes, thank you," I mumbled, relieved. The doctor went away and Phil and I looked at each other. I hadn't introduced him to Dr. Brandon. I hadn't known what to say.

"She's okay so far?" he asked, obviously seeking reassurance.

I nodded. "You heard the doctor. It just takes a long time."

We sat down, side by side in the waiting room, along with other waiting people. Phil smoked nervously, got up and walked around the room, sat down again. Somehow, his being there made me calmer. "Why don't you get us some coffee?" I suggested, more to give him something to do than anything. "There's a cafeteria on the second floor."

He fetched the coffee and we drank it silently. Every time a nurse appeared in the doorway, Phil jumped. Time dragged unbearably. It was almost an hour later when a nurse came to tell us that Evie was in the delivery room. After that I got up and paced the floor, too, and opened and shut the windows, oblivious to other people around me, even Phil. By the time the nurse came and called my name I was ready to scream with anxiety.

"Evie?" I asked fearfully.

"Your sister is fine," the nurse said crisply. "She had a rough time but she's all right."

"And the twins?"

She hesitated for just a fraction of a second and my heart did a long, sharp dive. "They're not twins," she said softly. "They're triplets. Two girls and a boy. "

"Triplets!" I gasped.

The nurse nodded. "Yes. The two girls are small, but they seem to be quite strong. The boy—" she paused.

I felt numb all over. I knew from the way she was choosing her words that something was wrong with the boy.

"He's very tiny," she said slowly, seriously. "Dr. Brandon will be out in just a moment to speak to you."

She left, and Phil and I stood there, stunned, not daring to speak. Phil's face was so pale, his expression so stricken, that I reached out impulsively for his hand. "Let's not jump to conclusions," I said firmly. "We'll see what Dr. Brandon says."

We didn't have to wait long. An elevator door opened and Dr. Brandon was with us, still in his surgical smock.

"The nurse told you the mother and both girls are fine?" he began, his eyes going to Phil's face.

"Yes, she told us," I said impatiently. "But the boy?"

Dr. Brandon took a deep breath. "It's too soon to tell. He isn't quite four pounds. With a baby that small there's often trouble with an undeveloped breathing capacity."

"You mean he'll die," I said flatly.

Dr. Brandon's expression didn't change. "I didn't say that. He's alive now—and there's a chance he might stay alive, but how good a chance we can't tell at this point. He also has a clubbed left foot, but that's relatively minor. We can fix that. I want you to stay here for awhile in case there should be a sudden change. Evie's under heavy sedation, but you can see the little girls now, if you like."

"May Phil come too, doctor?" I found myself asking. "He's—the babies' father."

Dr. Brandon's face hardened. "The mother hasn't named him as the father. Only the closest kin may see the babies. Come along, Marion."

As I followed Dr. Brandon down the hall, I could almost share the shame and humiliation Phil must be feeling, but I put it out of my mind. I had to see my little nieces. A doctor and a nurse were in the "preemie" room with the two little incubators but I was allowed to look through the glass. One baby was sleeping, but the other was waving a tiny shell-like hand. They were so sweet, so tiny my breath caught. The little boy, I thought, he's even smaller. Was it possible that he could be smaller than these two and still live? Wordlessly, I followed Dr. Brandon back into the hallway.

"May I see the boy?" I asked.

Dr. Brandon shook his head. "It would be best if you didn't, Marion. He isn't very pretty and it would just upset you. There'll be plenty of time to see him later."

There was nothing to do but return to the waiting room. The small hospital chapel was on the way; as I passed, I saw Phil kneeling, praying. Mixed emotions ran through me, then I walked on into the waiting room.

Hypocrite, I thought—why does Phil pray now? He wasn't thinking about God when he was sinning with Evie . . . And what was Evie thinking then, a voice whispered inside me. It wasn't all Phil's fault; Evie's no saint. But at least she's not a hypocrite, I answered the voice stubbornly. Who are you to judge? The voice whispered back. You don't really know Phil.

"Did you see them?" I jumped. I hadn't seen Phil come back into the waiting room.

"Yes. They're fine. But so tiny! You can't imagine how small they are." He sat down heavily beside me and put his face in his hands. "Phil, why don't you go home?" I asked softly. "There's nothing you can do here. I'll call you as soon as there's any news."

He looked up at me. "I have to stay here, too." There was no use in arguing with him. We sat quietly, drank coffee and looked at the clock. It was a quarter to four when a nurse came to say there was still no change in the little boy. Phil and I had breakfast in the cafeteria, and at eight I called my supervisor to say I couldn't work that day.

At nine, Phil's mother showed up. Mrs. O'Brian was a tall woman with red hair, turning gray. Her gaze was direct and steady, like Phil's, and her hand shake was firm.

"Is there anything I can do?" she asked in her sweet brogue.

"No," I, answered. "There's nothing any of us can do but wait."

"I see. In that case, I will wait with you. Phil, go home and clean up and go to work."

Their eyes met, held. "No, Mother." He answered, his voice as firm as hers. She didn't answer. She sighed and sat down and took out a bundle of knitting from a tote bag.

"Your mother's right, Phil," I said gently. "Please go. Try to get your mind on something else. Women are better at waiting than men."

He looked at me for a long moment. "All right," he said wearily. "I'll stay in the office all day, though. Call me."

"As soon as I hear anything," I promised. Phil left and Mrs. O'Brian and I were alone in the waiting room. She looked up from her knitting. Her dark dress was not stylish, neither were her shoes and stockings, but she sat straight as a ramrod. Her skin and eyes were beautiful. And her voice—gentle, sweet, so very kind.

"Is there nothing to be done for the mother?" she asked.

"No, she's fine," I answered quickly, thinking how strange it was that Mrs. O'Brian should be here. Evie would be furious if she knew.

A little later, a doctor I didn't know came to talk about the babies. The girls were still fine and the boy seemed to be a little stronger, but he was still in some danger. I thanked him and he left.

Mrs. O'Brian put down her knitting. "Shall I call Phil?" she asked.

"Yes, please do." I said. She went in search of a phone and I went down to the nurse's desk and asked about seeing Evie. They let me go right in. Evie was still a bit groggy, but she knew all about her son.

"Have they told you he's better this morning?" I asked eagerly.

"Yes, but they said it's still touch-and-go," she said cautiously. "But at least the girls are okay. I suppose I should go ahead with their adoptions . . ."

"Oh Evie, they're triplets!" I wailed softly. "Don't separate them—surely, there's a couple somewhere who'd want all three."

She pushed the hair back from her forehead. "Maybe—if they were all healthy. But we don't know about the boy. Besides, he's crippled."

"His foot can be fixed," I argued.

Her eyes met mine. "If he lives, that is. And even if he does, they can't operate on his foot for a long time. It might be a year. Oh Marion, don't you see?"

"No, I don't!" I said, my voice coming out sharp. Suddenly, Evie burst into tears. Alarmed, I bent to hug her.

"I don't know what to do," she sobbed, clinging to me. "I can't even think."

"That's why you shouldn't make a decision right now," I said soothingly. "My goodness, you just had the babies this morning! Wait until you're stronger and we know what's going to happen."

"All right, Marion," she agreed weakly, settling back on her pillow. "I am tired. I just want sleep."

Evie slept and Mrs. O'Brian and I waited. By late evening, when Phil came, the little boy was still gaining strength. By the next morning, Dr. Brandon was positively cheerful. The following day, everybody was doing so well I went back to work. Evie came home a week later, looking almost her old self. All three babies stayed in the hospital, of course.

Evie came home on a Friday so I had all weekend with her. Evenings, she rested while I visited the babies. Phil and Mrs. O'Brian were usually there. The two girls were in the regular nursery now and they could be seen during visiting hours.

There were several incidents with reporters, but Dr. Brandon came to my rescue and told them to leave me alone. An unmarried mother with triplets would have made a good story, I guess, but thanks to the hospital there was no publicity. Two weeks after Evie came home, Dr. Brandon said the baby girls could come home, too.

"This is on the condition that you have a nurse for awhile. Can you afford one? If not, I can arrange one through Family Services. Actually, a practical nurse will do."

"I think we can manage," I said happily. I hurried home to tell Evie. I think, inside, I was prepared for her reaction.

"No, we can't bring them here!" she insisted stubbornly. "Be

reasonable, Marion. You know it will be hard to give them up later if
take them now."

Her voice was firm and her eyes were determined. My happines
vanished. "But the boy—" I protested weakly.

"The boy is a different matter," she went on evenly. "I'll take hin
until his foot has been fixed and he's adoptable."

A desperation rose up from deep inside my being, a desperation a
strong as Evie's determination. "Evie, as long as there's a chance fo
those three babies to grow up together it's wrong to separate them."

Evie whirled on me, eyes flashing. "You listen to me, Marion
They're my babies—have you no heart? What are you trying to do t
me? Don't you know it'll kill me to give them up once I've seen them
held them in my arms . . ."

"Then don't give them up," I said quietly. "Keep them. Keep ther
all. I'll help you. Together, we can do it."

"No, I don't want them. You'd make all the sacrifices necessary t
keep them—but I can't. I'm not strong enough. I want a life of my own.

I took a long trembling breath, praying for the right words. "Al
right, then. Let Phil and Mrs. O'Brian take the girls until the boy i
strong enough to have his foot operated on. Phil and his mother visi
the babies every day; I trust them to take good care of the two girls."

Our eyes held for a long moment and then, finally, Evie's droppec
"Phil wouldn't give them up later," she said.

"He'd have to," I insisted. "You're the sole legal parent. Th
O'Brians would have no say in the matter."

Evie looked at me again, and this time I saw the defeat lurkin
behind her eyes. "Oh, Marion, I can fight the O'Brians, but not you
Let them take the girls for now, but with the understanding that it'
only until I decide."

I agreed quickly before she could change her mind. She didn't sa
any more about it that night. The next day I called Phil. I met him a
the hospital on Friday and he and his mother and a practical nurs
took the girls home.

When I got back to the apartment, Evie was out. Thinking she wa
only around in the neighborhood I went to the kitchen to start dinner

The silence of the apartment suddenly felt eerie. Feeling uneasy, I walked into our bedroom. All of Evie's things were gone! Then I saw a letter on the dresser. I opened it with trembling fingers.

"Dear Marion, I'm going far away so don't waste your time looking for me. I leave the babies to you and Phil. I just can't decide what is best for them and I only know what's right for me. I plan to start a new life someplace else. I know you'll be good to the babies. You might not believe this, but I do love you. Evie."

I leave the babies to you and Phil—yes, Evie knew I was in love with Phil, that I had loved him from the first day I'd seen him, that he blotted out the existence of all other men. Evie knew I wanted him for myself, the babies, too, not just because they were Evie's babies, but because they were Phil's, too. I sat at the kitchen table for a long time and then I got up to phone Phil.

The triplets start kindergarten this September. Tina and Terry are ready and eager, their blue eyes sparkling, blonde pigtails bouncing. Paul is more cautious. just a bit suspicious of the whole thing. Paul walks without a trace of a limp and he's much taller and heavier now than his two sisters. His eyes are grey like Phil's, and his hair sandy. The triplets call me mother, too, as my own son, Phil, Jr., does, but the truth of it is that all four children have lots of mothers. Phil's sisters are at the dating stage now; our big old house is full of young men courting, the chicken house is full of laying hens—and my days are full of unbelievable happiness. I think of Evie often. I see her every day in my little girls' faces. I feel Evie's love, too, and hope that wherever she is, she feels mine. Sometimes I wish I could tell her how happy we all are, but I think she knows. I really do think Evie knows. THE END

Ron Hogan Biography

Ron Hogan co-founded Lady Jane's Salon, a monthly reading series dedicated to romance fiction, and has been its primary host since 2009. He's also produced literary events throughout New York City, and was one of the first people to launch a book-related website, Beatrice.com. In addition to digging through the TruLoveStories archives for great stories, he publishes a digital magazine (also called Beatrice!) of interviews with some of today's best writers.

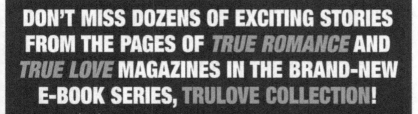

www.ingramcontent.com/pod-product-compliance
Lightning Source LLC
Jackson TN
JSHW020018141224
75386JS00025B/577